**PENGUIN
VITAE**

W HAT CLASSIC BOOKS would you place together on a shelf to represent the course of your
life? This is the question that sparks our hard-
cover series Penguin Vitae or, loosely translated, "Penguin of one's life." A diverse world
of storytellers from the past speak to us at piv-
otal chapters of our lives and connect a community of readers across time and generations.
Penguin Vitae invites readers to curate their
own personal Penguin Classics canon from this
series and to discover other seminal works of
timeless inspiration, intellectual engagement,
and creative originality. To enrich the reader's
experience of these gift editions, Paul Buckley
designs bold typographic covers inspired by
each work, with vibrant foil stamping and colored endpapers, contributing to Penguin's ac-
claimed history of innovative book design.

We hope you find yourself within Penguin
Vitae, discover something new, and share these
classic books with others.

ELDA ROTOR
Publisher
Penguin Classics

In a glass-enclosed city of absolute straight lines, ruled over by the all-powerful "Benefactor," the citizens of the totalitarian society of OneState live out lives devoid of passion and creativity—until D-503, a mathematician who dreams in numbers, makes a discovery: he has an individual soul. Set in the twenty-sixth century AD, Yevgeny Zamyatin's *We* is the archetype of the modern dystopia and the forerunner of works such as George Orwell's *1984* and Aldous Huxley's *Brave New World*. Suppressed for many years in Russia, it details the fate that might befall us all if we surrender to some collective dream of technology, and remains a resounding cry for individual freedom.

# WE

YEVGENY IVANOVICH ZAMYATIN (1884–1937) was
a naval architect by profession and a writer by nature. His favorite idea was the absolute freedom of
the human personality to create, to imagine, to love,
to make mistakes, and to change the world. This
made him a highly inconvenient citizen of two des-
potisms, the tsarist and the Communist, both of
which exiled him, the first for a year, the latter forever. He wrote short stories, plays, and essays, but
his masterpiece is *We*, written in 1920–21 and soon
thereafter translated into most of the languages of
the world. It first appeared in Russia only in 1988. It
is the archetype of the modern dystopia, or anti-
utopia; a great prose poem on the fate that might
befall all of us if we surrender our individual selves
to some collective dream of technology and fail in
the vigilance that is the price of freedom. George
Orwell, the author of *1984*, acknowledged his debt
to Zamyatin. The other great English dystopia of
our time, Aldous Huxley's *Brave New World*, was
evidently written out of the same impulse, though
without direct knowledge of Zamyatin's *We*.

CLARENCE BROWN (1929–2015) was the author of
several works on the Russian poet Osip Mandelstam
and the editor of *The Portable Twentieth-Century
Russian Reader*, which contains his translation of
Zamyatin's short story "The Cave."

MASHA GESSEN is the author of more than ten books, including the National Book Award–winning *The Future Is History: How Totalitarianism Reclaimed Russia* and *The Man Without a Face: The Unlikely Rise of Vladimir Putin*. A staff writer at *The New Yorker* and the recipient of numerous awards, including Guggenheim and Carnegie fellowships, Gessen teaches at Bard College and lives in New York City.

# YEVGENY ZAMYATIN

# WE

**TRANSLATED WITH AN INTRODUCTION AND NOTES BY**
Clarence Brown

**FOREWORD BY**
Masha Gessen

PENGUIN BOOKS

## PENGUIN BOOKS

An imprint of Penguin Random House LLC
penguinrandomhouse.com

Published in Penguin Books 1993
This edition with a foreword by Masha Gessen published in Penguin Books 2021

LIBRARY OF CONGRESS CATALOGING-IN-PUBLICATION DATA
Names: Zamíàtin, Evgeniï Ivanovich, 1884–1937, author. |
Brown, Clarence, 1929–2015, translator, writer of introduction. |
Gessen, Masha, writer of foreword.
Title: We / Yevgeny Zamyatin ; translated with an introduction and
notes by Clarence Brown ; foreword by Masha Gessen.
Other titles: My. Russian
Description: [New York] : Penguin Books, 2021. | Series: Penguin vitae |
Includes bibliographical references.
Identifiers: LCCN 2021036309 | ISBN 9780143136293 (hardcover)
Subjects: LCGFT: Dystopian fiction. | Novels.
Classification: LCC PG3476.Z34 M913 2021 | DDC 891.73/42—dc23
LC record available at https://lccn.loc.gov/2021036309

Printed in the United States of America
1st Printing

Set in Sabon LT Pro
Designed by Sabrina Bowers

# CONTENTS

# FOREWORD

I have an object to which I've given pride of place in every house I have lived in for many years. It's a wall hanging, of sorts, a two-by-three-foot glass display that contains a handprinted schedule for a day. It includes eight and a half hours of sleep; an hour each for breakfast, lunch, and dinner; a half hour of exercise; three hours of fresh air; and three hours of after-dinner board games and movie watching. Someone pilfered this beautiful object from a psychiatric ward in provincial Russia, to present to me as a gift. I never tire of looking at it, just as my daughter never tires of pointing out the entry "An hour of rest: 14:00–16:00." What a wondrous way to subvert the flow of time, by making an hour of rest stretch out for two.

Every year, when I read Yevgeny Zamyatin's *We* with my students, I wish the psychiatric-ward schedule were hanging in the classroom. I'd refer to it when I talk about the way Zamyatin imagined a regimented life but also when I talk about the way the book's existence seems to subvert the flow of time. Zamyatin wrote his dystopia in 1920, possibly revising it in 1921 or 1922. In other words, he was writing just a couple of years after the Bolshevik Revolution in Russia, completing the final draft before the Soviet Union took its own final form— before it built the first concentration camp or built the tyranny of bureaucracy, though not before it created its secret police and imposed censorship. Zamyatin, who was born in 1884, had been a revolutionary, indeed a Bolshevik, had been imprisoned and sent into internal exile in the Czar's Russia, had then moved to England, to return home half a year after the czar abdicated, ceding power to the Provisional Government.

It was September 1917 when he came back from England. A month later, the Bolsheviks overthrew the Provisional Government. It took them another few years to establish Soviet rule over most of what had been the Russian Empire, to expropriate most property, and even longer to establish a reign of terror. But by this time Zamyatin had already written a novel that described many of the specifics of that terror—and of other terrors of the twentieth century.

Zamyatin foresaw some of the specifics that have come to mark twentieth-century terror in our collective memory. People in *We* don't have proper names; they are marked by a combination of letters and numbers—like the inmates of Nazi camps. They wear identical clothes, their hair is uniformly shorn, their food is synthetic and purely utilitarian, and their homes are identical and transparent. Soviet life, with its enforced uniformity on the one hand and extreme scarcity on the other, looked like a less aesthetically pleasing version of this leveled existence. The people in the novel live according to a centralized schedule, a high-tech display that evokes my psychward timetable and specifies everything down to the hour of lovemaking—with a partner who will be assigned by the central authority. They speak an inverted language: the tyrant is called the Benefactor. The center of communal life is the execution, glorified, celebrated, and perfected: human life is reduced to a small amount of clean water and ash. Zamyatin imagined this twenty years before Nazi Germany began sanitized, industrial mass murder of people who had been reduced to numbers. Zamyatin's dystopia is a walled and domed city, and its inhabitants are unaware of the existence of a larger world; he imagined this years before the iron curtain sealed off the Soviet Union.

Zamyatin was writing *We* several years before the word "totalitarianism" appeared in political speech and a full three decades before political theorists defined and described totalitarianism. Yet he did more than predict some of the specific characteristics of totalitarianism—he predicted its defining condition: the destruction of the individual. Hannah Arendt, in *The Origins of Totalitarianism* and elsewhere, argued that totalitarianism was a novel form of government, distinct from the tyrannies that preceded it. The tyrants of the past demanded obedience, the outward performance of certain behaviors, while totalitarian regimes seek to subsume the entire person, to obliterate the core of the human being. Obedience is no longer enough, nor is the performance of love: the regime demands that and everything else, too. The contours of the self disappear, and humans meld into what Arendt called "one man of gigantic dimensions." Zamyatin found the word for it: "we."

*We* could not be published in Soviet Russia. It came out first in an English translation in 1925, then in Czech and in French. Following the Czech publication, Zamyatin was denounced by every journal and publishing house in the USSR and became a pariah. In 1931, he emigrated—by special dispensation, for by this point Soviet borders were effectively closed.

All of the foregoing is true, and all of it is obvious enough. If you have heard of *We*, you have heard that it was prescient and pioneering, and that it influenced Aldous Huxley and George Orwell, whose dystopian novels have, in turn, helped shape our understanding of the twentieth century and beyond. The contemporary Russian literary critic Dmitry Bykov, however, has argued that Zamyatin's predictions were off. "He was afraid of the wrong thing," Bykov said in a 2017 lecture. "He envisioned an exemplary totalitarian state, built on absolute reason, on logic . . . and an enforced totalitarian benevolence." Zamyatin's dystopia was clear, sterile, perfect—and hence soulless, and soul-killing. In reality, Bykov continued, it was not a tyranny of perfection that made twentieth-century totalitarianism so terrible: it was the tyranny of the worst.

To be sure, the horrors of the twentieth century were, as the philosopher Zygmunt Bauman argued, functions of modernity. The Holocaust ran on rails, timetables, and the technology that made mass, anonymized murder possible. Zamyatin was a man not only of words but also of science: he was educated as an engineer and worked in shipbuilding as one of the creators of a giant Russian icebreaker. He had a keen sense of the ways in which technology could transform human existence, and this, perhaps, enabled him to envision humans reduced to numbers, and to handfuls of ash. What he didn't foresee, as Bykov notes, is the irresistible appeal to the worst in human nature, the very appeal that links the darkest moments of the twentieth century to the autocrats and aspiring autocrats of the twenty-first century. They invite their followers to abandon conventions of dignity and expectations of morality and be their worst selves, together.

The regimes in Nazi Germany and the Soviet Union had enough similarities to enable scholars to create a new category that included them: totalitarianism. Both regimes relied on propaganda and terror; both treated their populations as dispensable. But there was one significant difference that continues to haunt us to this day. While Hitler openly appealed to the worst in humanity, the Bolsheviks built their state in the name of beautiful, humanistic ideas. They envisioned a state in which everyone was perfectly equal, everyone received according to need and contributed according to ability, and everyone existed in perfect harmony with the rest. Zamyatin's dystopia is consistent with these ideas, and prefigures their corruption. As both the son of an Orthodox minister and a Russian revolutionary, Zamyatin had a deep understanding, even love, for the ideals of communitarianism. When he imagined the ugly outcome of a relentless enforcement of these ideas, he used what he had surely once thought of as a beautiful word—"we" —to describe it.

In a world without personal boundaries, a world without deviation, conflict, serendipity, difference, a world without "I," there can be no "us." The "we" of *We* is a mass rather than a community of people. Arendt wrote about loneliness as the defining condition of totalitarianism. She drew a distinction between loneliness—a sense of isolation—and solitude, a condition necessary for thinking. One could be lonely in a crowd. But in Zamyatin's world of transparent houses and uniform lives, one could not have solitude.

Zamyatin imagined that if a totalitarian subject started thinking, feeling, pursuing his desires rather than following the master timetable and the Benefactor's orders, he would become unable to live within the "we": he would have to be fixed, executed, or expelled. In the novel, the protagonist, D-503, is diagnosed with having developed a soul—a condition that must be remedied so that he may be reintegrated into society. As Zamyatin's story is usually told, this is what happened to him, too: after the publication of *We* abroad, he was shut out of all Soviet institutions and was forced to ask Stalin to let him emigrate. That is the story I summarized above. It's neat, but it's not true.

Zamyatin's loss of professional and social standing preceded the publication of *We* abroad—indeed, it probably preceded the completion of the novel. Something had gone astray early on, and several years before *We* was published anywhere, Zamyatin was already feeling despondent. In 1921 he published an essay titled "I'm Afraid." He wrote about what he saw as an emergent Soviet system for choosing ideologically reliable writers and allowing only them to be published. He classified writers as "agile" and "not agile" and claimed that the latter group—those unable to pitch their words precisely to the expectations of the new regime—had been rendered silent.

> True literature can thrive only in places where literature is created not by obedient and reliable bureaucrats but by madmen, recluses, heretics, dreamers, rebels, and skeptics. Where a writer must be reasonable, faithful like a Catholic, useful in the present moment, where he cannot flail at everyone as Jonathan Swift did or smile at everything as Anatole France does, there can be no literature that is cast in bronze—there can only be the sort printed on paper, the newsprint sort that's read today and used to wrap bars of soap tomorrow.

Zamyatin thought, correctly, that his was the kind of writing that would live on long after the bar of soap had been used up and the writing in which it had been wrapped was forgotten. But this doesn't mean that he understood the system he was confronting. After several years of feeling like he was unfairly and inexplicably marginalized by the Soviet literary establishment, he set out to prove his ideological and writerly trustworthiness. He spent three years working on a play that he believed would restore his good name. In 1928, the play, *Attila*, was granted a reading before the Artistic Soviet of the Great Leningrad Drama Theater. Representatives of eighteen different city factories were present: laborers were now the ultimate authority in every area, including the arts.

They liked the play. One workman remarked that it reflected an ancient class struggle that mirrored contemporary reality. "Ideologically, this play is quite acceptable," this factory worker concluded. "This play is very impressive and does away with the idea that contemporary theater writing doesn't produce good plays." Another factory worker compared Zamyatin to Shakespeare and said, "The play is tragic, extremely saturated with action, and will engage the audience very much." A third laborer found that "all the episodes in the play were strong and fascinating." This was the contemporary equivalent of rave reviews—except, of course, in the era of state censorship reviews were supplanted by previews. Zamyatin thought he had succeeded: his nearly decade-long nightmare was over, the Soviet Union would recognize him as one of its own, and he would be allowed to serve the regime as a writer. Then the regional censorship authority banned the play. Did Zamyatin realize then that the ban had nothing to do with the content or style of his writing? Did he know that writers, like all other people, were subjected to random terror? Did he understand that his ideologically perfect offering was rejected precisely because totalitarianism had no use for transactional obedience, because it demanded unconditional surrender? It seems that he did not.

It makes so much sense—too much sense—to think that *We* was denied publication because it predicted some aspects of Soviet totalitarianism. More likely, though, it was banned primarily because Zamyatin himself had become taboo, because he had somehow fallen out of the community of Soviet writers. The system had expelled him before he rejected the system.

Zamyatin's trajectory does more than subvert the flow of time: it defies logic. This makes Zamyatin not only the original writer of totalitarianism but also one of its original victims. It also marks his biggest mistake as a writer of futurist fiction. In *We*, Zamyatin envisions the tyranny of rationality, a world of relentless causality. Every action has its predictable consequence. Work leads to progress. Progress leads to happiness. The sex act leads to children. Transgression leads to death. Even as Zamyatin's imagined totalitarianism breaks down, it does so in predictable ways. A breach in the wall leads to more life. The development of a soul destroys harmony. The amputation of the soul restores happiness. If only things were so clear.

Totalitarian terror is random. Nothing—not even an upside-down world, an inside-out world, a world that rewards the absence of soul and prizes the death of nature—can be as frightening as a world that makes no sense. True terror works by making everyone believe that they can be imprisoned, condemned, beaten, raped, executed anytime—punished for nothing and everything, without cause, warning, or recourse to justice. What ultimately dates *We*—what, in a sense, reaffirms our perception of time—is that in 1920, Zamyatin could not yet imagine a tyranny of chaos. Which is to say, he could not understand what was happening to him.

The rejection of his play *Atilla* in 1928, followed by a public-shaming campaign over the foreign publication of *We* the next year, robbed Zamyatin of all hope. He was now completely de-published in the Soviet Union. Not a single play of his was in production. His planned collected works were taken off the press. Even translations and academic critical articles, due to go to press, were suddenly canceled. Finally, he lost the last of his board memberships and copyediting gigs. As Zamyatin described it in his letter to Stalin, he was sentenced to a "literary death": he would not be published and he would not be allowed to play even supporting roles in the publishing world.

In his 1931 letter to Stalin, Zamyatin noted that the Soviet penal code provided for the possibility of replacing a death sentence with expulsion from the country. "If I truly am a criminal and deserve to be punished," he wrote, "then I dare suggest that my punishment should not be so severe as a literary death, and so I ask that my sentence be reduced to being sent outside the borders of the USSR, with my wife being granted the right to accompany me. But if I am not a criminal, then I ask that my wife and I be allowed temporarily, at least for a year, to go abroad, so that I may return as soon as it becomes possible in our literature to serve big ideas without serving little people."

Zamyatin got his permission to leave. He moved to Paris, where he lived for the next six years. He died in 1937, the year, it is generally believed, when Stalin's Russia carried out the greatest number of death sentences. A Russian academic lecturing on Zamyatin is likely to add the phrase "of natural causes" when mentioning the year of his death: without such a verbal notation, the audience might be expected to assume the opposite. Zamyatin died in Paris, two years before France was occupied by Nazi Germany, four years before the Holocaust. He died during the Soviet Great Terror, but he appears to have understood little about it. As an émigré, he was writing in Russian. He had become a member of the Union of Soviet Writers. He was, in all likelihood, still hoping to return home, to be a writer there. He still didn't know that the loneliness and lostness he had felt in the 1920s, the nagging feeling that nothing made sense and the obsessive need to extract reason from senselessness were the actual defining experiences of totalitarianism. The feeling of nonexistence permeates the book, but it is an expected, rule-bound nonexistence. A random, punitive, inexplicable nonexistence is not in the novel, perhaps because Zamyatin could not yet imagine it in 1920—or, perhaps, because he could never imagine it, even as he was experiencing it. *We* is a monument to both the possibilities of the human imagination and its limitations: Zamyatin could imagine a nightmare that wasn't, but not the one he was living.

MASHA GESSEN

# INTRODUCTION

*Zamyatin and the Persian Rooster*

*We* is a Russian novel that first saw the light of day in English in New York. If it were not a Russian novel, that publication history would be moderately spectacular, but under the circumstances it is merely unusual. Pasternak's *Doctor Zhivago*, Nadezhda Mandelstam's *Hope Against Hope*, and many another twentieth-century Russian classic have all come out first on foreign soil and in a language other than Russian.

Zamyatin writes in one place that he composed the novel *We* in 1920, but he was known for his habit of revising and polishing, and it seems likely that the final text was not completed until the fall of 1921.[1] It was widely discussed at the time. Zamyatin read parts of it and even the entire novel before various audiences, and the publication of the book was announced on more than one occasion. It was also announced that an English translation was under way, and this translation, by Gregory Zilboorg,[2] was to have the distinction of being the *editio princeps*. It was first published by Dutton in 1924.

Translations into other languages followed, but it is curious to explore the trail left by Zilboorg's pioneering work, which, though it was not in Zamyatin's own language, nevertheless seemed to enjoy all the rights of primogeniture. Ilya Ehrenburg, that indefatigable middleman of literary commerce between Russia and the West, appears to have been the instigator of the French translation. He wrote to Zamyatin on January 12, 1926, saying he'd gotten the manuscript from Vienna and wanted to bring it to the attention of several French publishers. "But for this the English translation is indispensable (the publishers don't know Russian and everyone here reads English)."[3]

The French *We* eventually appeared as *Nous autres*, translated by B. Cauvet-Duhamel, in 1929. I should add that it was the publishers who needed the English version from Ehrenburg in order to make up their minds. It was not needed by Cauvet-Duhamel, who evidently worked independently and from a Russian manuscript essentially the same as Zilboorg's. His version is by far the freest of those known to me, but that he did not depend upon Zilboorg is shown by his having correctly translated passages in which Zilboorg made mistakes. (For example: Zilboorg, p. 103: I am almost the only one *in this room*. Cauvet-Duhamel correctly translates: Je suis presque seul *à la maison*. p. 116.)

By this time, Zamyatin was in considerable trouble at home over these foreign editions of a book that could not get permission to come out in its own country and language. He was merely one of the first of a distinguished company of Soviet writers to suffer in this way.

What finally furnished a *casus belli* to his enemies at home was the publication of *We* in Prague. A Czech translation by Václav Koenig appeared in 1927 in the Brno newspaper *Lidové noviny*. Roman Jakobson, later a professor at Harvard and world famous as a literary theorist, was in Prague and had written to Zamyatin on August 16, 1926, to inform him of the forthcoming publication in Czech, and also to complain that his copy of the manuscript was very careless, though he thought the defects reparable. All the words in Latin characters had, for instance, been omitted (not uncommon, if a lazy typist on a Cyrillic keyboard will not take the trouble to pencil in Latin letters, of which there are quite a few in *We*). This would seem to indicate that Jakobson had in hand a Russian manuscript that differed in important ways from that used by Zilboorg. At any rate, he asked Zamyatin not for a more reliable Russian typescript but for a copy of Zilboorg's translation, of which he had only heard: "We therefore need at least one copy of the English book. Kindly inform us who the publisher was and when it appeared."[4] The same Czech translation came out that same year in book form.

Marc Slonim, a prolific Russian literary critic and later a professor at Sarah Lawrence College, was also in Prague in the late twenties, and he wished to bring the novel out in Russian in the important journal *Volya Rossii* (Russia's Will), which he edited there for the already numerous Russian émigré readership around the world. But, knowing that the publication in Russian of a Russian book on foreign soil, and in a journal opposed to the regime at home, would cause Zamyatin grief, Slonim took extraordinary steps to make it appear that his text had actually resulted from a retranslation from the Czech. This might protect Zamyatin from being charged with abetting the publication by supplying a Russian manuscript.[5]

The deliberately cryptic editorial note in *Volya Rossii* reads: "One of the most interesting works of modern literature, E. Zamyatin's novel *We*, depicting the life of people in the 26th Century, has not yet appeared . . . in Russian. Wishing to acquaint readers of *Volya Rossii* with the novel, we have taken advantage of the fact that a Czech translation of *We* has been published in the paper *Lidové noviny* in Brno. With the editor's gracious permission, we herewith present excerpts from the novel. For greater accuracy and approximation to the original, we have everywhere collated the Czech translation with the English, which came out in New York in 1925 [sic]."[6]

To enhance his deception, Slonim took the even more extraordinary (and deplorable) step of actually rewriting parts of the Russian manuscript in his possession. Of this thoroughly corrupt text only excerpts were actually published: twenty-two chapters, not all of them complete, of the forty in Zamyatin's novel. What use Slonim could have made of Zilboorg's English translation is not clear, but it seems to have played some part in this troubled appearance of *We*. Slonim might have saved himself the trouble. Zamyatin's detractors in the Soviet Union might have been wicked men, but they were not stupid, and no one believed that a Russian *We* had been reconstituted out of a Czech translation, helped along by an American translation.

This abridged Russian version, further camouflaged by the

editor's well-meaning mutilation of Zamyatin's text, hardly qualifies as the first appearance of *We* in its original language. For that long-postponed event it had to return to New York, where, twenty-eight years after its first English shadow had appeared, the genuine article was published in Zamyatin's own Russian words: *My* (New York: Izdatelstvo imeni Chekhova [Chekhov Publishing House], 1952).

That Russian text is the basis of this new English translation, and it is the one that was finally published, in 1988, on Russian soil.

Yevgeny Ivanovich Zamyatin was born on January 20, 1884, in the small provincial town of Lebedyan, which lay on the bank of the River Don 200 miles to the south of Moscow and which, for all its diminutive size, had a reputation thanks to Turgenev's story of the same name. He died in exile in Paris on March 10, 1937. Memoirists recall him as an infinitely citified man, dapper to a fault, and as elegant in manner as in dress. He might have struck his fellow Russians as "English" even if he had not spent some two years building Russian icebreakers in England during the First World War and acquiring a taste for London tailoring.

The point is that he combined in his person the two belligerents, the City and the Country, in the 200-Years War that preceded the establishment of OneState, the grimly germ-free capital of *We*. Lebedyan, defiantly redneck, was synonymous with a kind of rambunctious Russianism, whereas Leningrad (Petrograd when he was writing the novel there, and now St. Petersburg once again) was the least Russian and most cosmopolitan of all Russian cities. An extensive exile by the tsarist regime reacquainted him with solitary life in the remote countryside. And he spent his final years in Paris, Walter Benjamin's "capital of the Nineteenth Century."

The consciousness that presides over both sides in the novel—the immaculately mechanized Numbers of OneState and the wild natural people on the other side of the Green Wall—was by no means neutral. It was all on the side of the irruption of the natural and unplanned and spontaneous (the Country) into the dead routine of OneState. But this consciousness had itself been sufficiently polished by the international urbanity and culture of St. Petersburg to lend verisimilitude and sympathy to its deputy consciousness in the novel, the first-person voice of D-503, who is nothing if not a True Believer in every aspect of the City that Zamyatin hated.

It is perhaps better not to be too solemn about Zamyatin's wonderfully appealing novel. Its distinction as a work of art and its importance as a political statement about several peculiarly modern dilemmas will need little defense—its having constantly found a wide international audience ever since it first came out in 1924 seems an earnest of that. And for George Orwell, author of *1984*, and for certain others bent on creating their own dystopias, it appears to have been *the* crucial literary experience. But new readers, especially those devoted to highly sophisticated modern science fiction—the sort encapsulated in the *New York Times* television guide as "fast vivid sci-fi adventure about a ruthless cyborg programmed for assassination"—will scarcely be able to avoid, as an initial reaction, a sort of indulgent amusement. But Zamyatin himself called it both his most lighthearted and his most serious work, so it is okay to laugh at it so long as you remain alive to a seriousness that has not diminished over time.

There's a terrific Buck Rogers atmosphere to the whole thing, and I can't help feeling that illustrations from that venerable early sci-fi strip would be the best visual counterpoint to the text. I am thinking of the scene on board the INTEGRAL during the test flight of the space probe (designed and built by D-503) when I-330, who seems to our madly infatuated narrator to have grown a whole head taller, is described as looking, in her headphone helmet, like a winged Valkyrie. I had a strong recollection of the film of an early Buck Rogers serial that my father once brought home to install on our ancient two-reel home movie projector. The animation was hilariously bad. The spaceship jerked across the screen emitting perfect little doughnuts of speed-cloud, straight out of the comic strip. The animated figures were clad in armor, of course.

I recall that the breastplates jiggled so much they looked like brassieres gone berserk (my youngest brother said, "No, that is where they keep their hamsters!" and we all fell out of our chairs). Anyone who can read an evocation of erotic frenzy like *Blue sparks from her, and the scent of lightning, and my trembling gets faster and faster* with complete facial composure has, in my view, a problem. People walk about on the deck of the INTEGRAL during lift-off, undistracted by what Flann O'Brien's Sgt. Pluck would no doubt call "extravagant combustions of the most far-reaching kind."[7]

Hearing that I was about to undertake a new translation of Zamyatin's novel, a Russian friend ruefully wished me well, hoping that I might breathe new life into "that old post-modern monster." At the time, I took "postmodern" as little more than a nod toward contemporary cant. But the more I thought of it, the more it seemed to me that *We*, and all similar dystopias, are among the only works that truly deserve to be called postmodern. If "modern" means what any reader in any conceivable "today" regards as up-to-date opinion and style, then every imagined distant future will be irretrievably "post" all such notions.

But the novel as a form, whatever its ostensible setting, is always about the time in which it is written. Zamyatin's nightmare is a nightmare of the early twenties, and it is specifically the nightmare of a Russian who has spent time in the industrial north of England and read H. G. Wells, never forgetting his native Dostoevsky nor what he could see out the window.

Orwell's *1984* deals with the threat ripening even as he wrote (1948) within English Socialism, which he turned into "Ingsoc" for the oppressive world presided over by Big Brother. Russell Hoban's *Riddley Walker*,[8] set in a corner of England that had been bombed back into the Stone Age by a nuclear holocaust, is what it is because, at the time Hoban was writing, an American general had said his aircraft would do precisely that to villagers in Southeast Asia: bomb them back into the Stone Age. I imagine that Hoban simply wondered what this might be like, and gave a contemporary answer, though it was set in some hideously primitive future. Novels about the distant past are also about the day in which they are composed: They are about that day's conception of the distant past, that day's information and delusions, and nothing else.

In Zamyatin's time, when the Russian Bolsheviks were consolidating the revolution they had just taken over, human perfectibility was being talked about with utterly deadpan faces by platoons of well-meaning or malicious imbeciles. Part of man's bright future as a machine rested on the theories of an American efficiency expert named Frederick Winslow Taylor (1856–1915). This "father of scientific management" pioneered the time-and-motion studies that transformed industrial workers into maximally efficient adjuncts of the machines they were hired to operate. He was naturally seen as something of a messiah by management, while his name was universally execrated on the shop floor. Even so powerful a figure as Nadezhda Krupskaya, Lenin's consort in what was to become the modern world's most ruthless managerial class, wrote in praise of Taylor's theories. The novelist, meditating on where "Taylorism" might lead if taken to extremes, conceived of a *reductio ad absurdum* in which characters behave as nearly as possible as though they themselves were fail-safe pieces of hardware.

The reason why *We* could not appear in Russia until 1988 was that the Soviet cultural authorities, with an instinct for heresy second only to that of the Curia itself, immediately saw it as a travesty of the regime. Zilboorg promoted this reading in the preface to his 1924 translation in New York, and the political interpretation of *We* has been unquestioned ever since. Its being retrospectively read in the light of such an overtly political work as Orwell's *1984* has further institutionalized this estimate. I therefore think it is worth insisting at the very outset that the reception of Zamyatin's fable has always been far more political than the work itself.

The book is not even particularly Russian. There is something peculiarly apt about its having come out first in English translation, for once you remove the Russian language (and perhaps two minor characters, the *babushkas* who act as guardians of the Ancient House and D-503's building), what is left is a sort of generalized human society. Part of Zamyatin's point, surely, is that his nightmare state lacks the warm smell and taste of long human habitation, lacks any of the recognizable attributes of nationhood. Nothing is made, for instance, of the nationality of Taylor. OneState is not to be blamed on the Americans or the Bolsheviks or the industrial lords of Liverpool and Manchester. It is the fate toward which a thoughtless humanity is hurtling.

As for the inspiration of the novel, as opposed to the text that resulted, that seems far more English than Russian. It is when one sets *We* in the context of the subsequent dystopias by Huxley and Orwell that one realizes, in fact, how extremely English the roots of the novel are. Among his major productions, Zamyatin's short novel *Islanders* is what immediately precedes *We*. This obviously derives from his experiences during the two-year sojourn in the British Isles and is a parody of stuffy suburban English bourgeois life, which has already taken significant steps in the direction of OneState. Eliminate the proper names from the first paragraph of *Islanders*, and it sounds exactly as though it might have come from the novel *We*:

> Vicar Dooley was, of course, the well-known Dooley, the pride of Jesmond and author of the book *The Testament of Compulsory Salvation*. Schedules worked out according to the *Testament* were hung about the walls of Mr. Dooley's library. The schedule of the hours of ingestion; the schedule of the days of repentance (twice a week); the schedule for the utilization of fresh air; the schedule for charitable undertakings; and finally, among others, there was one schedule which for reasons of delicacy had no heading and touched specifically on Mrs. Dooley. Here the Saturdays of every third week were marked.[9]

This last item on Vicar Dooley's schedule (the reminder to engage in sexual congress with his wife) recalls not only the Table of Hours in OneState, with its sanitary provisions for the Sexual Hour, but also the opening of that most English of books, Laurence Sterne's *Tristram Shandy*, with its methodical attention to the same family matter.

As one might expect, the English authors are far more conscious of social class (in *We* there are no classes to speak of, only the Benefactor and everyone else). In fact, one of the underlying jokes is that the only one truly entitled to the pronoun "we" is the Benefactor, who makes royal use of it; the proles are merely encouraged to think that they are "we," just as they are encouraged to think that they actually vote. Far from being "we," they are merely "them." This is like the underlying joke of Gogol's masterpiece: The real "dead souls" are not those on the rosters of dead serfs but the serf-owners, the masters themselves.

That *We* has even a faintly English tone to it is not due, of course, to the Englishmen who followed it but to the Englishman, H. G. Wells, who preceded Zamyatin and everyone else in the peculiar genre in which they were all working. Zamyatin knew the works of Wells intimately. He edited a series of them for publication in Russian translation, and his preface to that enterprise is one of his most acute essays.[10] But if the visionary Wells gave everyone the idea, he was repaid by the usual black ingratitude. Zamyatin, Huxley, and Orwell all wrote savage satires of the idea of a scientific utopia.

Like *The Brothers Karamazov* and many another Russian novel, *We* involves the conflict not so much of individuals as of the ideas they embody. The individuals share with most other characters in dystopic fiction a certain schematic thinness of development. The warring ideas, however, impose themselves with a roundness and undeniability on every page.

There are two occasions when each idea receives its canonical statement from the mouth of each of the two real antagonists of the story, the Benefactor and I-330.

The Benefactor, the ancestor of Orwell's Big Brother, is the absolute ruler of OneState. That he united traits of Vladimir Lenin and Dostoevsky's Grand Inquisitor was obvious to the point of surgical pain for Zamyatin's contemporaries. He rules over a human society that is deemed to have achieved, with only negligible exceptions, absolute perfection. Men have finally become, if not actually machines, as machine-like as possible, utterly predictable and completely happy. All the messy inconvenience of freedom has been eliminated. Mere details, a final touch-up here and there, one last adjustment— these are all that remain. The Great Operation at the end (a sort of lobotomy for the removal of Man's last imperfection, the Imagination) is the final touch. That not every Number wishes to go under the knife is understandable, but (and here one hears the authentic voice of Dostoevsky's Grand Inquisitor) seeming cruelty can be the most genuine love of Mankind.

The Benefactor's opponent is I-330, a woman so liberated that even today one can only surmise what a jolt she must have delivered to the systems of her first readers. Gorgeous by nature, she is happy to enhance her beauty by the outlawed cosmetics and perfumes obtainable only by stealth. She drinks and smokes, activities known to the Numbers of OneState only through historical study. She enjoys sex but is not above using it as a weapon for the movement. She is big-hearted enough to find shelter for her rival, O-90, who wants to go through with the crime of bearing D-503's child. She is powerful enough to be the leader of a revolutionary underground, the Mephi. And she is courageous enough to endure the Benefactor's worst tortures and die rather than talk. She is also the philosophical voice of Zamyatin's favorite idea, the central thematic idea of the book.

When, some two years after We was finished, Zamyatin got around to putting this idea into essay form, he used the speech of I-330 as an epigraph. The essay is titled "On Literature, Revolution, Entropy, and Other Matters" (1923). The epigraph derives from Record 30, the philosophical core of the book. She stumps the mathematician and engineer D-503 by asking him to name the final number. To his objection that the number of numbers is infinite, she replies that so is the number of revolutions. There can be no final revolution. One imagines how sweetly this fell upon the ear of the Bolsheviks, whose first business, after commandeering one revolution, was to root out and destroy the slightest suspicion of a second.

The two forces at war, like the Country and the City, the

Mephi and OneState, are Energy and Entropy. Zamyatin's essay tends to be overrated as an essay simply because it is so splendid as a commentary on his masterpiece. For all its characteristic brevity and briskness, the essay manages to drop some weighty names: Louis XIV, Euclid, Lobachevsky, Galileo, Babeuf, Darwin, Lamarck, Schopenhauer, Dostoevsky, Nietzsche, Tolstoy, Gorky, Chekhov, and others. One eloquent name is suppressed, that of Heraclitus, possibly because it was Heraclitus who, some 500 years before Christ, gave the central idea of the essay its classical expression. Nothing is final. The only reality is change.

Zamyatin's merit is not to have discovered this, nor to have rehabilitated an old idea by dressing it in the latest fashion of the Second Law of Thermodynamics and Einsteinian Relativity, nor to have made the highly questionable if only metaphoric leap across the boundary from physical science to human social organization. His merit was and remains to have turned the idea into an enduring fable that immediately caught the imagination of the world and gave rise to others, like *1984*. *We* is indeed a clunky old postmodern monster, inhabited by women in headphones who look like radio Valkyries, but it has never lost its hold on the affection of readers, who have kept it constantly in print in dozens of languages ever since it appeared.

The translation in your hands is the latest of several English versions. I shall not undertake a detailed argument for proposing a new one at this time, though the discussion of two terms, one of them major and one minor, might serve as specimen motives for my trying anew to put *We* into English.

The minor term first. The inhabitants of OneState have only numbers, no names, and they all wear the same uniform, only the word "uniform," the author tells us, has been worn down by time to "unif." That's what Zamyatin writes in Russian, the Cyrillic equivalents of those four letters: u-n-i-f. All previous translators known to me have opted for "unif" in their English versions.

This struck me as wrong. I did not think an English speaker

(and an English translation has no other point than to make the characters English speakers) would naturally come up with "unif" as the worn-down stump of "uniform." So I made it "yuny," jettisoning the *f* (which seemed to me especially clumsy when clustered with an *s* in the plural: "unifs") and adding an initial *y* to make the pronunciation unmistakable.

When I was already near the end, locked in forever to this decision, I was listening one evening to John Sterling doing the play-by-play for a Yankees game over WABC in New York. There had been a rain delay, and the field was dotted with puddles. The right fielder Jesse Barfield was racing for a high fly that was obviously going to land somewhere near the warning track when he slipped on a slick spot. "And not only did he miss the ball," said the ever-playful John Sterling, "but he got his *yuny* wet!" I felt like grabbing a cab for the Bronx to throw my arms round his neck in gratitude. I had got it right: "Yuny" is the spontaneous and natural American reduction of "uniform."

The major term is the name of the state itself. What to do about that? The Russian name is *Yedinoe Gosudarstvo.* The last word, the noun, presents no problem: It means state. The meaning of the adjective clusters around the idea of singularity: one, single, united, unified, only. My predecessors have opted for United State or Single State or even The One State. All of these seem to me bad. Single State is a cliché for bachelorhood. United State is worse. The normal reader's eye involuntarily adds an *s.* It strikes me as significant that Alexandra Aldridge specifically warns her readers against this.[11] But even if they should heed the warning, readers might subconsciously associate Zamyatin's nightmare state with the actual United States. This country has been the fictional locale of enough dystopias already without inviting readers to place on this continent one that was not, I think, meant to be specifically American.

Consider again Russell Hoban's *Riddley Walker.* There is a mythical figure, the object of a cult, called Eusa who is worshipped or execrated, who is or is not to blame for the nuclear holocaust. Only this stump of a name suggests identification with the USA, but the allusion is definitely and operatively there in the fiction.

It is not there in Zamyatin's *We*. The realm of the Benefactor is as much the UK as it is the USA, as much Germany as it is Russia. Its name ought to be neutral. I've called it by the ugly name OneState. The writing of this name with no space and with the capital in the middle copies a current fashion, much in vogue among the computer elite, and even more among their agents of publicity, which I hope most readers will join me in detesting. But detesting OneState is, after all, a sign of mental and spiritual health.

Fatigued and disheartened by the uninterrupted viciousness of the campaign against him, the ever-unconventional Zamyatin simply wrote to the Benefactor, Iosif Stalin, saying that he'd done nothing to deserve death, and that for a writer to be denied every avenue to publication was the same thing as death. He therefore asked permission to go live abroad. Stalin, perhaps astonished or amused by such candor, and also no doubt on the advice of Gorky, granted the wish. Zamyatin quit his homeland forever in 1931.

In his Paris exile, he lived mostly apart from the large Russian community and wrote very little. He was only occasionally noticed. One interview he granted to the French press amused him to the extent of provoking in reply a sort of parodic self-interview, which lay unpublished in a Columbia University archive until Zamyatin's distinguished American biographer Alex Shane unearthed it and printed it (in Russian) in 1972.[12] Zamyatin, informing an imaginary French public about the current state of Soviet letters, said that the problem uppermost was still that of the individual personality versus the collective. He had, he said, written a novel, *We*, that was the first to expose this problem.

But he was reminded of the Persian rooster. "Once in the Caucasus I heard a Persian fairy tale about a rooster who had the bad habit of crowing an hour earlier than the others. This caused the owner of the rooster so much inconvenience that he chopped off his rooster's head. *We* turned out to be a Persian rooster. It was still too early to raise this problem, especially in such a form. So, after the novel was published (in various foreign translations) the Soviet critics hacked me about the head rather fiercely. But I must be solidly built, for my head, as you see, is still on my shoulders."

CLARENCE BROWN
PRINCETON, NEW JERSEY, 1992

# NOTES

1. Shane, A. M. *The Life and Works of Evgenij Zamjatin.* Berkeley: University of California Press, 1968, p. 38n.

2. Gregory Zilboorg (1890–1959) was born in Kiev. He trained as a psychiatrist, graduating from the Psychoneurological Institute in Petrograd in 1917. Zilboorg served as a doctor in the Russian Army during World War I and took part in the February Revolution of 1917. In 1919 he emigrated to the United States, where he studied for a time at Columbia University and occupied himself with literary translation. He later practiced psychiatry.

3. *Russian Literature Triquarterly,* 2 (1972), p. 469.

4. Zamyatin, *Sochineniya* [Works]. Moscow: Kniga, 1988, p. 526.

5. See Slonim's Preface to *We,* translated by G. Zilboorg. New York: Dutton, 1959.

6. *Volya Rossii* [Russia's Will], 1 (1927), p. 3. Quoted in Zamyatin, *Sochineniya* [Works]. Moscow: Kniga, 1988, p. 527.

7. In *The Third Policeman* (1967). This little-known and incomparably hilarious modern dystopia presents Hell as an idyllic Irish countryside presided over by demented bicycle policemen.

8. London: Jonathan Cape, 1980.

9. Zamyatin, "Ostrovityane" [Islanders], in *Izbrannye proizvedeniya* [Selected Works]. Sovetsky pisatel', 1989, p. 262.

10. For a translation of this essay see *A Soviet Heretic,* edited and translated by Mirra Ginsburg. Chicago: University of Chicago Press, 1970.

11. *The Scientific World View in Dystopia.* Ann Arbor: UMI Research Press, 1984, p. 37.

12. "Avtointerv'yu" [Autointerview], *Russian Literature Triquarterly,* 2 (1972), p. 464.

# SUGGESTIONS FOR FURTHER READING

Aldridge, Alexandra, *The Scientific World View in Dystopia*. Ann Arbor: UMI Research Press, 1984.

Brown, E. J., *"Brave New World, 1984, and We: An Essay on Anti-Utopia."* Ardis Essay Series, 4. Ann Arbor: Ardis, 1976. An earlier version appeared in *American Contributions to the Fifth International Congress of Slavists*, Vol. II. The Hague: Mouton, 1963.

Collins, Christopher, *Evgenii Zamiatin: An Interpretive Study*. The Hague, 1973.

Heller, Leonid (ed.), *Autour de Zamiatine*. Actes du colloque, Université de Lausanne, juin 1987. Lausanne: Editions de L'Age d'Homme, 1989.

Jackson, Robert Louis, *Dostoevskij's Underground Man in Russian Literature*. The Hague: Mouton, 1958.

Rhodes, C. H., "Frederick Winslow Taylor's System of Scientific Management in Zamyatin's *We*," *Journal of General Education*, 28 (1976), pp. 31–42.

Richards, D. J., *Zamyatin: A Soviet Heretic*. London, 1962.

*Russian Literature Triquarterly*, 2 (1972). Ann Arbor: Ardis.

Shane, A. M., *The Life and Works of Evgenij Zamjatin*. Berkeley: University of California Press, 1968.

Zamiatin, Eugene. *We*. Translated by Gregory Zilboorg. Introduction by Peter Rudy. Preface by Marc Slonim. New York: E. P. Dutton & Co., 1959.

Zamiatine, Eugène. *Nous autres*. Traduit par B. Cauvet-Duhamel. Preface de Jorge Semprun. Paris: Gallimard, 1971.

Zamyatin, Yevgeny. *Izbrannye proizvedeniya* [Selected Works]. Moscow: Sovetsky pisatel', 1989.

Zamyatin, Yevgeny. *My* [We]. New York: Chekhov Publishing House, 1952.

Zamyatin, Yevgeny. *Sochineniya* [Works]. Moscow: Kniga Publishers, 1988.

Zamyatin, Yevgeny. *A Soviet Heretic*. Edited and translated by Mirra Ginsburg. Chicago: University of Chicago Press, 1970.

# WE

# RECORD 1

*Announcement*

*The Wisest of Lines*

*An Epic Poem*

I am merely copying out here, word for word, what was printed today in the *State Gazette*:

> In 120 days from now the building of the INTEGRAL will be finished. Near at hand is the great, historic hour when the first INTEGRAL will lift off into space. A thousand years ago your heroic forebears subjugated the whole of planet Earth to the power of OneState. It is for you to accomplish an even more glorious feat: by means of the glass, the electric, the fire-breathing INTEGRAL to integrate the indefinite equation of the universe. It is for you to place the beneficial yoke of reason round the necks of the unknown beings who inhabit other planets—still living, it may be, in the primitive state known as freedom. If they will not understand that we are bringing them a mathematically infallible happiness, we shall be obliged to force them to be happy. But before taking up arms, we shall try what words can do.
>
> In the name of the Benefactor, all Numbers of OneState are hereby informed of the following:
>
> Everyone who feels himself capable of doing so is required to compose treatises, epic poems, manifestos, odes, or other compositions dealing with the beauty and grandeur of OneState.

This will be the first cargo transported by the INTE-
GRAL.

Long live OneState! Long live the Numbers! Long live
the Benefactor!

As I write this I feel my cheeks burning. Yes: to integrate
completely the colossal equation of the universe. Yes: to un-
bend the wild curve, to straighten it tangentially, asymptoti-
cally, to flatten it to an undeviating line. Because the line of
OneState is a straight line. The great, divine, precise, wise
straight line—the wisest of all lines . . .

I, D-503, builder of the INTEGRAL, I am only one of the
mathematicians of OneState. My pen, accustomed to figures,
is powerless to create the music of assonance and rhyme. I
shall attempt nothing more than to note down what I see,
what I think—or, to be more exact, what we think (that's
right: we; and let this WE be the title of these records). But
this, surely, will be a derivative of our life, of the mathemati-
cally perfect life of OneState, and if that is so, then won't this
be, of its own accord, whatever I may wish, an epic? It will; I
believe and I know that it will.

I feel my cheeks burning as I write this. This is probably like
what a woman feels when she first senses in her the pulse of a
new little person, still tiny and blind. It's me, and at the same
time it's not me. And for long months to come she will have to
nourish it with her own juice, her own blood, and then—tear
it painfully out of herself and lay it at the feet of OneState.

But I am ready. Like all of us, or nearly all of us. I am ready.

# RECORD 2

*Ballet*

*Harmony Squared*

*X*

It's spring. From beyond the Green Wall, from the wild plains out of sight in the distance, the wind is carrying the honeyed yellow pollen of some flower. This sweet pollen dries the lips—you keep running your tongue over them—and every woman you meet (and every man, too, of course) must have these sweet lips. This somewhat interferes with logical thought.

And then what a sky! Blue, unsullied by a single cloud (what primitive tastes the ancients must have had if their poets were inspired by those absurd, untidy clumps of mist, idiotically jostling one another about). I love—and I am sure that I am right in saying *we* love—only such a sky as this one today: sterile and immaculate. On days like this the whole world seems to have been cast of the same immovable and everlasting glass as the Green Wall, as all of our structures. On days like this you can see into the deep blue depth of things, you see their hitherto unsuspected, astonishing equations—you see this in the most ordinary, the most everyday things.

Here, take this for instance. Just this morning I was at the hangar where the INTEGRAL is being built—and suddenly I caught sight of the equipment: the regulator globes, their eyes closed, oblivious, were twirling round; the cranks were glistening and bending to the left and right; the balance beam was proudly heaving its shoulders; the bit of the router was squatting athletically to the beat of some unheard music. I suddenly saw the whole beauty of this grandiose mechanical ballet, flooded with the light of the lovely blue-eyed sun.

But why—my thoughts continued—why beautiful? Why is the dance beautiful? Answer: because it is *nonfree* movement, because all the fundamental significance of the dance lies precisely in its aesthetic subjection, its ideal nonfreedom. And if it is true that our ancestors gave themselves over to dancing at the most inspired moments of their lives (religious mysteries, military parades), that can mean only one thing: that from time immemorial the instinct of nonfreedom has been an organic part of man, and that we, in our present-day life, are only deliberately . . .

I'll have to finish this later: The intercom screen just clicked. I lift my eyes: O-90, of course. In half a minute she'll be here herself, coming to get me for our walk.

Dear O! It always struck me that she looks like her name: about ten centimeters shorter than the Maternal Norm, and therefore sort of rounded all over, and the pink O of her mouth, open to greet every word I say. And also, she has a sort of circular, puffy crease at her wrist, the way children have.

When she came in, my logical flywheel was still humming away inside me and the inertia carried me on to start talking about the formula I'd just come up with—the one containing us and the machines and the dance.

"Wonderful, isn't it?" I asked.

"Yes, wonderful. It's spring." O-90 smiled at me rosily.

There. How's that for you? Spring. She's right away on spring. Women. I didn't say a word.

We went down. The avenue was jammed. When the weather's like this, we usually take an extra walk during the Personal Hour after lunch. As usual, all the pipes of the music factory were singing the OneState March. The Numbers were marching along in step in neat ranks of four—hundreds and thousands of them in their sky-blue yunies* with the golden

---

*Probably from the old word *uniform*.

badge on each chest bearing each one's state number. And I, or rather we, our four, were one of the innumerable waves in that mighty flood. To my left was O-90 (if one of my hirsute ancestors from a thousand years back were writing this, he'd probably modify her with that funny word *my*); on my right were two Numbers I didn't know, a female and a male.

Blessedly blue sky, little baby suns on each badge, faces undimmed by anything so crazy as thought. Rays, you see. Everything made out of some kind of uniform, radiant, smiling matter. And the beat of the brass: Tra-ta-ta. Tra-ta-ta. Brass paces gleaming in the sun. And every pace carries you up higher and higher into the dizzying blue. . . .

And then, just the way it was this morning in the hangar, I saw again, as though right then for the first time in my life, I saw everything: the unalterably straight streets, the sparkling glass of the sidewalks, the divine parallelepipeds of the transparent dwellings, the squared harmony of our gray-blue ranks. And so I felt that I—not generations of people, but I myself—I had conquered the old God and the old life, I myself had created all this, and I'm like a tower, I'm afraid to move my elbow for fear of shattering the walls, the cupolas, the machines. . . .

And then there came a moment, a leap across the centuries, from + to –. I recalled (association by contrast, apparently), I suddenly recalled a picture in the museum: one of the avenues they had back then, after twenty centuries—a stunningly garish, mixed-up crush of people, wheels, animals, posters, trees, colors, birds . . . And they say it really was like that. It could have been like that. It all struck me as so unlikely, so idiotic, that I couldn't help it, I burst out laughing.

And suddenly there was an echo, laughter, from the right. I turned. Before my eyes were teeth—white, uncommonly white, sharp teeth—and a woman's face that I didn't know.

"I'm sorry," she said, "but the way you were looking at everything, it was inspired—like you were some god out of myth on the seventh day of creation. I think you believe you created me, too—you and nobody else. I'm very flattered."

All this with a straight face. I'd even say, with a kind of

respect (maybe she knows I'm the builder of the INTEGRAL). But I don't know—something about her eyes or brows, some kind of odd irritating X that I couldn't get at all, a thing I couldn't express in numbers.

For some reason this embarrassed and slightly confused me, and I started trying to make up some logical explanation for why I was laughing. It was perfectly clear that this contrast, this unbridgeable gulf between today and back then . . .

"Unbridgeable? But why?" (What white teeth!) "You could build a little bridge across the gulf. Just imagine: a drum, battalions, ranks—they used to have all that, too. So it follows that . . ."

"Well, yes, that's right!" I shouted. (This was an amazing example of mental crossover—she said almost in my very words exactly what I'd been writing before going to walk.) "You see? Even thoughts. That's because no one is *one* but only *one of*. We're so identical. . . ."

She said, "Are you sure?"

I saw the sharp angle her brows made when she lifted them toward her temples—like the sharp horns of an X, and for some reason I got confused again. I looked to the right, to the left . . . and . . .

She was to my right—slender, sharp, tough, and springy as a whip: I-330 (now I saw her number). To my left was O, completely different, everything about her round, with the babyish crease on her arm. And at the end of our group of four was a male Number that I didn't know. He bent in two places, like the letter S. We were all different. . . .

That one on the right, I-330, must have noticed my confused look.

"Yes . . . too bad!" she said with a sigh.

That "too bad" was absolutely called-for, no doubt about it. But again there was something in her face or her voice. . . .

So I said, very abruptly, which wasn't like me at all: "Nothing's *too bad*. Science is going forward, and it's clear that, maybe not right away, but in fifty or a hundred years . . ."

"Even the noses on everybody . . ."

"Yes, the noses!" I was practically shouting. "Once there's

some . . . never mind what reason for envy. Once I have a button nose and someone else has . . ."

"Well, now, if it comes to that, your nose is even rather *classical*, as they used to say in the old days. But as for your hands . . . No, come on now, show me, show me your hands!"

I can't stand people looking at my hands. They're hairy, shaggy, some kind of stupid throwback. I stuck out my hands and said with as steady a voice as I could manage: "A monkey's hands."

She looked at my hands and then at my face.

"Yes, there's an extraordinarily curious harmony." She weighed me with her eyes as if I were on a scale, and her brows once more looked like horns.

"He's assigned to me," said O-90, her mouth smiling rosily.

It would have been better if she'd not said anything, of course—that was completely beside the point. Besides, that dear O—how should I put this?—her tongue isn't set at the right speed. The mps (motions per second) of the tongue must always be a little less than the mps of thought, and never the other way round.

At the end of the avenue the clock on the accumulator tower was booming out 17:00. The Personal Hour was over. I-330 was walking away with that S-shaped male Number. His face was the kind that inspires a sort of respect, and I now saw that it was even a rather familiar face. I'd met him somewhere—can't recall just now.

In parting, I-330 smiled at me in the same X-like way and said, "Drop by to see me day after tomorrow in auditorium 112."

I shrugged and said, "If I get the order. For the auditorium you mention . . ."

Why she was so sure of herself, I couldn't see, but she said, "You'll get it."

This woman was just as irritating to me as an irrational term that accidentally creeps into your equation and can't be factored out. And I was glad to be alone with my dear O, even if not for long.

We went hand in hand across four lines of avenues. At the corner she was to go right, I left.

"I'd like so much to come to your place today and let the blinds down. Today—right this minute," said O, and shyly looked up at me with her round crystal-blue eyes.

She's a funny one. But what could I say? She was with me only yesterday, and she knows as well as I do that our next Sex Day is the day after tomorrow. It's just more of her thought getting ahead of itself, like a spark that fires too early in the ignition, which can do some harm at times.

Saying goodbye, I kissed her twice—no, I'll tell the truth— three times on those wonderful blue eyes of hers that not the least little cloud ever troubled.

# RECORD 3

*Jacket*

*Wall*

*The Table*

I've looked over what I wrote yesterday and I see it wasn't as clear as it should be. It's perfectly clear for any of us, I mean. But who knows? Maybe you unknown people who'll get my notes when the INTEGRAL brings them—maybe you've read the great book of civilization only up to the page our ancestors reached about 900 years ago. Maybe you don't even know the basics—like the Table of Hours, Personal Hours, Maternal Norm, Green Wall, Benefactor. It feels funny to me, and at the same time it's very hard to talk about all this. It's just as if a writer of the twentieth century, for instance, had to explain in his novel what he meant by "jacket" or "apartment" or "wife." Still, if his novel was translated for savages, there's no way he could write "jacket" without putting in a note.

I'm sure a savage would look at "jacket" and think, "What's that for? Just something else to carry." I think you'll probably look at me the same way when I tell you that not one of us, ever since the 200-Years War, has ever been on the other side of the Green Wall.

But, my dear readers, you'll have to do just a little thinking. It helps a lot. Because, you know, all human history, as far back as we know it, is the history of moving from nomadic life to a more settled way of life. So, doesn't it follow that the most settled form of life (ours) is by the same token the most perfect form of life (ours)? If people used to wander over the earth from one end to the other, that only happened in prehistoric times, when there were nations and wars and trade and discoveries of this and that America. But why do it now? Who needs it?

I'll admit that people did not take to this settled way of life right away and without any trouble. When the 200-Years War destroyed all the roads and the grass covered them over—during that first time it probably seemed very uncomfortable living in cities that were cut off from one another by all the tangled green stuff. But what of that? After man's tail fell off, it was probably some little while before he learned to shoo away the flies without a tail. I don't doubt that during that first time he probably missed his tail. But now—can you even imagine yourself with a tail? Or: Can you imagine yourself walking down the street naked—without your "jacket"? (Maybe you still run around in "jackets.") Well, it's the same here: I can't imagine a city that isn't girdled about with a Green Wall. I can't imagine a life that isn't clad in the numerical robes of the Table.

The Table—at this very minute, from the wall of my room, its purple figures on their golden ground are looking down at me sternly and tenderly, straight in the eyes. I can't help thinking of what the ancients called an "icon," and I feel like composing a poem or a prayer (which is the same thing). Oh, why am I not a poet, so that I might celebrate you properly, O Table, O heart and pulse of OneState!

All of us as schoolchildren (and you too, perhaps) used to read that greatest of all monuments of ancient literature that has come down to us, the *Railroad Timetable*. But set even this next to the Table, and what you'll see is graphite and diamond: They're both one and the same element—C, carbon—but how eternal, transparent, and brilliant is the diamond! Who doesn't catch his breath when he ruffles through the pages of the *Railroad Timetable*? But the Table of Hours—it turns each one of us right there in broad daylight into a steel six-wheeled epic hero. Every morning, with six-wheeled precision, at the very same hour and the very same minute, we get up, millions of us, as though we were one. At the very same hour, millions of us as one, we start work. Later, millions as one, we stop. And then, like one body with a million hands, at one and the same second according to the Table, we lift the spoon to our lips. And at one and the same second we leave for a stroll and go to the auditorium, to the hall for the Taylor exercises, and then to bed.

I'll be completely honest with you: Even we haven't yet solved the problem of happiness with 100 percent accuracy. Twice a day—from 16:00 to 17:00 and again from 21:00 to 22:00—the single mighty organism breaks down into its individual cells. These are the Personal Hours, as established by the Table. During these hours you'll see that some are in their rooms with the blinds modestly lowered; others are walking along the avenue in step with the brass beat of the March; still others, like me at this moment, will be at their desks. But I firmly believe—let them call me idealist and dreamer—but I firmly believe that, sooner or later, one day, we'll find a place for even these hours in the general formula. One day all 86,400 seconds will be on the Table of Hours.

I've read and heard a lot of unbelievable stuff about those times when people lived in freedom—that is, in disorganized wildness. But of all things the very hardest for me to believe was how the governmental power of that time, even if it was still embryonic, could have permitted people to live without even a semblance of our Table, without obligatory walks, without precisely established mealtimes, getting up and going to bed whenever it pleased them. Some historians even claim that in those days lights burned on the streets all night, people were out walking and driving on the streets all night long.

Now, that's something I simply cannot get through my head. No matter how limited their powers of reason might have been, still they must have understood that living like that was just murder, a capital crime—except it was slow, day-by-day murder. The government (or humanity) would not permit capital punishment for one man, but they permitted the murder of millions a little at a time. To kill one man—that is, to subtract 50 years from the sum of all human lives—that was a crime;

but to subtract from the sum of all human lives 50,000,000 years—that was not a crime! No, really, isn't that funny? This problem in moral math could be solved in half a minute by any ten-year-old Number today, but they couldn't solve it. All their Kants together couldn't solve it (because it never occurred to one of their Kants to construct a system of scientific ethics—that is, one based on subtraction, addition, division, and multiplication).

And then—isn't it absurd that a government (it had the nerve to call itself a government) could let sexual life proceed without the slightest control? Who, when, however much you wanted . . . Completely unscientific, like animals. And blindly, like animals, they produced young. Isn't it funny—to know horticulture, poultry keeping, fish farming (we have very precise records of their knowing all this) and not to be able to reach the last rung of this logical ladder: child production. Not to come up with something like our Maternal and Paternal Norms.

It's so funny, so improbable, that now I've written it I'm afraid that you, my unknown readers, will think I'm making wicked jokes. You might suddenly think I'm making fun of you and keeping a straight face while I tell you the most absolute nonsense.

But in the first place, I simply can't make jokes—the default value of every joke is a lie; and in the second place, OneState Science declares that ancient life was exactly as I have described it, and OneState Science cannot make a mistake. Besides, where could any governmental logic have come from, anyway, when people lived in the condition known as freedom—that is, like beasts, monkeys, cattle? What could you have expected from them, if even in our day you can still very occasionally hear coming up from the bottom, from the hairy depths, a wild, ape-like echo?

Only now and again, fortunately. These are, fortunately, no more than little chance details; it's easy to repair them without bringing to a halt the great eternal progress of the whole Machine. And in order to discard some bolt that has gotten bent, we have the heavy, skillful hand of the Benefactor, we have the experienced eye of the Guardians.

Which, now I think of it, reminds me about that Number yesterday with the double bend, like an S—I think I saw him once coming out of the Bureau of Guardians. Now I see why I had that instinctive feeling of respect for him, and why I felt so awkward when that strange I-330, in his presence . . . I must confess that I-330 . . .

That's the bell for sleep. It's 22:30. See you tomorrow.

# RECORD 4

*Savage with Barometer*

*Epilepsy*

*If*

Up to this point I have found everything in life clear (not for nothing do I seem to have a certain partiality for that very word *clear*). But today . . . I don't understand.

First: I did in fact get an order to be in that very auditorium 112, just as she had told me. Although the probability was something like:

$$\frac{1500}{10,000,000} = \frac{3}{20,000}$$

1500 is the number of auditoriums, and 10,000,000 the number of Numbers.

Second: It might be best, however, to go in order.

The auditorium. An immense sunlit hemisphere composed of massive glass sections. Circular rows of nobly spherical, smoothly shaved heads. I looked around with a slightly sinking heart. I think I was searching whether the pink crescent of my dear O's lips would not shine above the blue waves of the yunies. There . . . it looked like someone's very white, shiny teeth . . . but no, not hers. This evening at 21:00 hours O was to come to my place—it was perfectly natural that I'd want to see her here.

The bell. We stood up and sang the Anthem of OneState,

and on the platform appeared the phonolecturer, sparkling with wit and with his golden loudspeaker.

"Honored Numbers! Recently our archaeologists unearthed a book of the twentieth century. The author ironically relates the story of the savage and the barometer. The savage noticed that every time the barometer showed *Rain*, it did in fact rain. And, since the savage wanted it to rain, he found a way to let out just enough mercury so that the thing would point to *Rain*. [The screen showed a savage bedecked with feathers letting out some mercury: general laughter.] You laugh. But don't you think the European of that age was much more to be laughed at? Just like the savage, the European also wanted 'rain.' But *Rain* with a capital letter, algebraic *Rain*. But he stood in front of the barometer like a wet hen. The savage, at least, had more daring, more energy, and more—even if savage—logic. He was able to establish a connection between a cause and its effect. When he let that mercury out, he took the first step along the great path that . . ."

But at this (I repeat: I'm writing what happened, leaving nothing out) I became for a time impermeable to the vivifying stream pouring out of the loudspeaker. It suddenly struck me that I shouldn't have come (why "shouldn't," and how could I not have come, once I'd gotten the order?); it suddenly struck me that everything was empty, an empty shell. And I didn't manage to switch my attention back on until the phonolecturer had gotten down to his basic theme: to our music, to mathematical composition (the mathematician is the cause, the music the result), to a description of the recently invented musicometer.

". . . Simply by turning this handle, any one of you can produce up to three sonatas per hour. And how much labor such a thing cost your ancestors! They could create only by whipping themselves up to attacks of 'inspiration'—some unknown form of epilepsy. And here I have for you a most amusing example of what they got for their trouble—the music of Scriabin, twentieth century. This black box (a curtain was pulled aside on the stage, and there stood one of their ancient instruments), this black box was called a "grand piano," or even a

"Royal Grand," which is merely one more proof, if any were needed, of the degree to which all their music . . ."

And then . . . but again I'm not sure, because it might have been . . . no, I'll say it right out . . . because she, I-330, went up to the "Royal Grand." I was probably just dazzled by how she suddenly turned up, unexpectedly, on the stage.

She was wearing one of the fantastic costumes of ancient times: a tightly fitting black dress, very low cut, which sharply emphasized the whiteness of her shoulders and bosom, and the warm shadow that undulated in time with her breathing between her . . . and her blinding, almost wicked teeth. . . .

Her smile was a bite, and I was its target. She sat down. She began to play. Something wild, spasmodic, jumbled—like their whole life back then, when they didn't have even the faintest adumbration of rational mechanics. And of course those around me were right to laugh, as they all did. But a few of us . . . and I . . . why was I among those few?

Yes, epilepsy is a mental illness—pain . . . A slow, sweet pain—it is a bite—let it bite deeper, harder. And then, slowly, the sun. Not this one, not ours, shining all sky-blue crystal regularity through the glass brick—no: a savage, rushing, burning sun—flinging everything away from itself—everything in little pieces.

The one sitting next to me glanced to his left, at me, and giggled. For some reason I have a very vivid image of what I saw: a microscopic bubble of saliva appeared on his lips and burst. That bubble sobered me. I was myself once again.

Like everyone else, I heard nothing more than the stupid vain clattering of the strings. I laughed. Things became easy and simple. The talented phonolecturer had simply given us a too lively picture of that savage epoch—that's all.

After that, how pleasant it was to listen to our music of today. (A demonstration of it was given at the end, for contrast.) Crystalline chromatic scales of converging and diverging infinite series—and the synoptic harmonies of the formulae of Taylor and Maclaurin, wholesome, quadrangular, and weighty as Pythagoras's pants; mournful melodies of a wavering, diminishing movement, the alternating bright beats of the pauses according to the lines of Frauenhofer—the spectral analysis of the planet . . . What magnificence! What unalterable regularity! And what pathetic self-indulgence was that ancient music, limited only by its wild imaginings. . . .

We left through the broad doors of the auditorium in the usual way, marching four abreast in neat ranks. I caught a glimpse of the familiar double-bent figure somewhere to the side and bowed to him respectfully.

Dear O was to come in an hour. I felt a pleasant and useful excitement. Once home I passed quickly by the desk, handed the duty officer my pink ticket, and got the pass to use the blinds. We get to use the blinds only on Sex Day. Otherwise we live in broad daylight inside these walls that seem to have been fashioned out of bright air, always on view. We have nothing to hide from one another. Besides, this makes it easier for the Guardians to carry out their burdensome, noble task. No telling what might go on otherwise. Maybe it was the strange opaque dwellings of the ancients that gave rise to their pitiful cellular psychology. "My [sic] home is my castle!" Brilliant, right?

At 22:00 hours I lowered the blinds—and at that precise moment O came in, a little out of breath. She gave me her pink lips—and her pink ticket. I tore off the stub, but I couldn't tear myself away from her rosy lips until the very last second: 22:15.

Afterward I showed her my "notes" and spoke—rather well, I think—about the beauty of the square, the cube, the straight line. She listened in her enchantingly rosy way . . . and suddenly a tear fell from her blue eyes . . . then a second, a third . . . right on the page that was open (page 7). Made the ink run. So . . . I'll have to copy it over.

"Dear Dee, if only you . . . if . . ."

Well, what does that "if" mean? "If" what? She was singing the same old tune again: a child. Or maybe it was something new . . . about . . . about that other one. Though even here it seemed as though . . . But no, that would be too stupid.

# RECORD 5

*Square*

*Rulers of the World*

*Pleasant and Useful Function*

Wrong again. Again I'm talking to you, my unknown reader, as though you were . . . well, say, as though you were my old comrade R-13, the poet, the one with the African lips—everyone knows him. You, meanwhile, you might be anywhere . . . on the moon, on Venus, on Mars, on Mercury. Who knows you, where you are and who you are?

Here's what: Imagine a square, a splendid, living square. And he has to tell about himself, about his life. You see—the last thing on earth a square would think of telling about is that he has four equal angles. He simply does not see that, it's so familiar to him, such an everyday thing. That's me. I'm in the situation of that square all the time. Take the pink tickets and all that—to me that's nothing more than the four equal angles, but for you that might be, I don't know, as tough as Newton's binomial theorem.

So. One of the ancient wise men—by accident, of course—managed to say something very smart: "Love and hunger rule the world." *Ergo*: To rule the world, man has got to rule the rulers of the world. Our forebears finally managed to conquer Hunger, by paying a terrible price: I'm talking about the 200-Years War, the war between the City and the Country. It was probably religious prejudice that made the Christian savages

fight so stubbornly for their "bread."* But in the year 35 before the founding of OneState our present petroleum food was
invented. True, only 0.2 of the world's population survived.
On the other hand, when it was cleansed of a thousand years
of filth, how bright the face of the earth became! And what is
more, the zero point two tenths who survived . . . tasted
earthly bliss in the granaries of OneState.

But isn't it clear that bliss and envy are the numerator and
denominator of that fraction known as happiness? And what
sense would there be in all the numberless victims of the 200-
Years War if there still remained in our life some cause for
envy? But some cause did remain, because noses remained, the
button noses and classical noses mentioned in that conversation on our walk, and because there are some whose love many
people want, and others whose love nobody wants.

It's natural that once Hunger had been vanquished (which is
algebraically the equivalent of attaining the summit of material well-being), OneState mounted an attack on that other
ruler of the world, Love. Finally, this element was also conquered, i.e., organized, mathematicized, and our *Lex sexualis*
was promulgated about 300 years ago: "Any Number has the
right of access to any other Number as sexual product."

The rest is a purely technical matter. They give you a careful
going-over in the Sexual Bureau labs and determine the exact
content of the sexual hormones in your blood and work out
your correct Table of Sex Days. Then you fill out a declaration
that on your days you'd like to make use of Number (or Numbers) so-and-so and they hand you the corresponding book of
tickets (pink). And that's it.

So it's clear—there's no longer the slightest cause for envy.
The denominator of the happiness fraction has been reduced
to zero and the fraction becomes magnificent infinity. And the
very same thing that the ancients found to be a source of endless tragedy became for us a harmonious, pleasant, and useful

---

*This word has come down to us only as a poetic metaphor. It is not known
what the chemical composition of this material was.

function of the organism, just like sleep, physical work, eating, defecating, and so on. From this you can see how the mighty power of logic cleanses whatever it touches. Oh, if only you, my unknown readers, could come to know this divine power, if only you too could follow it to the end!

Strange—today I've been writing about the loftiest summits of human history, the whole time I've been breathing the purest mountain air of thought . . . but inside there is something cloudy, something spidery, something cross-shaped like that four-pawed X. Or is it my own paws bothering me, the fact that they've been in front of my eyes so long, these shaggy paws? I don't like talking about them. I don't like them. They're a holdover from the savage era. Can it really be true that I contain . . .

I wanted to cross all that out . . . because that's beyond the scope of these notes. But then I decided: No, I'll leave it in. Let these notes act like the most delicate seismograph, let them register the least little wiggles in my brainwaves, however insignificant. Sometimes, you never know, these are just the wiggles that give you the first warning . . .

But that's absurd, now. I really should cross it out. We've channeled all the elements of nature. No catastrophe can happen.

But now it's perfectly clear to me: That strange inner feeling just comes from my being like the square I spoke about earlier. And there's no X in me (there could not be)—I'm simply worried that there might still be some X in you, my unknown readers. But I have faith that you won't judge me too harshly. I have faith that you will understand how hard it is for me to write, harder than for any other writer in the whole extent of human history: They wrote for their contemporaries, others wrote for posterity, but nobody ever wrote for their ancestors or for people like their wild remote ancestors. . . .

# RECORD 6

*Accident*

*Damned "Clear"*

*24 Hours*

I repeat: I've imposed on myself the duty of writing without holding anything back. So, sad as it may be, I have to record here that apparently even we haven't yet finished the process of hardening and crystallizing life. The ideal is still a long way off. The ideal (this is clear) is that state of affairs where nothing ever happens anymore, but with us . . . Here, just have a look at this: Today I read in the *State Gazette* that two days from now there will be a Justice Gala in Cube Square. So that means that once again some Number has interfered with the progress of the great State Machine, again something unforeseen, unaccounted for in advance, has gone ahead and happened.

And what is more—something has happened to me. True, this happened during the Personal Hour—that is to say, during the time specially set aside for unforeseen circumstances—but still . . .

At about 16:00 hours (or to be precise, at 15:50) I was at home. Suddenly the phone rang.

"D-503?"

"Yes."

"You free?"

"Yes."

"It's me, I-330. I'll fly by for you and we'll go to the Ancient House, okay?"

I-330. That woman annoys me, repels me—almost scares me. But for that very reason I said: "Yes."

Five minutes later we were already in the aero, moving through the sky of the month of May, its blue majolica, and the light sun was zooming along behind us in its own golden aero, keeping up but never passing. But there ahead of us we could see the white cataract of a cloud, a stupid downy thing like the cheek of some antique "cupidon," and that somehow bothered me. The forward window was raised, and the wind dried your lips so that you kept running your tongue over them, which made you constantly think about lips.

Soon you could see in the distance the cloudy green spots—over there, beyond the Wall. Then your heart jumps into your throat, nothing you can do about it, and you sink down, down, down, like a steep fall downhill, and you're at the Ancient House. This entire strange, rickety, godforsaken structure is clad all about in a glass shell. Otherwise, of course, it would have collapsed long ago. At the glass door was an old woman, wrinkled all over, especially her mouth: nothing but wrinkles, pleats, her lips already gone inside, her mouth kind of grown over. And it was against all odds that she could speak. But she spoke.

"Well, my dears, have you come to see my little house?" And her wrinkles shone (that is, they probably folded together in such a way as to look like rays, but it made the impression of shining).

"Yes, Granny. Felt like it again," said I-330.

The wrinkles glowed. "What sun we have today! Isn't it something, though? Such a tease, such a tease . . . but I know. It's all right, you can go ahead by yourselves. I'd better stay here—in the sun."

Hm-m. My companion seems to come here often. I keep feeling I'd like to brush something off me, something bothering me. It's probably that same visual image that I can't shake off: that cloud on the smooth blue of the majolica.

As we were going up the wide, dark staircase, I-330 said: "I love her, that old woman."

"What for?"

"I don't know. Maybe for her mouth. Maybe for nothing at all. I just do."

I shrugged my shoulders. She went on with a sort of smile, or maybe it wasn't a smile: "I feel very guilty. It's clear that one shouldn't love 'just because' but 'because of.' All our natural impulses should be . . ."

"It's clear," I began, then caught myself at the word and stole a glance at I-330 to see whether she'd noticed.

She was looking down at something; her eyes were lowered like blinds.

I thought suddenly of how you walk along the avenue around 22:00 hours, and among the brightly lit cages there are some dark ones, with the blinds lowered. . . . What was going on there in her head, behind her blinds? Why had she phoned me today, and what was all this?

I opened a heavy, squeaking, solid door, and we found ourselves in a gloomy, untidy place (which they used to call an "apartment"). It contained that same strange "royal" instrument as well as a riot of colors and forms that were just as wild and disorganized and crazy as their music. The upper surface was a white plane; the walls were a dark blue; old books were bound in red, green, and orange; the candelabra was of yellow bronze; a statue of Buddha; and the lines of the furniture made lopsided ellipses that could never be accommodated in any conceivable equation.

I could hardly stand this chaos. But my companion, apparently, had a stronger constitution.

"This is my absolute favorite. . . ." And then she suddenly seemed to catch herself, and there was that incisive smile, those sharp white teeth, and she went on: "I mean to say, the absolute stupidest of their so-called 'apartments.'"

"Or to be more precise," I said, "of their states. Thousands of microscopic, eternally belligerent, merciless states, like . . ."

"Oh, yes, of course, that's clear . . ." said she, seemingly quite serious.

We walked through a room containing small beds for children (children were also private property in that era). And there were more rooms, flashing mirrors, gloomy chests, sofas covered in unbearably clashing fabrics, huge "fireplaces," an immense mahogany bed. What we have now—our splendid, transparent, eternal glass—could be seen nowhere except in their pathetic little rickety rectangular windows.

"And just think . . . here they loved 'just because,' they burned, they tormented themselves." Again, she lowered the blinds of her eyes. "What an idiotic, what a wasteful expense of human energy, don't you think?"

It was as though she were speaking with my voice, putting my thoughts into words. But her smile always contained that irritating X. There behind her blinds something . . . I have no idea what . . . was going on in her, something that made me lose all patience. I wanted to argue with her, yell at her (exactly that, yell), but I had to agree. It was impossible not to agree.

And now we stopped in front of the mirror. At that moment all I could see were her eyes. An idea hit me: The way the human body is built, it's just as stupid as those "apartments"— human heads are opaque and there's no way to see inside except through those tiny little windows, the eyes. She seemed to guess what I was thinking and turned around. "Well, here are my eyes. What do you think?" (Without actually saying this, of course.)

I saw before me two ominously dark windows, and inside there was another life, unknown. All I could see was a flame— there was some sort of "fireplace" inside—and some figures, that looked . . .

That would be natural, of course. What I saw there was my own reflection. But it was not natural and it did not look like me (apparently the surroundings were having a depressing effect). I felt absolutely afraid, I felt trapped, shut into that wild cage, I felt myself swept into the wild whirlwind of ancient life.

"You know what . . ." she said. "Go into the next room for a minute." Her voice came from there inside, from behind the windows of her eyes, where the fire was burning.

I went out and sat down. On a little bracket on the wall was a bust of one of their ancient poets, Pushkin, I think. His asymmetrical, snub-nosed face was looking straight at me with a barely detectable smile. Why am I sitting here? Why am I meekly putting up with this smile? And what is all this, anyway? What am I doing here? How did this ridiculous situation arise? That irritating, repellent woman . . . this weird game . . . ?

Inside, the door of the chest banged, there was the rustle of silk, and I had a hard time making myself not go in there and . . . I don't know what I was thinking: probably I meant to say some very sharp things to her.

But she'd already come out. She was wearing an old-fashioned dress, short, bright yellow, and had on a black hat and black stockings. The dress was made of a very thin silk—I could clearly see that the stockings were long and came way above her knees. And the neck was cut very low, with that shadow between her . . .

"Listen," I said, "it's clear that you want to show off your originality, but do you really have to . . ."

"It's clear," she broke in, "that to be original means to distinguish yourself from others. It follows that to be original is to violate the principle of equality. And what the ancients called, in their idiotic language, 'being banal' is what we call 'just doing your duty.' Because . . ."

I couldn't control myself: "Yes, yes, yes! That's exactly right! And you've got no business . . ."

She went up to the bust of the snub-nosed poet and, lowering the blinds to cover the wild fire behind the windows of her eyes, said something that, for once at least, struck me as completely serious (to calm me down, maybe). She said a very reasonable thing:

"Don't you think it surprising that people were once willing to put up with someone like this one here? And not only put up with him—they adored him. What a slavish mentality! Don't you agree?"

"It's clear . . . that is, I mean . . ." (Damn that "clear" I keep saying!)

"Oh, of course I understand. But the fact is, you know, that people like him were rulers with more power than those who actually wore the crown. Why weren't they isolated and wiped out? In our world . . ."

"Yes, in our world . . ." I had only begun when she burst out laughing. I didn't hear the laugh, only saw it with my eyes. I saw the curve of that laugh, ringing, steep, resilient, and lively as a whip.

I remember how I was trembling all over. I should have . . . I don't know . . . grabbed her, and—what? I don't remember. But I felt that I had to, I don't know, *do* something. What I did was mechanically open up my gold badge and look at the watch. It was 16:50.

"Don't you think it's time to go?" I said, as politely as I could.

"And suppose I asked you—to stay here with me?"

"Listen, do you . . . are you aware of what you're saying? In ten minutes I'm supposed to be in the auditorium. . . ."

". . . And it is the obligation of all Numbers to follow the prescribed course in art and the sciences," said I-330, mimicking my own voice. Then she raised the blinds, lifted her eyes, and I saw the fire burning behind those windows. "In the Bureau of Medicine there is a doctor I know . . . he's assigned to me . . . and if I ask, he'll make out a certificate for you, that you were sick. How about it?"

I understood. At last I understood where this whole game was leading.

"So that's how it is! And you know that what I should do, basically, like any honest Number, is head for the Bureau of Guardians immediately and . . ."

"And not just 'basically' [this with one of her smile-bites] . . . I'm really terribly curious: Are you or aren't you going to the Bureau?"

"You're staying?" I said as I reached for the handle of the door. The handle was made of brass, and my voice sounded to me like it was made of the same brass.

"Just a minute. . . . Do you mind?"

She went to the telephone, made a call, and spoke to some Number—I didn't catch who he was, I was so upset: "I'll wait

for you at the Ancient House," she shouted. "Yes, yes, I'll be
alone. . . ."

I turned the cold brass handle. "Will you let me take the
aero?"

"Oh, of course. Please."

At the entrance the old woman was dozing in the sun, like a
plant. Once more I was surprised that her mouth seemed to
appear out of some undergrowth and produce speech: "And
your . . . what's her name . . . she's staying on by herself?"

"Yes, by herself."

The old woman's mouth sank out of sight again. She shook
her head. Apparently even her feeble brain understood how
stupid and dangerous that woman's behavior was.

I got to the lecture precisely at 17:00. Just then for some reason it struck me that I'd told the old woman a lie: I-330 was
not alone there *now*. I didn't mean to, but I misinformed the
old woman; maybe that was what preyed on my mind and
kept me from hearing the lecture. No, she was not alone. That
was just the trouble.

After 21:30 I had a free hour. There was still time today to
go make my report to the Bureau of Guardians. But I was so
tired after that idiotic business. And then, too, you have two
days by law to make the report. I'd still have time tomorrow, a
whole twenty-four hours.

# RECORD 7

*An Eyelash*

*Taylor*

*Henbane and Lily of the Valley*

It's night. Green, orange, blue; a red "royal" instrument; a yellow-orange dress. Then, a bronze Buddha; suddenly it raised its bronze eyelids and juice started to flow, juice out of the Buddha. Then out of the yellow dress, too: juice. Juices ran all over the mirror, and the bed began to ooze juice, and then it came from the children's little beds, and now from me, too—some kind of fatally sweet horror. . . .

I wake up. Mild bluish light. The glass walls, the glass armchairs, the table were all glistening. This was reassuring. My heart stopped hammering. Juice? Buddha? What kind of nonsense . . . ? It was clear: I was sick. I never used to dream. They say in the old days it was the most normal thing in the world to have dreams. Which makes sense: Their whole life was some kind of horrible merry-go-round of green, orange, Buddha, juice. But today we know that dreams point to a serious mental illness. And I know that up to now my brain has checked out chronometrically perfect, a mechanism without a speck of dust to dull its shine . . . and now what? Now . . . what I feel there in my brain is just like . . . some kind of foreign body . . . like having a very thin little eyelash in your eye. You feel generally okay, but that eye with the lash in it—you can't get it off your mind for a second.

The cheerful little crystal bell in my headboard dings

7:00 A.M.: time to get up. To the right and left through the glass walls I see something like my own self, my own room, my own clothes, my own movements, and all repeated a thousand times. It cheers you up: You see yourself as part of an immense, powerful, single thing. And such a precise beauty it is: not a wasted gesture, bend, turn.

No doubt about it, that Taylor was *the* genius of antiquity. True, it never finally occurred to him to extend his method over the whole of life, over every step you take right around the clock. He wasn't able to integrate into his system the whole spread from hour 1:00 to hour 24:00. But still, how could they write whole libraries about someone like Kant and hardly even notice Taylor—that prophet who could see ten centuries ahead?

Breakfast is over. The OneState Anthem harmoniously sung. Harmoniously, four abreast, everyone to the elevators. Hum of the engines, hardly audible. Down, down, down. Heart nearly in your throat.

And then suddenly that stupid dream—or maybe some concealed function of that dream. Oh, yes, it was being in the aero yesterday, too—same descent. But all that's finished. Period. Good thing, too, that I was blunt and firm with her.

In the subway car I was speeding to where the elegant body of the INTEGRAL was gleaming on its stocks, shining in the sun and not yet alive with its own fire. With my eyes closed I was in a revery of formulas. Once more I mentally calculated the initial velocity needed to tear the INTEGRAL away from earth. Second by second, as the explosive fuel diminishes, the mass of the INTEGRAL changes. The equation is extremely complex, the values transcendental.

As though in a dream, while I was here in this world of hard figures, someone sat down beside me, someone brushed lightly against me and said: "Sorry."

I half opened my eyes, and at first I saw (associations carried over from the INTEGRAL) something flying into space: a head, and it was flying because on the sides it had ears like pink wings. Then the curve of a head bent over, a curved back, double curved, the letter S . . .

And through the glass walls of my algebraic world there was again that eyelash, something unpleasant, something that, today, I had to . . .

"Please, think nothing of it," I said, smiling at my neighbor and nodding to him. On his badge was a bright number: S-4711 (I could see why from the very first he was connected in my mind with the letter S—it was a visual impression beneath the threshold of consciousness). And his eyes flashed—two sharp drills whirling rapidly, screwing deeper and deeper down until they drilled to the very bottom and saw what I wouldn't even let myself . . .

Suddenly I knew what the eyelash was! He was one of them, one of the Guardians. What could be simpler—stop putting it off and tell him everything right now.

"I—er—you see—I was at the Ancient House yesterday . . ." My voice was strange, flat, squashed. I tried clearing my throat.

"So . . . that's excellent. That furnishes material for a lot of edifying conclusions."

"But, you see—I wasn't alone. I was with I-330, and what . . ."

"I-330. Good for you. Very interesting, talented woman. She has a lot of admirers."

But he, too—back during the walk—and maybe he was even assigned to her? No, I couldn't tell him. It was unthinkable. That was clear.

"Right! Right! You said it! Very . . ." My smile got wider and stupider, and it made me feel like a naked idiot.

The drills went right to the bottom of my soul and then turned around and drilled their way back up to the eyes. S smiled a double smile at me, bowed, and slipped away to the exit.

I hid behind the newspaper (it seemed to me everyone was looking at me), and soon I read something that upset me so much I forgot all about the eyelash, the drills, and everything. It was one short line: *Reliable sources report the discovery once again of signs pointing to an elusive organization whose goal is liberation from the beneficent yoke of the State.*

"*Liberation?*" Astonishing how the criminal instincts do survive in the human species. I choose the word *criminal* advisedly. Freedom and criminality are just as indissolubly linked as . . . well, as the movement of an aero and its velocity. When the velocity of an aero is reduced to 0, it is not in motion; when a man's freedom is reduced to zero, he commits no crimes. That's clear. The only means to rid man of crime is to rid him of freedom. And now when we'd only just managed to get rid of it (in the cosmic scale of things, centuries amount to "only just"), suddenly some pathetic morons . . .

No, I don't see why I didn't go immediately yesterday to the Bureau of Guardians. Today after 16:00 I'll go for sure.

At 16:10 I went out, and the first thing I saw was O standing on the corner, all pink with pleasure over running into me. "Now, she's got a simple round mind," I thought. "Just what I needed. She'll understand me and support me. But, wait . . . no, I don't need any support. I've got my mind made up."

The pipes of the Music Factory were harmoniously booming out the March—the good old daily March. You can't find words for how charming that is, that dailiness, that repetition, that mirror image.

O took my hand. "A walk . . . ?" Her round blue eyes open wide to me, those windows into the core of her being, and through them I enter in, nothing in my way, since there is nothing there—nothing, that is, strange or useless.

"No, no walk. I've got to . . ." and I told her where I was going. And to my surprise I saw the pink circle of her mouth turn into a pink crescent, with the corners turned down, as if she'd tasted something sour. I blew up.

"You women Numbers! You're so prejudiced it's hopeless. You absolutely cannot think abstractly. I'm sorry, but that's just stupid."

"You . . . you're going to the spies . . . ugh! And I was just going to bring you this bunch of lily-of the-valley from the Botanical Museum."

"Why 'And I'? Where do you get that 'And'? Just like a woman!" I grabbed her flowers (angrily, I admit it). "Okay. Take your lily-of the-valley, okay? Have a smell. Nice, right?

Now please try to follow just this little bit of logic, all right? Lily-of-the-valley smells nice . . . agreed. But you cannot say about smell—I'm talking about the concept *smell*—that it is good or bad, right? That you cannot, repeat NOT, do, right? There's the smell of lily-of-the-valley, and then there's the nasty smell of henbane: They're both of them smells. There were spies in the ancient state, and we have spies. That's right, spies; the word doesn't scare me. But what is clear is this. Their spies were henbane, ours are lily-of-the-valley. That's what I said: lily-of-the-valley!"

The pink crescent trembled. I understand now that I was wrong, but at the time I thought she was about to laugh. So I shouted even louder: "Yes! Lily-of-the-valley! And there's nothing funny. Nothing funny."

Smooth round globes of heads were floating past us—and turning to look. O gently took me by the arm: "What's got into you today? Are you sick?"

Dream—yellow—Buddha . . . It suddenly became clear to me that I ought to go to the Medical Bureau.

"You know you're right? I am sick." I said this very happily (which is an inexplicable contradiction—there was nothing to be happy about).

"So you should go to the doctor at once. You know very well it's your duty to be healthy—it's ridiculous even talking about it."

"O, darling, of course you're right. Absolutely right!"

I did not go to the Bureau of Guardians. I couldn't help it. I had to go to the Medical Bureau, where they kept me until 17:00.

And that evening (it doesn't matter, anyway, they're closed in the evening), that evening O came to my place. We didn't let the blinds down. We worked on some problems from an old book of problems—that calms you down and cleans out your thoughts. O-90 sat over the notebook, her head leaning toward her left shoulder, and making such an effort that her tongue was pushing her left cheek out. She looked like such a child, so charming. And so I felt good all over, clear, simple . . .

She left and I was alone. I took two deep breaths (which is

very good for you before going to sleep). And then all of a sudden I caught a whiff of something I didn't expect . . . something
that reminded me of something unpleasant. I soon found it. A
stem of lily-of-the-valley had been hidden in my bed. Immediately something rose up from the bottom, some whirlwind.
No, really, that was simply tactless of her . . . hiding that
flower on me. All right, then, I didn't go. But I'm not to blame
that I'm sick.

# RECORD 8

*The Irrational Root*

*R-13*

*Triangle*

How long ago was it? In my school years. That's when $\sqrt{-1}$ first happened to me. It's so clear it seems chiseled. I remember the bright globular auditorium, the hundreds of round boyish heads—and Pliapa, our math teacher. We nicknamed him Pliapa. He was already pretty much used up and falling apart by that time, and whenever the person on duty would connect the plug to him, the loudspeaker would always start with what sounded like "Plia-plia-plia-tshshsh" and only then we'd get the lesson. Once Pliapa told us about irrational numbers—and I remember how I cried, I beat my fists on the table and bawled: "I don't want $\sqrt{-1}$! Take it out of me, this $\sqrt{-1}$!" That irrational root grew in me like some alien thing, strange and terrifying, and it was eating me, and you couldn't make any sense of it or neutralize it because it was completely beyond *ratio*.

And now here's that $\sqrt{-1}$ again. I've looked over these records of mine, and it's clear to me that I've been fooling myself, I've been lying to myself, and all because I did not want to see that $\sqrt{-1}$. That's all nonsense about me being sick and so on. I could have gone there. A week ago I know I would have gone without a second thought. So why do I now . . . ? Why?

Same today. At 16:10 on the dot I was standing in front of the gleaming glass wall. Above me was the golden, sunny, pure shining of the letters on the Bureau's sign. Inside, through the glass, I could see a lot of light-blue yunies waiting in line. I could see faces glimmering like icon-lamps in an old church. These were people who had come to perform a heroic duty: They had come to lay on the altar of OneState their loved ones, their friends, even themselves. And as for me, I was dying to go to them, to be with them. And I couldn't. My feet were sunk deep in the glass pavement. I stood there looking stupid, unable to budge from the spot.

"Hey, mathematician! You're dreaming!"

I shuddered. The face looking at me had dark eyes, shiny from laughing, and thick African lips. It was the poet R-13, an old friend, and my rosy O was with him.

I turned around angrily (I think that if they hadn't interfered I'd have managed to tear that $\sqrt{-1}$ out of me with the meat still on it—I'd have gone into the Bureau). "I wasn't dreaming," I said, rather sharply. "I was admiring."

"Of course, of course! Listen, my friend, you've got no business being a mathematician. You're a poet . . . a poet! No, really, come over and join us poets. How about it? I'll fix it up for you in a minute."

R-13 chokes with excitement when he talks and the words come bursting out of him, out of those thick lips, in sprays. Every *p* is a fountain. The word *poets* is a real fountain.

"I have served and will continue to serve knowledge," I said, frowning. I don't like or understand jokes, and jokes are a bad habit with R-13.

"Knowledge! What does that mean? Your knowledge is nothing but cowardice. No, really, that's all it is. You just want to put a little wall around infinity. And you're afraid to look on the other side of that wall. It's the truth. You look and you screw up your eyes. You do!"

"Walls," I began, "walls are the basis of everything human. . . ."

R spluttered like a fountain. O gave her round pink little laugh. I waved my hand, meaning: Go on and laugh, who cares? I had no time for that. I had to get something to wash that damned $\sqrt{-1}$ down, to drown it out.

"You know what?" I proposed, "let's go to my place, let's sit around and work on problems" (I was thinking of that quiet hour we'd spent yesterday, and hoped we might have one today, too).

O glanced at R, and then turned her round, clear gaze on me, her cheeks taking on the tender, exciting color of our Sex Day tickets.

"But today . . . today I have . . . a ticket for him," she said, nodding toward R. "And he's busy this evening . . . so . . ."

He made a good-natured sound with his damp, shiny lips: "What's the problem? Half an hour's all we need, right, O? I don't really feel like working on your problems . . . but why don't we just go to my place and sit around?"

I was terrified of being left in my own company, or rather in the company of that new unknown me, who got my D-503 only by some weird coincidence. And so I went to his place, to R's. It's true that he is not a precise person, not rhythmical, and his logic is ridiculous, inside out, but still . . . we're friends. It wasn't by accident that he and I both chose that dear pink O three years ago. That somehow brought us even closer together than all our school years.

We went to R's room. To look at it, you'd think everything was just exactly like my place. Same Table on the wall, and the armchairs, table, chest, bed all made with the same glass. But R had hardly entered before he moved one of the easy chairs, then the other, and the planes were dislocated, everything slipped out of the prescribed correlation and became non-Euclidian. R will never change, never. In Taylor and in math he was always at the bottom of the class.

We talked about old Pliapa, about how we boys used to stick little thank-you notes all over his glass legs (we really loved old Pliapa). We talked about the law professor.* The law professor had a deafeningly loud voice, a real blast of sound came out of his loudspeaker, and we boys would bellow the texts along with him. We recalled how that crazy R-13 once chewed up some paper in his mouth and then rammed it down

*His subject was OneState law, of course, not the religious law that used to be taught in old schools.

the mouthpiece, and how with every text a spitball would shoot out. R was punished, of course. What he did was a dirty trick, of course. But now we laughed over it, our whole triangle laughed, all of us, including (I admit it) me.

"And what if the law professor had been a live human being, like teachers in the old world? What a panic . . ." And the $p$ meant a shower from the thick lips.

There was sun coming through the ceiling and walls—sunlight from above, from the sides, and reflected from below. O was sitting on R-13's lap, and there were little drops of sunlight in her blue eyes. I felt warmer and somewhat better. The $\sqrt{-1}$ eased off and lay quiet.

"Hey . . . how's your INTEGRAL doing? We flying off to enlighten the inhabitants of other planets anytime soon? You'd better get a move on if you don't want us poets to write more than your INTEGRAL can ever lift off with." Every day from 8:00 to 11:00 . . . R shook his head and scratched the back of it. From the rear his head looks like it has a little square suitcase attached to it. (It reminds me of an old painting called *In the Carriage.*)

This woke me up. "Oh, are you also writing something for the INTEGRAL? What about? What would you write about today, for instance."

"Today—nothing," he said. "Had other plans. . . ." Another $p$, another shower in my face.

"What plans?"

R frowned. "*What* what? Nothing. Okay, if you must know. It was a verdict. I had to put a verdict into verse. Some idiot . . . and one of us poets, too. For two years we sit next to each other and he seems okay. And then suddenly something snaps. 'I'm a genius!' he says. 'A genius . . . above the law!' And the stuff he wrote . . . ah, the hell with it."

His thick lips drooped and his eyes grew dull. R-13 jumped up, turned away, and fixed his gaze somewhere beyond the wall. I looked at that tightly locked little suitcase of his and wondered, "What thoughts are turning over now in that little case?"

There was a minute of awkward, asymmetrical silence. It wasn't clear to me what was going on, but something was.

"Thank goodness," I said, deliberately raising my voice, "the antediluvian times of all those Shakespeares and Dosto-evskys, or whatever you call them, are over."

R turned his head. The words spurted out of him like a fountain, as always, but I thought the twinkle in his eye was gone.

"Yes, my dear mathematician . . . thank goodness, thank goodness, thank goodness! We are the happiest of arithmetical means. . . . As you people put it: integrated from zero to infinity, from the cretin to Shakespeare. Right!"

I don't know why—it just seemed to come out of nowhere—but I thought of that woman, of her tone of voice. A very thin thread of some kind stretched between her and R. What kind of thread? I could feel the $\sqrt{-1}$ begin to stir in me again. I opened my badge: 16:25. They had 45 minutes left on their pink ticket.

"Well, time I was going," I said, and I gave O a kiss, shook hands with R, and went to the elevator.

I was already crossing to the other side of the avenue when I looked back: In the bright, sun-drenched mass of the glass building you could see here and there the gray-blue opaque cages where the blinds were down, the cages of rhythmic, Taylorized happiness. My eyes searched out R-13's cage on the seventh floor: He'd already lowered the blinds.

Dear O . . . dear R. There's something in him, too (why "too" I don't know, but let it stand as written), something in him, too, that isn't quite clear to me. Still, he, O, and I . . . we're a triangle, maybe not isosceles but still a triangle. If you want to put it in the language of our ancestors (a language that might be more understandable to you, my planetary readers), we're a family. And sometimes it is so good to rest, even if not for long, to lock yourself up in a strong simple triangle away from all that . . .

# RECORD 9

*Liturgy*

*Iambs and Trochees*

*Cast-Iron Hand*

A bright, triumphant day. On a day like today you forget about your weaknesses, your uncertainties, your illnesses, and everything is crystalline, steadfast, everlasting . . . like our new glass.

Cube Square. Sixty-six powerful concentric rings: the stands. And sixty-six rows: quiet faces like lamps, with eyes reflecting the shining heavens, or maybe the shining of OneState. Blood-red flowers: women's lips. Tender garlands of children's faces—down front to be near the action. A profound, strict, Gothic silence.

Judging by the descriptions that have come down to us, this is something like what the ancients felt during their "divine service." But they served their irrational, unknown God, whereas we serve something rational and very precisely known. Their God gave them nothing but eternal tormented searching. Their God couldn't come up with any smarter idea than sacrificing yourself, never mind why. But we, when we sacrifice to our God, OneState, we make a calm, rational, carefully considered sacrifice. Yes, this was the triumphant liturgy in celebration of OneState, a remembrance of the days and years that went into the crusade of the 200-Years War, the magnificent victory of all over one, of the whole over the part. . . .

There was one . . . standing on the steps of the Cube, the sunlight pouring down on him. His face was white, or no, not white, it was no color at all, his glass face, his glass lips. Just his eyes, dark, sucking, swallowing holes . . . and that terrifying world that he was only minutes away from. The gold badge with his number had already been taken. His hands were tied with a purple ribbon (ancient custom; the explanation seems to be that in old times, before this was done in the name of OneState, the condemned naturally thought he had a right to put up a fight, so his hands were usually chained).

And up above on the Cube, beside the Machine, was the figure of the one we call the Benefactor, dead still, like something made out of metal. From down here the face is hard to make out. All you can see is that the features are limited to strict, solemn, square lines. But as for the hands . . . It happens this way sometimes in photographs when the hands are too close, too much in the foreground, and they come out huge, they're all you can see, they cover up everything. These heavy hands, resting on the knees for the moment—it's clear that they're made of stone, and the knees can hardly bear up under their weight.

And suddenly one of these huge hands slowly rose . . . a slow, cast-iron gesture . . . and in answer to this raised hand a Number came from the stands and approached the Cube. This was one of the State Poets. It had fallen to his happy lot to crown the festivities with a poem. And there thundered out over the stands the divine bronze iambics, which were about him, the idiot with the glass eyes who was standing there on the steps waiting for the logical consequences of his stupidities.

. . . A conflagration. Houses swayed in the iambics, they burst upward in a liquid golden shower, then crashed. Green trees writhed in it, spewed drops of sap, left nothing but black skeletons like crosses. But Prometheus appeared (that's us, of course):

> And in machines, in steel, he harnessed fire,
> And chaos fettered he with hoops of Law.

All was new, made of steel: a steel sun, steel trees, steel people. Suddenly some madman "loosed the fire from its chains"—and everything was about to perish again. . . .

I have a poor memory for poetry, unfortunately, but one thing I do remember: You couldn't have picked more edifying and resplendent images.

Again the slow, heavy gesture, and a second poet stood on the steps of the Cube. I nearly rose from my seat: Could it be? No . . . those thick, African lips . . . it was him. Why didn't he mention that he was going to have the high . . . ? His lips trembled, they were gray. I can see that when you're face to face with the Benefactor, standing before the whole corpus of the Guardians, you'd be . . . but still, to be that nervous . . .

Trochees . . . cutting, rapid . . . sharp as an ax. About an unheard-of crime, about a blasphemous poem, one in which the Benefactor is called . . . but no, I can't make my hand write it.

Pale, not looking at anyone (this shyness was not like him), R-13 went down and took his seat. For one tiniest fraction of a second I thought I saw next to him someone's face . . . sharp, a dark triangle . . . and then it vanished at once. My eyes lifted up, and so did thousands of other eyes, up to the Machine. The inhuman hand made a third cast-iron gesture. And, shaken by some invisible wind, the criminal moves . . . a step . . . another . . . and takes the last step that he will make in life. He is face up to the sky, his head thrown back, on his final resting place.

Heavy, stone, like fate itself, the Benefactor made one full circle around the Machine and laid his huge hand on the lever. Not a rustle anywhere, not a breath. All eyes were on that hand. What a whirlwind of fire that must feel like—to be a weapon, to have the force of hundreds of thousands of volts. What a stupendous fate!

An instant. The hand fell, loosing the current. A sharp blade of unbearable light. A shudder in the pipes of the Machine, a crackling that you could hardly hear. The spread-eagled body was covered by a light, sparkling little puff of smoke, and then before our eyes it began to melt, and melt, and it dissolved so fast it was horrible. And then—nothing. A puddle of chemically pure water, which just a moment ago had been in a heart, red, beating up a storm.

This was all simple, we all knew about it. Dissociation of matter—check. Disengagement of the atoms of the human body—check. Still, every time it happened, it seemed like a miracle. It was a sign of the superhuman might of the Benefactor.

Up above, lined up in front of Him, were ten female Numbers with Hushed faces, their lips partly open with excitement, their bouquets of flowers blowing in the wind.*

According to the old custom, the ten women decorated with flowers the Benefactor's yuny, which was still damp from the spray. With the lordly stride of a high priest, He slowly descended, slowly passed through the stands—and in His wake were gentle white female hands raised aloft like branches and a million hosannas in unison. And then the same hosannas in honor of the corpus of Guardians, invisibly present somewhere in our midst, in our ranks. Who knows—maybe it was the Guardians that ancient man foresaw in his fantasy about the "archangels,"† both stern and tender, that were assigned at birth to every human.

Yes, there was something of the old religions, something cleansing, like storm and thunder, in this whole ceremony. You who are going to be reading this . . . have you ever known such moments? I'm sorry for you if you haven't.

---

*From the Botanical Museum, of course. I personally see nothing beautiful in flowers, nor in anything else that belongs to the savage world long ago banished behind the Green Wall. The only thing that is beautiful is what is rational and useful: machines, boots, formulas, food, and so on.

†See note p. 201.—*Trans.*

# RECORD 10

*Letter*

*Membrane*

*Hairy Me*

For me, yesterday was like the paper that chemists filter their solutions through: All the particles that were in suspension, all the unwanted stuff, stays on this paper. And when I went down this morning I felt I'd been freshly distilled, perfectly clear.

Down in the vestibule the controller was sitting at her little desk looking at her watch and jotting down the Numbers who were coming in. Her name is U . . . but maybe I'd better not give her numbers. I'm afraid I might write something bad about her. Though in fact she really is a quite decent old woman. The one thing I don't like about her is the way her cheeks hang down—they look like gills. (Though what's wrong with that?)

She made a scratch with her pen, and I saw myself on the page: D-503. And right next to it an inkblot.

I was just about to point this out to her when suddenly she raised her head and dribbled one of her inky little smiles at me: "Oh, yes. There's a letter for you, dear. You'll get it, you'll get it."

I knew that the letter, which she'd already read, still had to go through the Bureau of Guardians (I don't suppose there's any need to explain this natural procedure), and I'd get it by 12:00. But that little smile worried me. The drop of ink in it made my pure solution all cloudy. It got so bad that later on, at the building site of the INTEGRAL, I couldn't concentrate and even made a computational error, something that never happens with me.

At 12:00 I had to face the pinkish-brown gills and the little smile again and finally got to hold my letter in my own hands. I don't know why, but I didn't read it right away. I stuck it in my pocket and hurried off to my room. I opened it, skimmed through it quickly, and sat down. It was an official notification that I-330 had been assigned to me and that today at 21:00 hours I was to report to her at . . . and the address was given.

No. After all that had happened, after I'd gone out of my way to make it perfectly clear to her how I felt. What's more, she didn't even know if I'd been to the Bureau of Guardians or not. She had no way of knowing I'd been sick. Or at least that I couldn't . . . And in spite of everything . . .

A dynamo was whirling and humming in my head. Buddha . . . yellow . . . lily-of-the-valley . . . pink crescent moon. Yes, and what about . . . How about O, who was supposed to drop by today? Should I show her this notification about I-330? I don't know. She wouldn't believe it. (And how could anybody believe it, anyway?) She wouldn't believe that I had nothing to do with it, that I was completely . . . And I knew there'd be a hard, stupid, totally illogical conversation. Oh no, spare me that. Let's just settle the whole thing mechanically: I'll simply send her a copy of the notice.

I was hurrying to stick the notice in my pocket when I caught sight of my horrible, ape-like hand. I remembered how I-330 had taken my hand that time on the walk and looked at it. Surely she couldn't really . . .

And then it was 20:45. A white night. Everything greenish, glassy. But it was some other kind of glass, sort of fragile, not ours, not real glass. It was a thin glass shell, and under the shell was twisting, hurrying, buzzing. And I wouldn't have been surprised if the cupolas of the auditoriums had suddenly shot up into the air in slow, round puffs of smoke, and the old moon had given me an inky smile like that woman at her little desk this morning, and the blinds had suddenly gone down in every building, and behind the blinds . . .

I felt strange. I felt my own ribs, like they were iron rods, and they were in the way, they were actually in the way of my heart, it was too close, there wasn't enough room. I was standing in front of the glass door with the golden numbers I-330. She was bent over her desk writing something, her back to me. I went in.

"Here you are," I said, and I handed her the pink ticket. "I got the notice today and I'm reporting for duty."

"How punctual you are! Just a minute—do you mind? Have a seat, I'll just finish this."

She lowered her eyes again to what she was writing. And what, I wondered, was there inside her head, behind the lowered blinds? What would she say, and what was I to do, after that minute? How could you know, how compute it, when every bit of her came from . . . *there*, from the land of dreams?

I watched her without saying a word. My ribs were iron rods, there was no room. . . . When she talks, her face is like a quick, flashing wheel—you can't see the separate spokes. I saw a strange configuration: Her dark eyebrows pulled up high toward her temples, they made a sardonic sharp triangle; and the two deep lines running from her nose to the corners of her mouth made another, this time with the point up. And these two triangles somehow canceled each other out, made an unpleasant, irritating X on her face, like a cross. Her face was crossed out.

The wheel began to turn, the spokes blurred together: "You didn't really go to the Bureau of Guardians, did you?"

"I was . . . I couldn't. I was sick."

"Yes. Well, it's about what I expected—something was bound to stop you, no matter what [sharp teeth, smile]. But now you are . . . in my hands. You remember: *Any Number failing to report within 48 hours to the Bureau is to be considered . . .*"

My heart was beating so hard that the rods bent. Like a kid—I'd gotten caught like a dumb kid. I kept my dumb mouth shut. And I felt I was trapped hand and foot.

She stood up and stretched herself lazily. She pressed a button, and the blinds on all sides went down with a light rushing noise. I was cut off from the world—and one on one with her.

I-330 was somewhere behind my back near the wardrobe. Her yuny made a rustling noise and fell. I listened. My whole body listened. And I recalled . . . no. Something flashed by my mind for the hundredth part of a second.

I recently had to work out the curvature of a new type of street membrane (these membranes, elegantly decorated, are now on all the avenues and record street conversations for the Bureau of Guardians). And I remembered: It was a concave, pink, trembling tympanum—a strange creature with only the one organ—an ear. I was at that moment such a membrane.

Now the button at the collar snapped, then the one on the breast, then lower . . . The glassy silk rustled from her shoulders, round her knees, onto the floor. I heard—and I could hear clearer than I could see—how one foot, then the other, stepped out of the pile of bluish-gray silk.

The tightly stretched membrane trembles and records the silence. No, make that the sharp striking of a hammer on rods, with interminable pauses. And I hear, I see, that behind me she's thinking for a second.

—There . . . those were the wardrobe doors . . . that was . . . some sort of lid closing . . . and still silk and more silk . . .

"There now . . . it's okay."

I turned around. She had on a light dress of an old-fashioned cut, saffron-yellow. This was a thousand times more evil than wearing nothing at all. Through the thin material you could see two pointed tips that glowed pink like coals seen through ashes. Her knees were tender, round. . . .

She was sitting in a low armchair. On the little square table in front of her was a flask full of some poisonous-looking green stuff. Two tiny stem glasses. In the corner of her mouth something was giving off fumes, a thin little paper tube, which the ancients used for smoking (can't remember at the moment what it was called).

The membrane was still trembling. Inside me the hammer

was beating the rods, now heated red-hot. I clearly heard every single blow . . . but, what if she heard them, too?

But she went on calmly smoking and calmly glancing at me and . . . knocked off some ashes on my pink ticket.

As nonchalantly as possible, I asked: "Listen, if that's how it is, how come you registered for me? And why'd you have me come here?"

Pretended not to hear. Poured herself a drink and sipped it.

"Charming liqueur. Have some?"

This was when I finally understood: It was alcohol. All that had happened yesterday flashed before me: the stone hand of the Benefactor, the unbearable blade of light, and up there on the Cube, the spread-eagled body with the head thrown back. I shuddered.

"Listen," I said, "you know it yourself, *whoever shall poison himself with nicotine, and especially with alcohol, need expect no mercy from OneState. . . .*"

"To destroy a few quickly makes more sense than to allow the many to ruin themselves, to degenerate, etc., etc. That is indecently true."

"Yes . . . indecently."

"And just you take this little grouplet of truths, all naked and bald, and let them out on the street. . ∴. No, really, just imagine. Take that most constant of all my admirers—you know who I mean—and let him divest himself of that lie known as clothing, let him appear in his true form before the public. . . . Oh, my god!"

She laughed. But I could see quite clearly that lower of her two triangles, the sorrowful one, the two deep lines from her nose to the corners of her mouth. And somehow these lines made me understand something: that double-bowed, hunchbacked, wing-eared . . . he'd embraced her . . . and just as she was now . . . he'd . . .

By the way, right now I'm trying to convey the feelings I had at that time, which were not normal. Now, though, when I am writing this, I realize perfectly that all that was as it should be, that he's just as entitled to happiness as every other honest Number, and it wouldn't be fair . . . but that's all clear enough.

I-330's very strange laughing went on for a long time. Afterward she looked hard at me, right into me, and said, "But the main thing is that I'm not worried about you. You're so nice. Oh, I'm certain you would not even think of going to the Bureau and informing about my drinking liquor and smoking. You'll be sick, or you'll be busy, or you'll be . . . I don't know what. What is more, I'm certain that right now you are going to drink some of this charming poison with me. . . ."

Her tone was so impudent, so full of mockery. I definitely felt: Now I hate her again. But why *again*? I always hated her.

She drained one of the little glasses of green poison, stood up, and, glowing pink through the saffron, took several steps that brought her up behind my chair.

Suddenly her arm crept round my neck, lips touched lips, went deeper, things got even scarier. . . . I swear, this was a total surprise for me, and maybe that's the only reason why . . . Because I could not have . . . I now understand this with absolute clarity . . . I could not possibly have desired what happened next.

Unbearably sweet lips (the liqueur, I suppose) . . . and I tasted a swallow of burning poison, and another, and another, and I broke free of the earth, a free planet, whirling furiously, down, down, along some orbit yet to be calculated.

The rest I can describe only approximately, only with the help of more or less close analogies.

Somehow this never entered my head before, but this is really how it is: We on this earth are walking the whole time above a boiling crimson sea of fire, hidden down there in the bowels of the earth. But we never think of it. And then suddenly the thin shell beneath our feet seems to turn to glass, and suddenly we see. . . .

I became glass. I saw into myself, inside.

There were two me's. One me was the old one, D-503, Number D-503, and the other . . . The other used to just stick his hairy paws out of his shell, but now all of him came out, the shell burst open, and the pieces were just about to fly in all directions . . . and then what?

Like grasping at a straw with all my strength, I grasped the arms of the chair and asked, just to hear what that old me sounded like: "Where . . . where'd you get this . . . poison?"

"Oh, this? Just a doctor. One of my . . ."

"*My!* One of *my*!? Who?"

It was that other me. He suddenly jumped out and started screaming: "I won't stand for it! I don't want anyone but me to . . . I'll kill anyone who . . . Because I lo . . . I . . ."

I saw it. I saw how he grabbed her with his hairy paws, tore the thin silk from her, sank his teeth . . . I remember it clearly: his teeth.

I don't remember how it happened, but I-330 slipped away. And then (her eyes were behind those damned blinds) she was standing there, her back against the wardrobe, listening to me.

I remember I was on the floor hugging her legs, kissing her knees. And I was begging, "Now, right now, this minute . . ."

The sharp teeth, the sharp mocking triangle of her brows. She leaned over and undid my badge, not saying a word.

"Yes! Yes, darling . . . darling." I started throwing my yuny off. But she, still without saying a word, brought the watch in my badge right up to my eyes. In five minutes it would be 22:30.

That put a chill on me. I knew what it meant to show yourself on the street after 22:30. All my madness seemed to be blown away from me all of a sudden. I was me again. One thing was clear: I hated her, I hated her, I hated her!

Without saying goodbye or looking back, I rushed out of the room. Pinning my badge back on as I ran down the steps (taking the emergency stairs for fear of running into somebody in the elevator), I ran out onto the empty avenue.

Nothing was out of place—the usual simple, customary, normal scene: glass buildings shining with lights, pale glass sky, the greenish quiet night. But underneath this quiet cool glass something wild, crimson, and hairy was silently rushing along. And I was racing along, fighting for breath, trying not to be late.

Suddenly I felt that the badge I'd stuck back on so hastily was coming off—it came off, and clattered as it hit the glass sidewalk. I bent over to retrieve it, and in the momentary silence I heard someone's footsteps behind me. I turned.

Something small and bent was rounding the corner, or at least that's how it seemed to me at the time.

I took off as fast as I could and heard nothing but the wind rushing past my ears. At the entrance I stopped: The clock showed one minute remaining before 22:30. I listened hard— no one back there. Stupid . . . I'd imagined the whole thing. Effect of the poison.

That night was torture. The bed under me rose and fell and rose again—sailing along a sinusoid. I kept repeating to myself: "At night the Number's duty is to sleep. This is just as much an obligation as work during the day. It is required so that one can work during the day. Not to sleep at night is unlawful." And still I could not, I just could not.

I'm done for. I'm in no condition to fulfill my obligations to OneState. I . . .

# RECORD 11

~~~

*No, I Can't . . .*

*Skip the Contents*

Evening. A light mist. The sky is covered over with some milky gold fabric, and you can't see what's up there, beyond, higher. The ancients knew what was up there: their magnificent, bored sceptic—God. We know that it's a crystalline blue, naked, indecent nothing. Now I don't know what's there. I've learned too much. Knowledge that is absolutely sure it's infallible—that's faith. I had a firm faith in myself, I believed I knew everything about myself. And now . . .

I'm in front of a mirror. And for the first time in my life, I swear it, for the very first time in my life, I get a clear, distinct, conscious look at myself; I see myself and I'm astonished, like I'm looking at some "him." There I am—or rather, there he is: He's got straight black eyebrows, drawn with a ruler, and between them, like a scar, is a vertical crease (I don't know if it was there before). Gray, steel eyes, with the circle of a sleepless night around them; and behind that steel—it turns out I never knew what was there. And from that "there" (a "there" that is here and at the same time infinitely far away)—I am looking at myself, at him, and I am absolutely certain that he, with his ruler-straight eyebrows, is a stranger, somebody else, I just met him for the first time in my life. And I'm the real one. I AM NOT HIM.

No. Period. That's all nonsense, all those stupid sensations . . .

they're phantasms, they come from being poisoned yesterday. Poisoned with what, the swallow of green poison, or her? It doesn't matter. The only reason I'm writing this down is to show how human reason, even very sharp and exact human reason, can get crazily confused and thrown off the track. This same reason, which has managed to make even infinity, the terror of the ancients, easily digestible by using . . .

The intercom screen clicks. I see the numbers *R-13*. Good— I'm even glad. For me right now, being alone would . . .

## 20 MINUTES LATER.

On the surface of the paper, in the two-dimensional world, these lines are right next to each other, but in another world . . . I'm starting to lose my feel for figures: 20 minutes could be 200 or 200,000. And it's just as weird to sit here calmly, reasonably, thinking over every word, and write down what just happened between R and me. It'd be just the same as you sitting down in the chair next to your own bed, crossing your legs, and looking with some curiosity at yourself, your very own self, twisting and turning on that bed.

When R-13 came in, I was completely quiet and normal. I was quite sincere when I began to carry on about what a magnificent job he did of putting the verdict into trochees and how it was his poem more than anything that made mincemeat of that lunatic and destroyed him.

"And I'll even say this," I wound up, "if I got the job of making schematic drawings of the Benefactor's Machine, I would somehow, without fail, I would somehow work your trochees into that drawing."

Suddenly I notice R's eyes have gone dull and his lips gray.

"What's the matter with you?"

"What do you mean, what? It's just . . . just that I'm bored. You'd think the verdict is all there is. I don't want to hear about it anymore, that's all. I don't want to."

He frowned and scratched the back of his head, that little

suitcase of his with the strange baggage that I can't understand. A pause. Then he suddenly located something in that little bag, pulled it out, unfolded it, smoothed it out, and jumped up, his eyes all shiny and laughing:

"But for your INTEGRAL I *am* writing something! For that I *am* writing!"

His old self again: His lips smacked, he sprayed you, the words welled up in him.

"Paradise," he began, and the *p* meant a spray. "The old legend about Paradise—that was about us, about right now. Yes! Just think about it. Those two in Paradise, they were offered a choice: happiness without freedom, or freedom without happiness, nothing else. Those idiots chose freedom. And then what? Then for centuries they were homesick for the chains. That's why the world was so miserable, see? They missed the chains. For ages! And we were the first to hit on the way to get back to happiness. No, wait . . . listen to me. The ancient God and us, side by side, at the same table. Yes! We helped God finally overcome the Devil—because that's who it was that pushed people to break the commandment and taste freedom and be ruined. It was him, the wily serpent. But we gave him a boot to the head! Crack! And it was all over: Paradise was back. And we're simple and innocent again, like Adam and Eve. None of those complications about good and evil: Everything is very simple, childishly simple—Paradise! The Benefactor, the Machine, the Cube, the Gas Bell, the Guardians: All those things represent good, all that is sublime, splendid, noble, elevated, crystal pure. Because that is what protects our nonfreedom, which is to say, our happiness. Here's where the ancients would stand around discussing things, weighing this and that, racking their brains: Is it ethical, unethical? . . . Well, you get the point. What I'm saying is, there's this great poem of Paradise, right? Extremely serious in tone, of course . . . You understand, don't you? Isn't it something?"

What was not to understand? I remember thinking: "He looks dumb and asymmetrical, but how straight his mind thinks." That's why he's so close to me, to the real me (I still

regard the former me as the real one; this present me is of
course nothing but some illness).

R must have read my thoughts from my expression. He
threw his arms around my shoulders and started laughing.

"Oh, you . . . Adam! Oh, and by the way, about your
Eve . . ."

He rummaged about in his pocket, brought out a small
notebook, and began turning the pages.

"Day after tomorrow . . . no, in two days, O has a pink
ticket to come to your place. How's that with you? Same as before? Do you want her to . . . ?"

"Yes, sure. That's clear. . . ."

"I'll tell her. Because you see . . . she's . . . shy. Honestly, what
a story. Me? I'm just a pink-ticket item with her, but you . . .
And she's not telling who that fourth one is that crawled into
our triangle. Come on, you old lecher . . . tell us who it is. Confess!"

Inside me a curtain went up, and . . . the rustle of silk, a
green bottle, lips . . . and apropos of nothing, out of the blue,
the words—if I'd only held them in!—burst out of me: "Tell
me, did you ever by any chance try nicotine or alcohol?"

R bit his lips and gave me a sideways glance. I could hear his
thoughts as clearly as if he'd said it: "You are a friend, all right,
but still . . ." What he actually said was:

"Well, how to put it . . . ? Me personally—no. But I did
know one woman . . ."

"I-330!" I shouted.

"What . . . ? You, too? Are you with her, too?" He burst out
laughing, choked, and spluttered.

The way my mirror was hung, I could see myself in it only
across the table. From where I was sitting in the armchair, all I
saw was my forehead and eyebrows.

And what the real me saw in the mirror was a skewed pranc-
ing line of eyebrows and what this real me heard was a wild,
disgusting shout: "What do you mean *too*?! What is this *too*?
No, wait . . . I demand an answer!"

Negro lips stretched, eyes bulging. . . . I, the real I, grabbed
the other me, wild, hairy, panting, by the neck, and said to R:

"Forgive me, for the Benefactor's sake! I'm sick, no sleep, don't know what's wrong with me. . . ."

The thick lips smiled fleetingly: "Yes, yes, I understand! I know all about that—theoretically, of course. Goodbye!"

From the door he bounced back like a black ball to the table and tossed a book onto it: "My latest. Meant to leave it and nearly forgot. Bye!" (Wet *B*) Bounced out.

Alone—or with "him," the other me. Sitting legs crossed in the chair, I watch with curiosity, from some other "there," my own self tossing on the bed.

Why, why, for three whole years, were O and I such good friends, only to have one word about her, I-330, spoil . . . ? Maybe that nonsense about love and jealousy is not just in stupid old books. And me, of all people! Equations, formulas, figures, and now . . . I don't get it. None of it. Tomorrow I'll see R and tell him that I . . .

That's a lie. I won't. Not tomorrow, not the day after— never. I can't. I don't want to see him. Finished! End of our triangle.

I'm alone. Evening. A little foggy. Milky-gold cloth over the sky. What's beyond it? If only one could know. And know who I am, what I am.

*Limitation of Infinity*

*Angel*

*Reflections on Poetry*

I keep on thinking I'm getting well, that I can get well. I slept like a rock. None of those dreams or any other sign of illness. Dear O is coming to me tomorrow, and everything's going to be like a circle: simple, correct, within certain limitations. The word doesn't scare me—*limitation*. The highest thing in Man is his reason, and what the work of reason comes down to is the continual limitation of infinity, dividing infinity up into convenient, easily digestible portions: differentiation. This is exactly what constitutes the divine beauty of my element, mathematics. And this beauty is precisely what that woman will never understand. But never mind that . . . I don't know what made me think of her.

These thoughts come to me in time with the measured, metrical beat of the subway wheels. In my head I was keeping time with the wheels and with R's poetry (the book from yesterday) when I sensed that somebody from behind was carefully bending over my shoulder and looking at the open page. Not turning around, just with the corner of my eye, I see the pink wings of the protruding ears, the double bend . . . him! I didn't feel like disturbing him, so I pretended not to notice. How he turned up, I don't know. I don't think he was in the car when I got on.

This occurrence, completely insignificant in itself, had a

very good effect on me. It strengthened me, I'd say. It's so nice
to feel that someone's keeping a sharp eye on you, kindly protecting you from making the slightest mistake, the slightest
misstep. This may sound sentimental, but the same analogy
occurs to me: the guardian angels that the ancients dreamed
about. So much of what they merely dreamed about has materialized in our life.

At the moment when I sensed the guardian angel behind my
back, I was enjoying a sonnet titled "Happiness." I don't think
I'd go wrong in saying that this is a thing of rare beauty and
deep thought. Here are the first four lines:

> *Forever enamoured are two plus two,*
> *Forever conjoined in blissful four.*
> *The hottest lovers in all the world:*
> *The permanent weld of two plus two. . . .*

And so on in the same vein, about the wise, permanent happiness of the multiplication table.

Every genuine poet is bound to be a Columbus. America
had existed for ages even before Columbus, but only Columbus was able to find it. The multiplication table existed for
ages before R-13, too, but only R-13 was able to find a new El-
dorado in that virgin forest. No, really: Does there exist any
happiness that is wiser, more cloudless, than what can be
found in that marvelous world? Steel rusts. The ancients' God
created ancient—that is, prone to error—man, and so erred
himself. The multiplication table is wiser and more absolute
than the ancient God. It never—repeat, never—makes a mistake. And there's nothing happier than figures that live according to the elegant and eternal laws of the multiplication table.
No wavering, no wandering. Truth is one, and the true path is
one. And that truth is two times two and that true path is
four. And wouldn't it be absurd if these two happily, ideally
multiplied twos started thinking about some kind of freedom,
that is, about some mistake? For me it's axiomatic: R-13 has
latched onto the most fundamental, the most . . .

At this point I again felt, first on the back of my neck and then on my left ear, the warm, tender breath of my guardian angel. He'd evidently noticed that the book on my knees was shut and my thoughts far away. So what? I'm ready right this minute to spread the pages of my brain open for his inspection: This is just a peaceful, joyous feeling. I remember that I even turned around, I deliberately looked him right in the eyes, as though asking for something, but he did not understand, or didn't feel like understanding, and didn't ask me anything. But I've still got this: You, my unknown readers, you will be told everything (right now you are just as dear, as close, and as unapproachable, as he was at that moment).

Here was the path I had to take: from the part to the whole. The part was R-13. The magnificent whole was our Institute of State Poets and Writers. How could it have happened, I wondered, that the ancients did not immediately see how completely idiotic their literature and poetry was. The immense majestic power of the artistic word was squandered for absolutely nothing. It's simply ridiculous—everybody wrote about whatever popped into his head. It's just as stupid and ridiculous as the fact that the ancients let the ocean go on dumbly beating against the shore around the clock, and the millions of kilogrammeters locked up inside the waves went for nothing but kindling lovers' emotions. We've taken the waves' sweet nothings and turned them into electricity . . . taken a mad crashing foaming beast and turned it into a domestic animal. In just the same way we've tamed and saddled what used to be the wild nature of poetry. Poetry today is not some impudent nightingale's piping—poetry is government service, poetry is usefulness.

Take our famous "Mathematical Rhymes"—if we hadn't had them in school, could we possibly have conceived such a sincere and tender love for the four rules of arithmetic? And the "Thorns," that classical image. The Guardians are the thorns on the rosebush, protecting the gentle State Flower against all rude contact. Who could be so stony-hearted as to resist the sight of innocent children's lips murmuring, like a prayer, the lines:

*Ninny, Ninny, grabbed a rose,*
*Got a thorn stuck in his nose,*
*Served him right, the silly imp!*
*Ninny, Ninny, home did limp.*

And how about the "Daily Odes to the Benefactor"? Who can read them without bowing his head reverently before the selfless labor of this Number of Numbers? Or the terrible, blood-red beauty of the "Flowers of Judicial Verdicts"? Or the immortal tragedy, "Late for Work"? Or the bedside book of "Stanzas on Sexual Hygiene"?

The whole of life, in all its complexity and beauty, has been etched into the gold of words.

Our poets no longer soar into the Empyrean; they've come down to earth. They go along in step with us to the stern mechanical march of the Musical Factory. Their lyre consists of the morning hum of electrical toothbrushes, the spark's ominous snap in the Machine of the Benefactor, the grandiose echo of the OneState Anthem, the intimate sound of the crystal bright chamber pot at night, the exciting clatter of lowering blinds, the merry voices of the latest cookbook, and the barely audible whisper of the street membranes.

Our gods are here below, with us, in the Bureau, in the kitchen, in the shop, in the toilet. The gods have become like us—ergo, we've become like gods. And we're headed your way, my unknown planetary readers, we're coming to make your life divinely rational and precise, like ours.

## RECORD 13

*Fog*

*Familiar "You"*

*An Absolutely Inane Occurrence*

I woke at dawn and my eyes took in a pink, strong firmament. Everything was good and round. O would come in the evening. I was already well . . . no doubt of that. Smiling, I fell asleep.

The morning bell sounds. I get up, and everything is totally different: through the glass of the ceiling, the walls, everywhere, all over, throughout everything—fog. Insane clouds of it, now heavier, now lighter, now closer, and there's no more telling earth from sky, everything flying, melting, falling, nothing to grab hold of. There are no more buildings. The glass walls have dissolved in the fog like salt crystals in water. Looking from the pavement you'd see the dark figures of people in the buildings like particles suspended in some delirious, milky solution. They hang down low and then higher, and then still higher, on the tenth floor. And smoke everywhere, like some fire raging in complete silence.

Precisely at 11:45 I deliberately glanced at the clock so as to grab hold of the figures—the figures, at least, would save me.

At 11:45, before going, in accordance with the Table of Hours, to my regular physical labor, I ran by my room for a second. Just then the phone rang. The voice was a long, slow needle into my heart.

"Oh good, you're at home. I'm glad. Wait for me on the corner. We'll go . . . but you'll see where we're going."

"You know very well that I'm going to work right now."

"You know very well that you're going to do as I tell you. Goodbye. See you in two minutes."

Two minutes later I was standing on the corner. I had to show her that she was not in charge of me—OneState was. "Do as I tell you." And she was sure I would—you could hear it in her voice. Well, now I was going to have it out with her for sure.

Gray yunies woven out of damp fog hastily swam into existence near me, and the next minute dissolved in the fog. I didn't take my eyes off the clock. I was the second hand, sharp and trembling. Eight minutes passed. Ten. Three minutes to twelve, two . . .

I knew it. I was already late for work. How I hated her. But I had to show her. . . .

On the corner in the white fog. Blood. Cut with a sharp knife. It was her lips.

"It looks like I've kept you waiting. Anyway, it doesn't matter. You're already late."

How I . . . But she was right. It was already too late.

I looked silently at her lips. All women are lips, nothing but lips. Some are pink, supple, round—a ring, a tender shield against the whole world. And then these: A second ago they didn't exist, and now suddenly, made by a knife, the sweet blood still dripping . . .

Closer—she leaned against me with her shoulder, and we made one, she blended into me—and I knew: This is how it has to be. I knew this with every nerve, every hair, with the sweet pain of every heartbeat. And what a joy it was to give in to this *has to be*. A piece of iron probably feels just as glad to submit to the precise, inevitable law and clamp onto a magnet. A stone thrown up in the air hesitates for a moment and then plunges down headlong to the earth. And after the final agony a man is glad to breathe his last—and die.

I remember that I smiled in a vacant way and, for no particular reason, said, "Foggy . . . very."

"You like the fog?"

She'd switched to the familiar form of "you"—an ancient, forgotten form . . . the "you" a master used to his slave. It was slowly sinking into me, but sharp: Yes, I am a slave, and that is also how it *has to be*, also good.

"Yes, good," I said aloud to myself. And then to her, "I hate the fog. I'm afraid of the fog."

"That means you love it. You're afraid of it because it's stronger than you, you hate it because you're afraid of it, you love it because you can't master it. You can only love something that refuses to be mastered."

Yes, that's right. And that's why, that's exactly why I . . .

The two of us walked along as one. Somewhere a long ways off through the fog you could hear the sun singing, everything was supple, pearly, golden, pink, red. The whole world was one immense woman and we were in her very womb, we hadn't yet been born, we were joyously ripening. And it was clear, unshakably clear, that all of this was for me: the sun, the fog, the pink, the gold—for me.

I didn't ask where we were going. It didn't matter, just so we were going, going, ripening, burgeoning and supple. . . .

"Well, here we are," said I-330, stopping at an entrance. "The person on duty just now happens to be one. . . . I spoke about him when we were in the Ancient House."

Trying not to lose that thing that was ripening, I read the sign from a distance, with my eyes only: "Bureau of Medicine." I understood everything.

Glass room full of golden fog. Glass rows of colored bottles and jars. Wires. Bluish sparks in tubes.

And a little man, extremely thin. He was like something cut out of paper, and no matter which way he turned, he was nothing but profile, sharp and chiseled. His nose, a flashing blade; his lips—scissors.

I couldn't hear what I-330 was saying to him. I looked at how she was saying it. And I felt myself smiling blissfully, helplessly. The blades of the scissor-lips flashed and the doctor said, "Yes, yes. I understand. A most dangerous disease—I don't know one more dangerous." He gave a laugh. With his thin paper hand he quickly wrote something down and gave it to I-330. Wrote something else, gave it to me.

These were notes certifying that we were sick, that we could not show up for work. I was stealing my labor from OneState. I was a thief. I was headed for the Benefactor's Machine. But I was indifferent to all that, it was far away, as though in some book. I took the sheet of paper without a moment's hesitation. I knew—my eyes, my lips, my hands, all knew that this is how it *had to be*.

In a half-empty garage at the corner we took an aero. As before, I-330 sat at the wheel, shoved the starter to "Forward," we lifted off the ground and floated away. And it all followed along after us: the pink-gold fog, the sun, the razor-thin profile of the doctor, suddenly so dear and close. Everything used to revolve around the sun; now I knew it all revolved around me—slowly, blissfully, squinting its eyes.

The old woman was at the gates of the Ancient House. Same dear, sunken mouth, with wrinkles like rays. Probably sunken all these days, and only now opened up and smiled.

"Ah, you scamp! None of this working like everybody else . . . but it's okay. If anything happens, I'll run and tell you. . . ."

The heavy, squeaking, opaque door closed, and at that instant my heart opened, painfully and wide, still wider—all the way open. Her lips met mine, I drank, drank, tore myself away, silently looked into the eyes opened wide on me . . . and again . . .

The half-light of the rooms, blue, saffron-yellow, dark green morocco, the Buddha's golden smile, gleaming mirrors. And my old dream, so understandable now: everything saturated with the golden-pink juice, and now at any moment it will spill over and splash . . .

It was ripe. Helplessly, like iron and magnet, sweetly yielding to the immutable precise law, I emptied myself into her. There was no pink ticket, no accounting, no OneState, there was no me. There were only the dear, sharp, clenched teeth, there were the golden eyes opened wide on me, and through them I slowly penetrated inside, deeper and deeper. And there was silence. Only in the corner, thousands of miles away, drops were dropping into the basin and I was the universe, and between one drop and another were eras, epochs . . .

Throwing on my yuny, I bent over I-330 and, for the last time, took her in with my eyes.

"I knew that . . . I knew you," said she, very softly. She got up quickly, put on her yuny, and her smile-bite.

"Well, fallen angel. Now you're ruined," she said, reverting to the formal *you*. "No, aren't you afraid? Well, goodbye! You'll get back on your own, right?"

She opened the mirrored door that was in one wall of the wardrobe. Over her shoulder she looked at me and waited. I left obediently. But I'd no more than stepped over the threshold when suddenly I had to feel her pressed against me with her shoulder, only for a second, with her shoulder, that's all.

I rushed back into the room where she (I thought) was still buttoning up her yuny in front of the mirror. I ran in—and stopped. I can see it now: The old ring on the key of the wardrobe door was still swinging, but I-330 was gone. There was nowhere she could have gone, there was only one exit from the room, but still she was gone. I rummaged through everything, I even opened the door of the wardrobe and ran my hands through the ancient motley dresses. No one.

I feel a little awkward, my planetary readers, when I tell you about this totally improbable thing that happened. But what can you do if that really is the way it happened? The whole day from the earliest morning—wasn't it full of the most improbable things, wasn't it just like that ancient sickness called dreaming? And so what difference does it make, one absurdity more or less? Besides, I am certain that sooner or later I'm going to be able to fit any absurdity into a syllogism. I find that comforting, and I hope it comforts you.

How full I am! If only you knew how full I am!

# RECORD 14

*"Mine"*

*Forbidden*

*Cold Floor*

Still about what happened yesterday. During the Personal Hour before bedtime yesterday I was busy and couldn't make a note here. But all that seems carved into me—and especially (this is probably carved in forever) that unbearably cold floor. . . .

O was supposed to come to me in the evening—it was her day. I went downstairs to the duty desk to get my pass for lowering the blinds.

"What's the matter with you?" the duty officer asked. "You look sort of, I don't know, today . . ."

"I . . . I'm sick. . . ."

As a matter of fact, that was the truth. Of course I'm sick. The whole thing is sickness. And just then it hit me: I had the certificate. I felt in my pocket. There it was, it rustled. Which meant . . . it all . . . really happened.

I handed the slip of paper to the duty officer. I could feel my cheeks start to burn. I didn't have to look at the duty officer to see that he was looking at me with surprise.

And it was already 21:30. In the room to my left the blinds were down. In the room to the right I see my neighbor. He's bent over a book, his bumpy, hillocky bald spot and forehead making a huge yellow parabola. And I keep pacing and pacing. I'm in torment. How can I, after all that . . . with her, with O? And from the right I definitely feel eyes on me, I can clearly make out wrinkles on that forehead—a string of yellow lines. And it somehow seems that those lines are about me.

At 22:45 in my room: a rosy whirlwind of joy. A strong ring of rosy arms around my neck. And then I feel how the ring is weakening, weakening . . . it breaks . . . the arms drop . . .

"You aren't the same, not how you were before. You aren't mine!"

What savage terminology—"mine." I was never . . . But I suddenly caught myself: It occurred to me that I wasn't before, true, but now . . . Because now I wasn't living in our rational world. I was in the ancient delirious world, the world where minus one has roots.

The blinds fall. There, behind the wall to the right, my neighbor knocks his book off the table onto the floor, and in the last little momentary crack between the blinds and the floor I see his yellow hand grab the book. And everything in me longs to reach out and grasp that hand. . . .

"I thought . . . I wanted to meet you today during the walk. There was a lot I had . . . I needed to tell you so much. . . ."

Poor, dear O! Her rosy mouth . . . the rosy crescent with its horns turned downward. But I can't tell her everything that happened, if only because that would make her an accomplice of my crimes. Because I know she doesn't have the strength to go to the Bureau of Guardians, and, consequently . . .

O was lying on the bed. I was kissing her slowly. I kissed that naive little puffy crease on her wrist. Her blue eyes were closed. The rosy crescent was slowly opening up like a flower . . . and I kissed her all over.

Suddenly I had an intense feeling of the emptiness of everything, how it had all been abandoned. I couldn't, it was impossible. I needed to, but I couldn't. My lips turned cold at once.

The rosy crescent began to tremble, faded, became contorted. O pulled the cover over her, wrapped herself in it, and turned her face into the pillow. . . .

I sat on the floor next to the bed, a desperately cold floor, and said nothing. The punishing cold from beneath me rose higher and higher. There is probably the same mute cold up there, in the silent blue interplanetary spaces.

"Please understand me . . . I didn't mean . . ." I mumbled. "I tried with all my might . . ."

It was true. I, the real me, did not want . . . But still, what words could I use to tell her? How explain to her that the piece of iron did not want . . . but the law was implacable, precise . . .

Lifting her head out of the pillow, O said, her eyes still shut, "Go away." But as she was crying this came out: "O-way." And this stupid detail also etched itself into me.

Cold through and through, turning numb, I went out into the hall. There beyond the wall was a barely visible wisp of fog. But by night it would probably come down again and cover everything. What would that night bring?

O slipped past me without a word and went to the elevator. The door banged shut.

"Wait a minute!" I yelled. I was terrified.

But the elevator was already humming down, down, down . . .

She had taken R from me.

She had taken O from me.

And yet . . . and yet . . .

# RECORD 15

*Bell*

*Mirror-Like Sea*

*My Fate to Burn Forever*

As soon as I enter the hangar where the INTEGRAL is being built, the Second Builder comes toward me. His face is the same as always: round, white, a porcelain plate. And—serving something irresistibly tasty on this plate—he says:

"Yesterday, while you were so good as to be sick, while the boss was away, so to speak, we had here what you might call an event."

"An event?"

"Yes! The bell rang, they knocked off work, everybody started to leave the hangar, and—wait for it—the man on the door caught a fellow with no number. How he got in I'll never understand. They took him to Operations. Poor baby, they'll pull it out of him there, how and why he . . ." (a delicious smile).

Our best and most experienced physicians work in Operations, under the direct supervision of the Benefactor himself. They have all sorts of apparatus, the main instrument being the famous Gas Bell. This is essentially the old school experiment: A mouse is placed under a glass dome, a pump gradually rarefies the air in the dome . . . and so on. But the Gas Bell is of course a much improved piece of equipment, it uses various gasses; and then, too, this is not making fun of some poor little helpless animal, this has a high purpose, the security of

OneState—in other words, the happiness of millions. About five centuries back, when the work in Operations was only just getting under way, there were certain idiots who compared Operations with the ancient Inquisition. But that's just as stupid as equating a surgeon doing a tracheotomy with a highway robber. They might both be holding the same knife in their hand and doing the same thing—cutting a living human being's throat open—but one of them is a benefactor and the other's a criminal, one has a + sign and the other a – sign.

All this is too obvious, all this you can see in one second, one spin of the logical machine. And then all of a sudden the gear teeth snag on that minus sign—and something totally different swims up to the surface: that key ring still swinging on the wardrobe door. The door had obviously just slammed, but she, I-330, was not there. She'd vanished. There was no way the machine could handle that. A dream? But I can still feel it, that incomprehensibly sweet pain in my right shoulder, I-330 pressing against my right shoulder, beside me in the fog. "You love the fog?" Yes, the fog, too. I love everything. And everything is supple, new, surprising, everything is . . . okay.

"Everything's okay," I said aloud.

"Okay?" The round porcelain eyes popped. "I mean, what's okay about this? If that guy with no number managed . . . then they must be . . . everywhere, all around, all the time, they're here, they're around the INTEGRAL, they . . ."

"Who is *they*?"

"How should I know who? But I feel them—you know? All the time."

"Have you heard about this new operation they're supposed to have developed—the one where they cut out the imagination?" (I had in fact recently heard something like this.)

"Yes, I know. Why do you bring that up?"

"Because, if I were you, I'd go see about having that done."

Something sour as a lemon materialized on the plate. Dear little man. The remotest hint that he might have an imagination was quite insulting to him. But what am I saying? A week back, and I'd probably have been insulted, too. But not now. Because now I know that I have one, that I'm sick. And I also know I don't feel like getting well. I just don't feel like it, that's all. We mounted the glass steps of the stairway. You could see everything below like the palm of your hand.

Those of you reading these notes, wherever you are, you've got the sun above you. And if you were ever as sick as I am now, you know what the sun is like in the morning, or how it might be, you know that rosy, transparent, warm gold. And even the air is a little pink, and everything's saturated with the tender blood of the sun, everything's alive; soft and alive—the stones; warm and alive—the iron; the people alive and every one of them smiling. It might be that an hour later everything will vanish, in one hour the last drop of rosy blood will be gone, but for the time being everything's alive. And I see something pulsing and surging in the glass juices of the INTEGRAL. I see the INTEGRAL thinking about its great and terrifying future, about the heavy burden of inescapable happiness that it will carry there, upward, to you, the unknown ones, to you who seek eternally and never find. You will find, you will be happy. It is your duty to be happy. And you don't have long to wait.

The hull of the INTEGRAL is almost ready: an elegant, elongated ellipsoid made of our glass—as everlasting as gold, as resilient as steel. I saw them inside fastening the transverse ribs, or framers, and the lengthwise stringers to the glass body; aft, they were putting in the base for the giant rocket engine. One blast every three seconds. Every three seconds the mighty tail of the INTEGRAL will spew out flame and gasses into cosmic space, and then off it will fly, the fiery Tamerlane of happiness. . . .

I watched the men below, how they would bend over, straighten up, turn around, all in accordance with Taylor, smoothly and quickly, keeping in time, like the levers of a single immense machine. Pipes glistened in their hands: With fire they were cutting, with fire they were soldering the glass partitions, angle bars, ribs, gussets. I watched the gigantic cranes, made of clear glass, slowly rolling along glass rails and, just like the men, obediently turn, bend, and insert their cargo into the innards of the INTEGRAL. They were the same, all one: humanized, perfected men.

It was the sublimest, the most moving beauty, harmony, music. . . .
I wanted to go down there at once, to them, to be with them!

And there I'd be: shoulder to shoulder with them, welded to
them, caught up in the steel rhythm, the measured movements,
the firm round ruddy cheeks, the mirror-smooth brows, un-
clouded by the insanity of thought. I was sailing on a mirror-
like sea. I was at rest.

Suddenly one of them turned to me serenely and said: "Well,
how's it going today? Feeling better?"

"Better? What . . . ?"

"I mean, you weren't at work yesterday. We thought you
might be down with something serious. . . ." Clear brow, innocent, childlike smile.

The blood rushed to my face. I could not lie to those eyes, I
could not. I said nothing. I was sinking.

From above—gleaming, round, and white—the porcelain
face appeared from a hatch: "Hey! D-503! Mind coming here
for a minute? We've got a tight frame here with the consoles,
and the junction nodes are showing pressure up to . . ."

Not waiting for him to finish, I rushed off in his direction—
I was running away in disgrace, to escape. I didn't have the
strength to raise my eyes. I was dazzled by the flashing glass
steps beneath my feet, and each step made me feel more hopeless: I had no business being here, a criminal, a poisoned man.
Never again was I to blend into the precise mechanical rhythm,
never to sail on the serene and mirror-like sea. My fate was to
burn forever, to rush hither and yon, searching for some corner to hide my eyes—forever, until I found the strength at last
to go through . . .

And then a frozen spark shot through: So much for me, I no
longer mattered, but it would have to be about her, too, and
she . . .

I crawled out of the hatch onto the deck and stopped: I
didn't know where to go now, I didn't know why I'd come
here. I looked up. There the sun, exhausted by noon, was
dimly rising. Down below was the INTEGRAL, gray-glassed
and dead. The rosy blood had run out—I knew I was imagining

all this, that everything was the way it was before, but still, it was clear. . . .

"What's the matter with you, 503? Are you deaf? I've been calling and calling. . . . What's the matter?" It was the Second Builder, who must have been shouting right in my ear for a long time.

What is the matter with me? I've lost the rudder. The motor is roaring for all it's worth, the aero is trembling and racing along, but there's no rudder—and I don't know where it's headed: downward to crash into the earth any second, or upward . . . to the sun, to fire . . .

# RECORD 16

*Yellow*

*Two-Dimensional Shadow*

*Incurable Soul*

Haven't written here in several days. I don't know how many: All the days seem like one. All the days have one color, yellow, like desiccated, hyper-heated sand, and there isn't a shred of shade, nor a drop of water, and no end of the yellow sand. I can't manage without her—but she, ever since she mysteriously vanished from the Ancient House . . .

Since then I've seen her only once on the walk. Two, three, four days ago . . . I don't know. All the days are the same. She appeared once, momentarily, and filled the empty yellow world for a second. Hand in hand with her was the double-bent S, who came only to her shoulder, and the paper-thin doctor, and a fourth Number—only his fingers stuck in my memory: They stuck out of the sleeves of his yuny like bundles of rays . . . extremely thin, white, and long. I-330 raised her hand and waved to me, then she bent across S's head and said something to ray-fingers. I could hear the word "INTE-GRAL," and then all four looked back at me, and then they were lost in the gray-blue sky and I was left with the yellow, dried path.

She had a pink ticket to come to my place that evening. I stood in front of the intercom screen and with mixed tenderness and hatred implored it to click so that the white slot would hurry and light up with "I-330." The elevator doors clanged and every sort came out—pale, tall, pink, dark—but not her. She didn't come.

And it may be that right now, at 22:00, at the very minute when I'm writing this, she's got her eyes closed and is pressing her shoulders against someone and saying, "You like it?" Who? Who is he? That one with the ray-fingers? Or the thick-lipped sprinkler, R? Or S?

S . . . How come not a day passes that I don't hear his flat feet behind me, squelching along as though walking through puddles? Why is he behind me every day, like a shadow? In front, to the side, behind, this gray-blue, two-dimensional shadow. People walk through it, step on it, but it's always right there all the same, next to me, attached by an invisible umbilical cord. Maybe she's the umbilical—I-330? I don't know. Or maybe they, the Guardians, already know that I . . .

Let's say they told you that your shadow could see you, see you all the time. You understand. And suddenly you have this strange feeling that your arms are somebody else's, they're in your way, and I catch myself swinging my arms like an idiot, out of step with my own feet. And suddenly you've absolutely got to look behind you, but you can't look behind you, it's impossible, your neck's in a vise. So I run, I run faster and faster, and my very back senses my shadow running after me, faster and faster, and there's nowhere, nowhere, I can hide from it. . . .

I'm in my room, I'm finally alone. But now there's something else: the phone. I pick up the receiver again: "Yes, may I speak to I-330, please." There's more of the slight noise in the receiver, someone's footsteps, in the hallway, past the doors of her room, and silence. . . . I throw the receiver down . . . and that's it, I can't go on. I've got to go there, to her.

That was yesterday. I ran over there, and for a whole hour, from 16:00 to 17:00, I wandered around the building where she lives. Numbers were passing in rows. Thousands of feet raining down in time, a million-footed leviathan, heaving, was floating past. But I am alone—cast up by the storm on an uninhabited island, and I search and search with my eyes through the gray-blue waves.

Any minute now, from somewhere—the sharp sardonic

angle of eyebrows raised toward temples, and the dark windows of the eyes and there, inside, a burning hearth and someone's shadows moving. And I'm headed straight there, inside, and I call her (by the intimate "you"): "But surely you know— I can't do without you. So why this . . . ?"

She is silent. Suddenly all I hear is silence. Then suddenly I hear the Musical Factory and I understand that it's already past 17:00, that they all left long ago, that I'm alone, I'm late. All around is a glass desert suffused with the yellow sun. In the smooth glass surface I see, like a reflection in water, the shiny walls turned upside down, and I too hang there upside down, a ridiculous figure.

I've got to go at once, right this minute, to the Medical Bureau and get a certificate that I'm sick, or else they'll take me and . . . But that might even be the best thing. Just stay here and wait quietly until I'm seen and they take me to Operations—to end it all right away, pay my debt immediately.

A light rustling noise and the shadow with the double curve stood before me. I didn't have to look to sense the two steel-gray drills quickly boring into me. With all my strength I managed to smile and say (you had to say something): "I . . . I've got to go to the Medical Bureau."

"So what's the matter? Why are you standing there?"

Turned upside down like an idiot, hanging by my feet and burning with shame, I said nothing.

S said sternly: "Follow me."

I went obediently, swinging the useless arms that belonged to someone else. I couldn't raise my eyes. The whole time I was walking in a wild world turned on its head. There were machines bottom up and people like those at the other end of the earth with their feet glued to the ceiling, and down below was the sky, clamped onto the thick glass of the pavement. What hurt most, I remember, was that this was the way I was to see it for the last time in my life—upside down, not the way it should be. But I couldn't raise my eyes.

We stopped. There were steps in front of me. One step more, and I'd see figures in white coats, doctors, and the huge silent Bell. . . .

Finally, with all the effort of a spiral drive mechanism, I tore my eyes away from the glass beneath my feet—and suddenly my face is flooded with the golden letters MEDICAL. . . . Why had he brought me here and not to Operations, why had he spared me? At the moment, this didn't even cross my mind. I was over the threshold in one bound and slammed the door behind me and . . . took a deep breath. I felt I hadn't breathed since early morning, that my heart had not beat—and only now for the first time I took a breath, only now the floodgates in my chest opened. . . .

There were two of them. One, shortish, with legs like mileposts, used his eyes as though they were horns to toss the patients. The other was extremely thin, had lips like scissors and a nose like a blade. It was him.

I threw myself toward him as though we were relatives, right onto the scissors, muttering something about insomnia, dreams, a shadow, a yellow world. The scissor-lips flashed a smile.

"You're in bad shape. It looks like you're developing a soul."

A soul? That strange, ancient, long-forgotten word. We sometimes used expressions like "soul-mate," "body and soul," "soul-destroying," and so on, but soul . . .

"That's . . . very dangerous," I murmured.

"Incurable," the scissors snipped.

"But . . . what is really going on? I don't . . . I can't understand."

"You see . . . how can I put this? You're a mathematician, right?"

"Yes."

"Okay . . . take a flat plane, a surface, take this mirror, for instance. And the two of us are on this surface, see, and we squint our eyes against the sun, and there's a blue electric spark in the tubing, and—there—the shadow of an aero just flashed by. But only on the surface, only for a second. But just imagine now that some fire has softened this impenetrable surface and nothing skims along the top of it any longer—everything penetrates into it, inside, into that mirror world that we peer into with such curiosity, like children—and I assure you, children aren't so dumb. The plane has taken on mass, body, the world, and it's all inside the mirror, inside you: the sun, the wash from the aero's propeller, and your trembling lips, and somebody else's, too. And, you understand, the cold mirror reflects, throws back, while this absorbs, and the trace left by everything lasts forever. Let there be only once a barely noticeable wrinkle on somebody's face, and it's in you forever; once you heard a drop fall in silence—and you hear it right now."

"Yes, yes . . . that's right," I said, and I grabbed his hand. "I just heard it. From . . . the faucet of a washbowl . . . drops slowly dropping in silence. And I knew that would be forever. But, still, why a soul all of a sudden? There wasn't one for such a long time, and now suddenly . . . How come no one else has one, and I . . . ?"

I held on all the harder to that thinnest of hands. I was terrified of losing my lifebelt.

"Why? But why don't we have feathers? Or wings? Nothing but the shoulder blades where wings would be attached? Why, because we no longer need wings. We've got aeros. Wings would only be in the way. Wings are for flying, but we have nowhere to fly to, we've already flown there, we've found it. Isn't that right?"

I nodded my head, in a daze. He looked at me and gave a sharp laugh, like a lancet. The other one, hearing this, stamped out of his consulting-room on his milepost legs and tossed me and my thin doctor on the horns of his eyes.

"What's going on? A soul? Did you say, a soul? What the hell! Next thing you know we'll have cholera again. What did I tell you? [He tossed the thin one on his horns.] I told you so. . . . We should operate on all of them, on the imagination. Extirpate the imagination. Surgery's the only answer . . . nothing but surgery. . . ."

He pulled on some X-ray glasses, walked around me for a long time, peered through the bone of my skull into my brain, and kept on jotting down stuff in his notebook.

"Extremely, extremely curious! Listen—would you by any chance agree to our . . . preserving you in alcohol? For

OneState that would be an extraordinary . . . it would help us ward off an epidemic. That's of course if you have no special reasons to . . ."

"But you see," said he, "Number D-503 is the builder of the INTEGRAL. And I'm sure it would violate . . ."

"Ah," muttered the other, and milestoned it back to his consulting-room.

The two of us were left alone. The paper-thin hand lay lightly and caressingly on mine. The face in profile leaned over to me, and he whispered: "I'll tell you this as a secret, between us. You aren't the only one who has it. It's no accident my colleague mentioned an epidemic. Just think a moment—haven't you yourself noticed someone else with something like this . . . very like it, very close . . . ?" He fixed me with his gaze. What was he hinting at? Who? Surely he couldn't mean . . .

"Listen . . ." I jumped up from the chair. But he'd already begun talking loudly about something else: ". . . And as for the insomnia, these dreams of yours, I can only advise one thing— that you spend more time walking. Start right away tomorrow, and take a walk early in the morning, say, over to the Ancient House, for instance."

He pierced me again with his eyes and gave his thinnest smile. And it seemed to me that I saw, very clearly, wrapped up in the thin fabric of that smile, a word . . . a letter . . . a name, the only name . . . Or was that again just imagination?

I could hardly wait for him to write me a certificate of illness for today and tomorrow, after which I shook hands with him, firmly, saying nothing, and ran outside.

My heart was light and fast as an aero, and it was carrying me up and up. I knew that some sort of happiness was waiting for me tomorrow. But what sort?

# RECORD 17

~ ~

*Through Glass*

*I Died*

*Hallways*

I'm totally confused. Yesterday at the very moment when I thought I'd worked it all out, found the value of every X, new unknowns turned up in my equation.

The coordinates of the whole business all begin, of course, with the Ancient House. The X, Y, and Z axes that recently began serving as the basis of my whole world all start there. I was walking along the X-axis (59th Avenue) toward the place where the coordinates start. What happened yesterday turns in me like a gaudy whirlwind: the upside-down houses and people, the tormentingly strange hands, the flashing scissors, the keen drops falling in the washbowl—that's how it was, or how it was once. And all this, tearing my flesh apart, is twirling there, beneath the surface melted by fire, where the "soul" is.

In obedience to the doctor's prescription I deliberately did not choose to walk along the hypotenuse but took the other two legs of the triangle. Now I'd reached the second of them, the curving road that runs along the base of the Green Wall. From out of the boundless green ocean beyond the Wall a savage wave of roots, flowers, branches, leaves rushed at me, rose up on its hindquarters, would have swamped me, would have turned me, a man, that most delicate and precise of mechanisms, into . . .

But fortunately, between me and the wild green ocean was

the glass of the Wall. O, mighty, divinely delimited wisdom of walls, boundaries! It is perhaps the most magnificent of all inventions. Man ceased to be a wild animal only when he built the first wall. Man ceased to be a wild man only when we built the Green Wall, only when, by means of that Wall, we isolated our perfect machine world from the irrational, ugly world of trees, birds, and animals. . . .

Through the glass, dim and foggy, the blunt muzzle of some beast looked at me, its yellow eyes insistently repeating one and the same thought, incomprehensible to me. We looked each other in the eye for a long time—through those shafts connecting the surface world to that other beneath the surface. And then a little thought wormed its way into my head: "And what if yellow-eyes, in his stupid, dirty pile of leaves, in his uncalculated life, is happier than us?"

I waved my hand, the yellow eyes blinked, backed off, vanished in the foliage. Pathetic creature! How ridiculous—him happier than us! Happier than me—that could be, all right. But then I'm simply an exception, I'm sick.

And then, I . . . I already see the dark red walls of the Ancient House—and the dear old woman's sunken mouth. I rush toward her as fast as I can: "She here?"

"She who?"

"Who?! I-330, of course . . . We came together that time . . . in the aero. . . ."

"Ah, yes . . . Yes, yes, yes . . ."

Wrinkle-rays around her lips, shifty rays in her eyes, which bored into my insides, deeper and deeper, until she finally brought out: "Okay, I guess she's here. Came not long ago."

Here. At the old woman's feet I noticed a bush of silvery bitter wormwood (the courtyard of the Ancient House is a museum, too, which they maintain in the prehistoric form). The wormwood had stuck out a twig to the old woman's hand and she was caressing the twig, and a yellow stripe of sunlight lay across her knees. And for one second: I, the sun, the old woman, the wormwood, the yellow eyes—we all blended into one, were all bound forever by veins through which flowed one common, stormy, magnificent blood.

I'm ashamed to write about this now, but I promised to hold absolutely nothing back in these notes. So here goes: I bent over and kissed that sunken, soft, mossy mouth. The old woman wiped it away and laughed.

I set off at a run through the familiar, slightly cramped, echoing rooms and, for some reason, went straight to the bedroom. I was already at the double doors and had grasped the handle before I suddenly thought: "And suppose she's not alone in there?" I stopped and listened. But all I could hear was . . . a kind of thudding, and not in me but somewhere near me . . . my heart.

I went in. The wide bed, still made. The mirror. Another mirror in the wardrobe door, and in the keyhole there—the key with the ancient ring. And nobody.

I called softly: "I-! You here?" And then even softer, with my eyes closed, not daring to breathe, as if I were on my knees in front of her: "I- . . . ! Darling!"

All was quiet. Only water dripping fast from the faucet into the white basin of the washbowl. Right now I can't say why, but that annoyed me. I gave the handle a hard turn and went out. She wasn't here. That was clear. So that meant she was in some other *apartment*.

I ran down the wide gloomy stairs to the floor below and tried one door, a second, a third: all locked. Everything was locked with the single exception of that one apartment, "ours," and there was no one there.

All the same, I headed back there, I myself don't know why. I walked slowly, I had trouble walking, the soles of my shoes had suddenly turned to cast iron. I distinctly remember thinking: "It's a mistake to consider the force of gravity a constant. Which means that all my formulas . . ."

Just at this point, there was an explosion. All the way downstairs I heard a door slam and someone's feet pounding across the flagstones. Suddenly I was light again, nearly weightless, and rushed to the banisters, where I leaned into one word, one shout, trying to put everything into it . . . "You!"

I froze. Down there, inscribed in the dark square of the shadow cast by the window sash, was the head of S, its winglike ears swinging.

I arrived like lightning at one single naked conclusion, without premises (even now I don't know the premises): "He must absolutely not see me, not for anything."

And pressing myself against the wall, I crept upstairs on tiptoe to the unlocked apartment.

A second's pause by the door. He was dully clumping up the stairs, toward me. Everything was riding on the door! I pleaded with the door, but it was wooden, it creaked, it squeaked. Things flew past in a whirlwind—green, red, the yellow Buddha—and I stood before the mirrored door of the wardrobe: my pale face, eyes intent, lips . . . Through the noise of my blood I hear the door squeak again. . . . That's him, him.

I grabbed for the key of the wardrobe door, and the ring started swinging. That reminded me of something—another momentary, naked conclusion without premise. Or only a part of a conclusion: "That time I-330 . . ." I quickly open the wardrobe door, I'm inside, in the dark, I shut it tight behind me. I take one step, and something gives beneath my feet. I slowly, softly floated off in some downward direction. Everything went black. I died.

Later on when I came to write down all these strange happenings I rummaged about in my memory and in books and now I understand, of course. That was the condition of temporary death, familiar to the ancients and, so far as I can tell, completely unknown among us.

I have no idea how long I was dead, probably not more than five or ten seconds, but a certain amount of time passed before I was resurrected and opened my eyes. It was dark and I felt myself going down, down. . . . I put out my hand, grabbed, and scratched a rough wall that was flying past, which left blood on my finger—obviously this was not just some game of my sick imagination. But what was it, then?

I could hear my unsteady breathing, coming out as though it were a dotted line (I'm ashamed to admit all this—but everything was so sudden and confusing). A minute passed . . . two . . . three . . . and I was still falling. Finally there was a soft bump. Whatever it was that had been falling beneath my feet was now still. Groping about in the dark, I found some sort of handle, gave it a push, a door opened, there was a dim light. I turned and saw behind me a small square platform that was going up very fast. I made a dash but was too late. I was cut off here. Where *here* was, I did not know.

A corridor. A thousand pounds of silence. Lightbulbs on the curved vaults made an endless, twinkling, swaying dotted line. It looked a little like the "tubes" of our subways, only much narrower and not made of our glass but some other ancient material. I had a momentary image of the caves where people are supposed to have hidden out during the 200-Years War. . . . But anyway, it was time to go.

I reckon that I walked about twenty minutes. I turned right and the corridor got wider, the lights brighter. There was some kind of vague humming sound. It could have been machines or it could have been voices . . . I couldn't tell . . . only I was standing next to a heavy opaque door and that's where the humming was coming from.

I gave a knock, and then a second knock, louder. It got quiet behind the door. There was a clank, and the door began to open, very slow and heavy.

I don't know which of us was more stunned—I was looking at my thin, blade-nosed doctor.

"You? Here?" he said, and his scissor-lips clicked. And as for me, it was like I'd never known a single human word. I said nothing, just looked at him, and understood absolutely nothing of what he was saying to me. Probably that I had to get out of there, because then he pushed me with his flat paper belly to the end of that better-lighted corridor, and gave me a shove in the back.

"Excuse me, I wanted, I thought that she, that I-330 . . . But behind me . . ."

"Stay here." The doctor cut me off and disappeared.

Finally! Finally she was here nearby . . . and who cared where this *here* was? The familiar saffron-yellow silk, the bite-smile, the eyes hidden behind blinds . . . My lips, my hands, my knees were all trembling . . . and an idiotic thought crossed my mind: "Sound is vibration. Trembling ought to make a noise. How come I can't hear it?"

Her eyes opened to me—wide open—I entered. . . .

"I couldn't stand it any longer! Where were you? Why . . ." I said, never taking my eyes off her for a second. What I was saying sounded delirious, quick, disconnected, and maybe I wasn't even saying it, just thinking it. "The shadow . . . behind me . . . I died . . . out of the wardrobe . . . Because that doctor of yours . . . he speaks with scissors, says I've got a soul . . . says it's incurable. . . ."

"An incurable soul! You poor thing!" I-330 burst out laughing. And her laughter splashed all over me, the whole delirium passed, and little sequins of laughter were flashing and how . . . how wonderful it all was.

The doctor unfolded himself from around the corner again—the wonderful, magnificent, paper-thin doctor.

"Well . . ." said he, stopping next to her.

"It's okay, okay! I'll tell you later. He just happened . . . Tell them I'll be back in . . . fifteen minutes."

The doctor flashed off around the corner. She waited. There was a dull sound of the door closing. Then very, very slowly I-330, thrusting her sharp sweet needle deeper and deeper into my heart, pressed against me with her shoulder, her arm, her whole body, and we went, she and I, she and I, two as one . . .

I don't remember at what point we turned into the dark, and in the dark how we went up endless steps in complete silence. I couldn't see but I knew she was walking along just as I was, with eyes closed, blind, head thrown back, biting her lips, and listening to the music—the music of my barely audible trembling.

I woke up in one of the countless niches in the courtyard of the Ancient House. There was some kind of earthen fence—the bare rocky ribs and yellow teeth of some dilapidated walls. She opened her eyes and said, "Day after tomorrow at 16:00." Then she left.

Did all this really happen? I don't know. I'll find out day after tomorrow. The only actual evidence is that the skin is scraped away on the tips of the fingers of my right hand. But today at the INTEGRAL the Second Builder assured me that he himself had seen me accidentally touch a sanding wheel with those fingers—so that's all it was. Who knows—maybe that was it. It's very possible. I don't know. I don't know anything.

# RECORD 18

*Logical Labyrinth*

*Wounds and Plaster*

*Never Again*

Yesterday I lay down and instantly sank to the bottom of sleep, like a ship overloaded and overturned. Issueless depth of heaving green water. At length I swam slowly up from the bottom, and somewhere about halfway to the top I opened my eyes. I see my room, the morning still green and rigid with cold. On the mirrored door of the wardrobe a shard of sun hits me in the eyes. This stops me from putting in exactly all the hours of sleep prescribed by the Table. The best thing would be just to open the door of the wardrobe. But I feel all wrapped up in a spiderweb, with spiderwebs in my eyes, and I haven't got the strength to get up.

I get up anyway, open the—and suddenly I see, behind the door, all pink, struggling out of the clothes on the rack: I-330. By now I was so used to the most unexpected things happening that, so far as I remember, I was not even the least bit surprised. I asked no questions. I just got into the wardrobe at once, slammed the mirrored door shut behind me, and then—panting, quickly, blindly, greedily—became one with I-330. I see it plainly even now: In the dark, through a crack in the door, a sharp ray of sunlight shatters on the floor like lightning, then on the wall of the wardrobe, then higher . . . and then this cruel flashing blade falls on I-330's open, naked throat . . . and I find this so horrible that I can't stand it, I scream . . . and once more I open my eyes.

My room. Same green frozen morning. A shard of sun on the wardrobe door. I'm in my bed. A dream. But my heart is still beating wildly, shuddering, spurting. The tips of my fingers, my knees, are numb. There can be no doubt: This did happen. And now I don't know dream from waking. Irrational magnitudes are growing up through everything that is stable, customary, three-dimensional, and all around me something rough and shaggy is replacing the firm, polished surfaces. . . .

The bell to get up is still a long way off. I lie in the bed thinking . . . and a logical chain, extraordinarily odd, starts unwinding itself.

For every equation, every formula in the superficial world, there is a corresponding curve or solid. For irrational formulas, for my $\sqrt{-1}$, we know of no corresponding solids, we've never seen them. . . . But that's just the whole horror—that these solids, invisible, exist. They absolutely inescapably must exist. Because in mathematics their eccentric prickly shadows, the irrational formulas, parade in front of our eyes as if they were on a screen. And mathematics and death never make a mistake. And if we don't see these solids in our surface world, there is for them, there inevitably must be, a whole immense world there, beneath the surface.

I jumped up without waiting for the bell and began to run around my room. My mathematics, up to now the only lasting and immovable island in my entire dislocated life, had also broken loose and floated whirling off. So does this mean that that stupid "soul" is just as real as my yuny, as my boots, even though I can't see them now (they're behind the mirror of the wardrobe door)? And if the boots are not a disease, why is the "soul" a disease?

I looked for it but I found no way out of this wild logical thicket. This was a tangle every bit as unknown and terrifying as that behind the Green Wall. These were creatures just as extraordinary and incomprehensible, and they said as much with no words. I imagined that I saw through some kind of thick glass the square root of minus one—infinitely huge and at the same time infinitely small, scorpion-shaped, with that hidden but always sensed sting of a minus sign. . . . But maybe that is nothing except my "soul," like the legendary scorpion of the ancients, which would deliberately sting itself with everything that . . .

The bell. Daylight. None of this died or vanished—it was simply covered over by the light of day; just the way visible objects don't die but are concealed at night by the darkness of night. A light shimmering fog in my head. Through the fog, long glass tables are visible. Spherical heads are slowly, silently chewing in time with one another. From a distance a metronome is ticking through the fog, and I mechanically chew to the familiar caress of its music, counting, along with everyone else, up to fifty: fifty statutory chews for each mouthful. And, still mechanically beating out the time, I go downstairs, and, like everyone else, check off my name in the book as one leaving the premises. But I sense that I'm living separately from everyone else, alone, surrounded by a soft, soundproof wall, and that my world is on my side of this wall.

But how about this? If this world is only mine, how come it is in these notes? How come these stupid "dreams," wardrobes, endless corridors are here? I am crushed to see that instead of the elegant and strict mathematical poem in honor of OneState, it's turning out to be some kind of fantastic adventure novel. Oh, if only this really were just a novel instead of my actual life, filled with X's, $\sqrt{-1}$, and degradations.

On the other hand, maybe it's all for the best. You, my unknown readers, are most likely children compared to us (we were after all reared by OneState and have consequently attained the highest summits possible for man). And like children, you will only swallow all the bitter stuff I have to give you if it is carefully coated with a thick syrup of adventure.


## EVENING.

Do you know this feeling? When you're in an aero speeding up through a blue spiral, the window open, the wind whistling, and there's no earth, you've forgotten the earth, the earth is just as far from you as Saturn or Jupiter or Venus? That's how I'm living now. The wind is in my face and I've forgotten about the earth, I've forgotten about dear rosy O. But earth exists all the same, and sooner or later I've got to glide down and land on it, and I'm just shutting my eyes to the day on my Sexual Table with O-90's name on it. . . .

This evening the distant earth sent me a reminder of itself.

In order to carry out the doctor's orders (I sincerely, sincerely want to get well), I roamed for two whole hours in the desolate glass grid of the avenues. Everyone was in the auditoriums, in accordance with the Table, and only I alone. . . . It was basically an unnatural sight. Picture this: a human finger, cut off from its body, its hand . . . a separate human finger, running hopping along, all hunched over, on a glass sidewalk. I am that finger.

And what is strangest of all, most unnatural of all, is that the finger hasn't got the slightest desire to be on the hand, to be with the others; either like this, all alone, or . . . Well, look, there's no point any longer in my trying to hide it: either alone or with her, with that woman, to empty my whole self into her through a shoulder, through clasped hands . . .

The sun was already setting when I got back home. The rosy ashes of the evening were already on the glass of the walls, on the gold of the spire of the accumulator tower, on the voices and the smiles of the Numbers I passed. Isn't it odd that the dying rays of the sun fall at precisely the same angle as those coming to life in the morning, but everything is completely different, there's a different rosiness, now it's very quiet, with a touch of bitterness, but in the morning it will be once again loud and ebullient?

But now, downstairs in the vestibule, U, the woman on duty, has just reached under a pile of envelopes covered with rosy ash, pulled out a letter, and handed it to me. I repeat: She's a very respectable woman, and I'm sure she is very well disposed toward me.

Still, every time I see those cheeks hanging down like fish gills, I somehow don't like it.

As she handed me the letter with her gnarled hand, U gave a sigh. But this sigh caused hardly a stir in the curtain separating me from the world. My concentration was 100 percent focused on the trembling envelope in my hand, which, I had no doubt, contained a letter from I-330.

At this point came a second sigh, one so pointed, with a double line beneath it, that I tore myself away from the envelope. Between the gills, and through the shy jalousies of her lowered lids, I saw a tender, embracing, blinding smile. And then:

"You poor, poor thing . . ." She said this with a triple-underlined sigh and a barely detectable nod at the envelope (the contents of which she naturally knew as part of her duty).

"No, really, I . . . I mean, why?"

"No, no, dear. I know you better than you know yourself. I've had my eye on you for a long time now, and I see that you're in need of someone to go arm in arm with you through life, someone who's spent long years studying life."

All swaddled in this smile, I have the feeling it is the plaster for the wounds with which this letter trembling in my hand is about to cover me. Finally, very quietly, through the shy jalousies, she says: "I'll think about it, dear, I'll think about it. And don't worry . . . if I feel that I have enough strength . . . but no, I'll still have to think it over first. . . ."

Great Benefactor! Don't tell me that's going to be my fate. . . . Don't tell me she's trying to say that . . .

My eyes dazzle, there are thousands of sinusoids, the letter leaps. I walk over to the light, to the wall. Over there the sun is setting, and a sad, dark rose ash of denser and denser light is falling on me, on the floor, on my hands, and on the letter.

The envelope is torn open, a quick glance at the signature, and a wound: not from I-330, not from her . . . it's from O. And another wound: In the bottom right corner of the paper is a stain where the ink has run, where a drop of something fell. . . . I can't stand smudges, ink or any other kind, it doesn't matter. And I know that, before, this would have just been unpleasant to me, unpleasant for the eyes, this unpleasant spot. But now . . . how come this grayish little spot is like a raincloud, making everything darker and more leaden? Or is this just more "soul"?

### THE LETTER

You know . . . or maybe you don't know . . . I don't know how to write this—but never mind: Now you know that there will never be a day for me, or a morning, or a springtime, without you. Because for me R is nothing more than . . . but you don't care about this. At any rate, I'm very grateful to him. I don't know what I would have done, alone, without him, these last few days. During these days and nights I've lived through ten or maybe twenty years. My room has seemed round and not square, and endless, round and round and all the same, with no doors anywhere.

I can't live without you—because I love you. Because I see, I understand, that you don't need anybody, anybody on earth, except her, that other one, and . . . look, that's just it, if I love you, then I have to . . .

I just need two or three more days to try and put the pieces of myself back into some semblance of the former O-90—and then I'll go and fill out the form myself, that I'm withdrawing my registration for you, and you'll be better off, you'll be fine. I'll never come again. Goodbye.

O.

Never again. It's better that way, of course. She's right. But why, why . . .

# RECORD 19

*Third-Order Infinitesimal*

*A Sullen Glare*

*Over the Parapet*

There in that strange corridor with the wavy dotted line of dull lightbulbs . . . or no, not there . . . later, when she and I were in that out-of-the-way niche in the courtyard of the Ancient House . . . she said, "Day after tomorrow." That "day after tomorrow" is today, and everyone's sprouted wings, the day is flying, and our INTEGRAL already has its wings on: They've finished installing the rocket engine, and today we put it through a test run. What magnificent, powerful blasts, and for me each one was a salute to her, to the only one, and to this day.

At the first pass (= shot) some ten or so Numbers from our hangar were caught napping beneath the engine exhaust—absolutely nothing was left of them but some sort of crumbs and soot. I'm proud to note down here that this did not cause a second's hitch in the rhythm of our work, no one flinched; and we and our work teams continued our rectilinear and circular movement with exactly the same precision as though nothing had happened. Ten Numbers—that is scarcely one hundred-millionth part of the mass of OneState. For all practical purposes, it's a third-order infinitesimal. Innumerate pity is a thing known only to the ancients; to us it's funny.

And it's funny to me that yesterday I was capable of wasting time thinking about—and even noting down in these pages—some pathetic gray spot, some ink-blot. That's the same "softening of the surface" that ought to be diamond-hard, like our walls (cf. the old saying: "like peas against a wall").

16:00 hours. I didn't go for the extra walk. Who can tell? She might take a notion to come right this minute, with everything ringing in the sunshine.

I'm practically alone in the building. Through the sunny walls I have a long view—to the right, left, and down—of empty rooms hanging in the air, repeating one another like mirror reflections. And only along the bluish staircase, hardly inked in by the sun, an emaciated gray shadow slips slowly upward. Now you can even hear the footsteps, and I can see through the door, I can feel that the plaster-smile has been stuck on me. Then it goes past, to another stairwell, and down.

Click of the intercom screen. I throw myself at the narrow white slot . . . and I see some Number I've never heard of (male, since it began with a consonant). Elevator hum. Doors slam. In front of me is a Number whose forehead seems to have been carelessly tilted down over his eyes. Very odd impression, as though he were speaking from underneath his brow, where his eyes are located.

"A letter for you, from her." This from beneath the brow, from behind the curtain. "She asked that everything, without fail, be done as it's written here."

Then a searching look round, still from beneath the brow, the curtain. But there's no one here, I tell you—let's have the letter! One more look round, he sticks the envelope in my hand, and leaves. I'm alone.

No, I'm not alone. From the envelope falls a pink ticket and, barely detectable, her scent. It's her, she's coming, she'll come to me. To the letter, quick, to read it with my own eyes, to really believe it all the way. . . .

What? It can't be! I read it again, leaping across the lines: "Ticket . . . and be sure to let the blinds down, as though I really were with you. . . . I need them to think that I . . . I'm very, very sorry. . . ."

The letter's in shreds. A second's glance in the mirror. I see my broken, distorted eyebrows. I take the ticket, to shred it like the letter. . . .

"She asked that everything, without fail, be done as it's written here."

My hands weakened, relaxed. The ticket fell out of them onto the table. She is stronger than me, and it looks as though I'm going to do as she wants. But still . . . I don't know. We'll see. Tomorrow is still a ways off. The ticket's on the table.

My broken, distorted eyebrows are in the mirror. If only I had a doctor's certificate for today, too, to go walk and walk forever around the Green Wall and then come drop in the bed, down to the bottom of it. . . . But I've got to go to auditorium No. 13, I've got to screw myself up tight, to sit through two hours, two whole hours, not moving . . . when I need to scream and stamp my feet.

A lecture. It's very strange that the gleaming apparatus emits not the usual metallic voice but a kind of soft, shaggy, mossy voice. A female voice. Her image as she was in life flits before my mind's eye: a little bent old woman, like that one at the Ancient House.

The Ancient House . . . and all at once everything shoots up from underneath like a fountain and I have to screw myself as tight as I can to keep from drowning the whole auditorium with a scream. Soft, shaggy words. They go through me, leaving behind only one thing . . . something about children, about child husbandry. Like a photographic plate, I register it all with a mad precision that seems to come from someone else, somewhere outside me: a golden sickle of reflected light on the loudspeaker; beneath this, a child, a living illustration, reaching toward the sickle; the hem of its tiny yuny is stuck in its mouth; tightly clenched fist, the little thumb squeezed inside; light, downy shadow; a little crease on the wrist. Like a photographic plate I register it: Now there's a bare leg hanging over the side, the toes making a rosy fan to step on the air, and in one moment, one moment more, the child will fall on the floor. . . .

And there's a woman's scream. Onto the stage she sweeps with the diaphanous wings of her yuny, grabs the child, brushes the puffy crease at the wrist with her lips, moves it to the center of the table, comes down from the stage. On my internal plate is an impression: rosy mouth-crescent, horns downward, blue saucer-eyes brimming to the edge. It's O. And I feel as I do when reading an elegant formula—a sudden sense of the necessity, the rightness of this trivial incident.

She took a seat a little ways behind me and to the left. I looked back. She obediently took her eyes away from the table with the child, turned her eyes toward me, into me, and again: The three of us—she, I, and the table on the stage—we were three points, and through these points were drawn three lines, projections of some unavoidable, some still-hidden events.

I head home at dusk along the green street, already big-eyed with streetlamps. I could hear myself ticking all over, like a clock. And any minute now my hour hand is going to pass a certain figure on the dial and I'll do something that I'll never be able to take back. She needs someone or other to think that she's with me. But I need her, and what do I care about her "needs"? I don't want to be someone else's blinds. I don't want it, and that's that.

Behind me I hear the familiar squelching footsteps, like someone walking through puddles. I don't even look around any longer—I know it's S. He'll follow me right up to the entrance, and then probably he'll stand there below on the sidewalk and drill upward with his gimlet eyes to my room, until the blinds go down to cover up someone's crime.

He, the Guardian Angel, had brought things to a point. I made up my mind: I'd had enough. I decided.

When I went up to my room and turned on the light, I couldn't believe my eyes: O was standing beside my table. Or rather, she was hanging there, the way an empty dress hangs when it's been taken off. Inside that dress there was no spring left in her, no spring in her arms, her legs, her sagging voice.

"I . . . I'm here about my letter. You got it? Yes? I have to know the answer, I have to know it today, now."

I shrugged my shoulders. I took pleasure, as though it were all her fault, in staring into her blue eyes, brimming with tears. I took my time answering. I enjoyed inserting each separate word into her as I said: "Answer? What do you expect? You're right. Absolutely. In everything."

"That means . . ." She tries to cover a slight tremble with a smile, but I see it. "Well, very good! I'll . . . I'll go now."

And she went on hanging over the table, her eyes, feet, and hands sagging. *Her* crumpled pink ticket is still lying on the table. I hurry to unfold this manuscript of mine—*We*—and hide the ticket with its pages (more from myself, maybe, than from O).

"Look—I'm writing it all down. Already 170 pages. . . . It's turning out to be sort of surprising. . . ."

Her voice . . . or the shadow of it: "You remember how . . . on page 7 . . . I let a tear fall . . . and you . . ."

The little blue saucers had silent, hurried tears running over the brim and down along her cheeks, and hurried words brimmed: "I can't, I'm leaving right now. . . . I'll never come again, that's best. Only I'd like . . . I must have a child from you. Give me a child and I'll leave, I'll leave!"

I saw that under her yuny she was trembling all over, and I felt now I, too . . . I clasped my hands behind my back and smiled. "What? You suddenly feel like going on the Benefactor's Machine?"

Then her words flooded onto me as over a dike: "So what! At least I'll get to feel it—I'll feel it inside me. And maybe for only a few days . . . see it. Just once to see its little fold, here, like that one, there on the table. Just one day!"

Three points: her, me, and there on the table the little fist with the puffy fold. . . .

Once when I was a child, I remember, they took us to the Accumulator Tower. On the very top flight I leaned over the glass parapet. Down below the people were dots, and a sweet excitement ticked in my heart: "What if . . ." Then I gripped the railing all the tighter; now—I leapt over.

"It's what you want? And you're perfectly aware that . . ."

Her eyes were closed as if she were looking right into the sun. A moist, radiant smile. "Yes, yes! It's what I want!"

I reached under the manuscript and grabbed *her* ticket and ran down the stairs to the duty desk. O had grabbed at my hand and shouted something, but what it was I understood only when I got back.

She was sitting on the edge of the bed with her hands tightly clasped between her knees.

"That . . . that was her ticket?"

"What difference does it make? Yes . . . hers."

There was a cracking noise. Probably O had just shifted on the bed. She was sitting with her hands in her lap, not saying anything.

"Well? We're wasting time . . ." I said, and I grabbed her arm hard and red spots (bruises tomorrow) showed on her wrist, at the place she's got that puffy babyish fold.

That was the last of it. Then the lights were turned off, thoughts sputtered out, darkness, sparks—and me, over the side of the parapet and down. . . .

# RECORD 20

*Discharge*

*Idea Material*

*Zero Cliff*

Discharge is the most suitable definition. That's what that was, I now see: like an electrical discharge. These last few days my pulse has been getting drier and drier, quicker and quicker, more and more tense—the poles closer and closer, making this dry crackling sound. One millimeter more, and there'll be an explosion. After which: silence.

Inside me right now it's very quiet and empty, the same as in the building when everyone's left and you're lying all alone, sick, and you can hear this clear, precise, metallic beating of your thoughts.

Maybe this "discharge" cured me, finally, of that torment called my "soul," and I'm just like all the rest of us again. Now at least I don't feel any pain when I see O in my thoughts standing on the steps of the Cube, when I see her under the Gas Bell. And if she gives them my name there in Operations— so be it. My last act will be to put a pious and grateful kiss on the Benefactor's punishing hand. In my relationship with One-State I have that right, to undergo punishment, and this right I will not give up. None of us Numbers ought, none dares, to refuse that one right that we have, which means it is the most valuable.

. . . There's a quiet, clear metallic sound to my thoughts' clicking; an unknown aero is carrying me away into the blue heights of my favorite abstractions. And here in this purest, most rarefied air, I see my reflection "on operative right" pop with a slight bang like a tire blowing out. And I see clearly that it was nothing more than a throwback to the ancients' idiotic superstition, their idea about one's "right."

There are ideas made of clay, and there are ideas sculpted for the ages out of gold or out of our precious glass. And to determine what material an idea is made of, all you have to do is let a drop of powerful acid fall on it. Even the ancients knew one such acid: *reductio ad finem.* That's what they seem to have called it. But they were afraid of this poison. They preferred to see at least some kind of heaven—however clay, however toylike—to this blue nothing. But we are grown-ups, thanks be to the Benefactor, and don't need toys.

Look here—suppose you let a drop fall on the idea of "rights." Even among the ancients the more grown-up knew that the source of right is power, that right is a function of power. So, take some scales and put on one side a gram, on the other a ton; on one side "I" and on the other "We," OneState. It's clear, isn't it?—to assert that "I" has certain "rights" with respect to the State is exactly the same as asserting that a gram weighs the same as a ton. That explains the way things are divided up: To the ton go the rights, to the gram the duties. And the natural path from nullity to greatness is this: Forget that you're a gram and feel yourself a millionth part of a ton.

You, plump, rosy-cheeked Venusians, and you Uranites, sooty as blacksmiths—in my blue silence I can hear your grumbling. But understand this: All greatness is simple. Understand this: Only the four rules of arithmetic are unalterable and everlasting. And only that moral system built on the four rules will prevail as great, unalterable, and everlasting. That is the ultimate wisdom. That is the summit of the pyramid up which people, red and sweating, kicking and panting, have scrambled for centuries. And looking down from this summit to the bottom, we see what remains in us of our savage ancestors seething like wretched worms. Looking down from this summit, there's no difference between a woman who gave birth illegally—O—and a murderer, and that madman who dared aim his poem at OneState. And the verdict is the same for them all: premature death. This is the very same divine justice dreamt of by the people of the stone-house age, illuminated by the rosy naive rays of the dawn of history: Their "God" punished abuse of Holy Church exactly the same as murder.

You Uranites, stern and black as early Spaniards, you who were wise enough to do some burning at the stake, you are silent; I think you're with me. But you rosy Venusians . . . among you I hear something about torture, executions, a return to the age of barbarism. I'm sorry for you, old dears. You aren't up to philosophical-mathematical thinking.

Human history ascends in spirals, like an aero. The circles vary, some are gold, some are bloody, but all are divided into the same 360 degrees. It starts at zero and goes forward: 10, 20, 200, 360 degrees—then back to zero. Yes, we've come back to zero—yes. But for my mind, thinking in mathematics as it does, one thing is clear: This zero is completely different, new. Leaving zero, we headed to the right. We returned to zero from the left. So instead of plus zero, we have minus zero. Do you understand?

I see this zero as some kind of silent, huge, narrow, knife-sharp cliff. In ferocious, shaggy darkness, holding our breath, we pushed off from the black night side of the Zero Cliff. For centuries, like some new Columbus, we sailed and sailed and rounded the whole earth, and at last, Hurrah! A salute! All hands on deck and lookouts aloft! In front of us is the new, hitherto unknown side of the Zero Cliff, lit by the polar effulgence of OneState, a blue massif, the sparks of a rainbow, the sun, hundreds of suns, billions of rainbows. . . .

So what if nothing but the breadth of a knife blade separates us from the other dark side of the Zero Cliff? A knife is the most permanent, the most immortal, the most ingenious of all of man's creations. The knife was a guillotine, the knife is a universal means of resolving all knots, and the path of paradox lies along the blade of a knife—the only path worthy of the mind without fear. . . .

# RECORD 21

*An Author's Duty*

*Swollen Ice*

*The Most Difficult Love*

Yesterday was her day, and again she didn't come, and again she sent me an incoherent note, explaining nothing. But I am staying calm, absolutely calm. If I'm still doing just as the note told me to do, if I'm still taking her ticket down to the duty desk and then lowering the blinds and sitting alone in my room—it isn't because I don't have the strength to go against her wishes. That's ridiculous! Of course not. It's just that with the blinds down I'm protected against any sticking-plaster smiles and can write these pages in peace—that's one. And two: I'm afraid that if I lose her, I-330, I might lose the only key to explain all the unknowns (that story with the wardrobe, my temporary death, and so on). And explaining them— I now feel myself duty-bound to do it, if only because I am the author of these records, to say nothing of the fact that the unknown is in general the enemy of man, and *Homo sapiens* is not fully man until his grammar is absolutely rid of question marks, leaving nothing but exclamation points, commas, and periods.

And so, in obedience to what strikes me as my authorial duty, I took an aero today at 16:00 and set off once again for the Ancient House. There was a strong headwind. The aero had a hard time butting its way through the dense thicket of air, the transparent branches whistling and whipping. The city below looked like light-blue blocks of ice. Suddenly there was a cloud, a quick slash of shadow, and the ice turned leaden and began to swell, the way it does in spring when you're standing on the bank waiting for it to burst at any moment and rush whirling away, but minutes pass one after the other and the ice just lies there and you yourself start to swell, your heart starts beating wildly and faster (but . . . why am I writing about this, and where do these strange feelings come from? Because, really, there isn't any icebreaker that could break through this life of ours, this extremely transparent and permanent crystal).

There was no one at the entrance to the Ancient House. I went round it and saw the old woman, the gatekeeper, standing beside the Green Wall. She was shielding her eyes with her hand and looking up. There above the Wall were the sharp black triangles of some sort of birds that were cawing and throwing themselves into the attack, striking their breasts against the strong fence of electric waves, being thrown back, and again flying over the Wall.

I see quick slanting shadows on her face, overgrown with wrinkles, as she steals a quick glance at me. "There's nobody here—nobody, nobody! That's right! And no use you going in. Right. . . ."

What does she mean, no use? And what's got into her, anyway—to consider me nothing more than someone's shadow? And maybe you're all nothing but my shadows. Wasn't I the one that used you to populate these pages, which only a little while ago were white quadrangular deserts? Without me, would you ever have been seen by any of those that I am going to lead along behind me down the narrow paths of these lines?

I didn't say any of this to her, of course. I know from personal experience what a torment it can be if you plant a doubt in someone's mind that he is reality—and three-dimensional reality, not some other kind. All I did was remark dryly that her only concern was to open the door, and she let me into the courtyard.

It was empty. Quiet. The wind was far away, over there beyond the walls, the way it was that day when the two of us, walking like one, shoulder to shoulder, emerged from the corridors below—if in fact that ever really happened. I was walking under some kind of stone arches where the sound of my footsteps bounced off the damp vaults and fell behind me, like someone that kept walking right on my heels. The yellow walls with their red brick lesions watched me through the dark square spectacles of the windows, watched me opening the squealing doors of the barns, peering into corners, dead ends, nooks and crannies. There was a gate in the fence, and beyond it a wasteland, a relic of the Great 200-Years War, where bare stone ribs came up out of the ground, the yellow grimacing jaws of walls, an ancient stove beneath a vertical stovepipe, a ship turned to everlasting stone among stone and brick waves of yellow and red.

It seemed to me I'd already seen these very same yellow teeth once before, but dimly, as though on the bottom, through fathoms of water. And I began to search. I kept falling into holes, I stumbled on rocks, rusty paws kept grabbing the sleeves of my yuny, salty drops of sweat slid across my forehead into my eyes.

Not there! That lower exit from the corridors I could not locate anywhere—it didn't exist. But maybe it was better that way. It made it even more likely that all this was one of my stupid "dreams."

I was tired, covered with dust and some kind of spiderweb, and was already opening the gate to return to the main courtyard, when suddenly, from behind me, there was a rustling noise, the sound of squelching footsteps, and I found myself facing the pink ear-wings and double-twist smile of S.

With a squint he drilled into me with his eyes and said: "Out for a stroll, are you?"

I said nothing. My hands were bothering me.

"Well, how are you? Feeling any better now?"

"Yes, thank you. I seem to be getting back to normal."

He released me by raising his eyes. His head tilted back, and for the first time I noticed his Adam's apple.

Not very far above, about 50 meters, aeros were humming. From the slow, low-level flight, and the black elephant trunks of spy-tubes that they'd let down, I recognized them as belonging to the Guardians. Except there weren't the usual two or three of them, but about ten or twelve (sorry, but I have to make do with these approximations).

I got up the courage to ask: "How come there're so many today?"

"How come? Hm . . . a real doctor starts treating a man while he's still well, the one who's not going to be sick until to-morrow, the day after, a week later. Prophylactic, it's called."

He nodded and slouched off across the stone flags of the courtyard. Then he turned and said to me, over his shoulder: "Be careful!"

I was alone. It was quiet. Empty. High up above the Green Wall the birds were dashing about. The wind was blowing. What did he mean by that?

The aero took me quickly along the current of air. Cloud shadows, light and heavy. Below, light blue cupolas, cubes of frozen glass, turning the color of lead, swelling . . .

## EVENING.

I opened my manuscript in order to write down in these pages a few thoughts that seem to me useful (for you, readers) about the great Day of Unanimity, which is already close. And what I saw was that I can't write just now. I keep on listening all the time to how the wind is beating against the glass walls with its dark wings, I'm looking around all the time, waiting. For what? I don't know. And when the familiar brownish-pink gills turned up in my room, I was very glad, I'll be honest about it. She sat down, modestly arranged the fold of her yuny that had fallen between her knees, quickly plastered her smiles all over me, one for each hurt place, and I felt wonderful, held tight.

"I came into the classroom today, you see [she works at the Childrearing Plant], and there was a caricature on the wall. Oh, yes, I assure you! They drew me as some kind of fish. Maybe I really do . . ."

"Oh, no, of course not," I hastened to say (up close, as a

matter of fact, she has nothing remotely like gills, and my crack about gills—that was completely uncalled for).

"Oh, well, it's not important in the long run. But it was just the act itself, you know. Of course I called the Guardians. I love the children very much, and I think that cruelty is the highest, the most difficult kind of love, if you see what I mean."

Did I ever! It could not have chimed in better with the thoughts just running through my head. I couldn't resist and read her a section from my Record 20, beginning with the words: "There's a quiet, clear metallic sound to my thoughts' clicking. . . ."

Even without looking I could see the brownish-pink cheeks trembling. Then they moved closer and closer to me, and I felt in my hands her dry, hard, even somewhat bristly fingers.

"Give that to me! Give it to me! I'll have it phonocopied and make the children learn it by heart. We're the ones who need that much more than your Venusians—right now, tomorrow, and the day after."

She gave a look round and said, very quietly, "Did you hear? They say that on the Day of Unanimity . . ."

I jumped up. "What? What are they saying? What's going to happen on the Day of Unanimity?"

The cozy walls had vanished. I felt myself instantly thrown outside, out there, where the huge wind was tossing about above the rooftops and the slanting clouds of twilight were falling lower and lower. . . .

U threw her arms firmly and resolutely round my shoulders (though I noticed that her fingerbones were like tuning forks, vibrating to my alarm).

"Sit down, dear, and don't get excited. What won't people say? Anyway, I'll be right beside you that day—only if you need me, of course—I'll get someone else to mind my school-children, and I'll be with you, because you're also a child, dear, and you need . . ."

"No, no." I waved my arms. "Not for anything. Then you'd really think I'm some kind of baby, that I can't manage alone. . . . Not for anything!" (I admit, I had other plans for that day.)

She smiled. The unwritten message of this smile appeared to be: "Oh, what a stubborn boy!" Then she sat down, her eyes lowered, her embarrassed hands once again smoothing out the fold of yuny that had fallen between her knees. Let's change the subject.

"I think I've got to make up my mind . . . for your sake. . . . No, I beg of you, don't hurry me, I've got to think it over. . . ."

I was in no hurry. Although I understood that I ought to be happy and that there was no greater honor than to crown someone's waning years with the gift of oneself. . . .

That whole night I heard wings of some kind, and I walked about trying to protect my head with my arms from those wings. Then there was a chair, but not like one of our chairs now—this one was old-fashioned, made of wood. And I'm moving my legs like a horse (right foreleg and left hind leg, left foreleg and right hind leg). Then the chair runs right up to my bed and jumps in. And I make love to the wooden chair. It was uncomfortable. It hurt.

Amazing. Is it really impossible to think up some means of curing this dream sickness, or at least to make it rational, maybe even useful?

# RECORD 22

*Frozen Waves*

*Everything Tends to Perfection*

*I Am a Microbe*

Imagine this: You're standing on a bank, and the waves rise up right on time, then, when they've crested, suddenly they stop, they freeze solid. That's just how terrifying and unnatural this was, too, when our walk, prescribed by the Tables, suddenly went haywire, this way and that, and stopped. According to our chronicles, the last time anything like this happened was 119 years ago when a meteorite came crashing out of the sky and landed, screaming and smoking, right in the midst of our walk.

We were walking the same as always, that is to say, just like the warriors you see on Assyrian monuments: a thousand heads with two fused, integrated legs, with two integrated arms, swinging wide. Down at the end of the avenue, where the Accumulator Tower was making its grim hum, a rectangle was coming toward us: The front, back, and two sides consisted of guards, and in the middle were three people with the gold numbers already gone from their yunies, and the whole thing was clear to the point of pain.

The huge clockface at the top of the tower—that was a face, leaning out of the clouds and spitting out the seconds and waiting. It couldn't care less. And then, right on the dot at 13:06, something crazy happened in the rectangle. It was all very close to me, I could see every smallest detail, and I very clearly remember a long thin neck and a tangle of twisted little light blue veins at the temples, like rivers on the map of some unknown little world, and this unknown world, it seemed, was a young man. He probably noticed someone in our ranks, got up on his tiptoes, craned his neck out, and stopped. One of the guards snapped him with the bluish spark of an electric knout. He gave out a thin squeal, like a puppy. This brought another neat snap, about one every two seconds—squeal, snap, squeal. . . .

We walked on as before in our measured, Assyrian walk, and I looked at the elegant zigzag of the sparks and thought: "Everything in human society is endlessly perfecting itself . . . and should perfect itself. What an ugly weapon the ancient knout was—and what beauty there is in . . ."

But at this point, like a nut flying off a machine at top speed, a lithe, slender female figure tore off out of our ranks screaming, "That's enough! Don't you dare . . . !" and pitched right into the midst of the rectangle. This was like the meteor 119 years ago. The whole walk froze, and our ranks were like the gray crests of waves instantly immobilized by a flash frost.

For one second I stared at her like all the others as something that had dropped out of nowhere: She was no longer a Number, she was simply a person; she existed as nothing more than the metaphysical substance of the insult committed against One-State. But then some one of her movements—turning, she twisted her hips to the left—and all at once I knew: I know her, I know that body resilient as a whip—my eyes, my lips, my hands know it—in one moment I was absolutely sure of it.

Two of the guards moved to cut her off. A still-bright mirror-like patch of pavement showed me that now, any moment, their trajectories would cross, they would grab her. My heart swallowed hard and stopped, and, never stopping to think whether one could or not, whether it was stupid or not, I dashed for that point. . . .

I could feel a thousand eyes popping with horror on me, but that only added more desperate giddy strength to the hairy-handed savage that had leapt out of me, and he ran all the faster. Two steps more, and she turned around. . . .

What I saw was a trembling face with lots of freckles and reddish eyebrows. It wasn't her. It wasn't I-330.

Wild, bursting joy. I feel like shouting something like, "Go on! Grab her!" but all I can hear coming out of me is a whisper. Then I feel a heavy hand take me by the shoulder, they're holding me, they're taking me somewhere, I'm trying to explain to them . . .

"Wait a minute, listen, you've got to understand, I thought she was . . ."

But how was I going to explain my whole being, this whole disease that I've been jotting down in these pages? So I shut up and went along peacefully. A leaf torn off a tree by a sudden gust of wind falls peacefully downward, but on the way it twists and catches at every twig, offshoot, branch that it knows. That is just how I caught at each silent, spherical head, at the transparent ice of the walls, at the light blue needle of the Accumulator Tower as it thrust up into the clouds.

At that moment, when a blank curtain was on the point of separating me forever from that whole splendid world, I see a little way off over the mirrored pavement a large familiar head and a pair of waving pink winglike arms. And I hear the familiar flat voice:

"I consider it my duty to state that Number D-503 is ill and in no condition to control his emotions. And I am convinced that he was carried away by a perfectly natural outrage. . . ."

"Yes, yes!" I jumped in. "I even shouted: Grab her!"

"You shouted nothing." This from just behind me.

"Yes, but I meant to . . . I swear by the Benefactor, I meant to."

I was instantly pierced by the cold gray eye-drills. I don't know whether he could see into me and tell that this was (almost) the truth, or whether he had some sort of secret aim to spare me once again for a while, but all he did was write out some note and hand it to one of the men holding me—and I was free once more, or rather, I was once more confined within the orderly, endless Assyrian ranks.

The rectangle containing the freckled face and the temple with the geographical map of blue veins disappeared round the corner, forever. We march on, one million-headed body, and each one of us harbors that humble happiness that also, probably, sustains the life of molecules, atoms, and phagocytes. In the ancient world, this was understood by the Christians, our only (if very imperfect) predecessors: Humility is a virtue, pride a vice; *We* comes from God, *I* from the Devil.

So here am I, in step with everyone else, and yet separate from all of them. I'm still trembling all over from the recent excitement—like a bridge that one of the ancient iron trains has just rumbled over. I feel myself. But it's only the eye with a lash in it, the swollen finger, the infected tooth that feels itself, is conscious of its own individual being. The healthy eye or finger or tooth doesn't seem to exist. So it's clear, isn't it? Self-consciousness is just a disease. ·

Maybe I'm no longer a phagocyte calmly going about the business of devouring microbes (with blue temples and freckles). Maybe I'm a microbe, and maybe there are thousands more of them among us, pretending like me to be phagocytes. . . .

This thing that happened today was really not so important, but just suppose it were only the beginning, only the first meteor of a whole shower of thundering hot rocks poured down by infinity onto our glass paradise?

# RECORD 23

*Flowers*

*Dissolution of a Crystal*

*If Only*

They say there are flowers that bloom only once every hundred years. Why shouldn't there be some that bloom only once every thousand, every ten thousand years? Maybe we just haven't heard about them up to now because this very day is that once-in-a-thousand-years.

So here I am, drunk with joy, going down the stairs to the duty desk, and before my very eyes, quickly, silently, thousand-year buds are popping open all around me, everywhere, and armchairs are blossoming, and shoes, golden badges, light-bulbs, someone's dark long-lashed eyes, the faceted columns of the banisters, a handkerchief lost on the stairs, the table of the one on duty, and above the table the gentle cheeks of U, brown with spots. It's all unusual, new, tender, pink, moist.

I hand U the pink ticket, and above her head, through the glass wall, the moon hangs blue and fragrant from some invisible branch. I point to it triumphantly and say: "The moon . . . you understand?"

U glances at me, then at the number on the ticket, and I see that familiar movement of hers, so charmingly modest, when she adjusts the folds of her yuny between the angles of her knees.

"You don't look normal, dear. You look sick. Because sick

and not normal are the same thing. You're destroying yourself, and no one is going to tell you that—no one."

That "no one" was of course equal to the number on the ticket, I-330. Dear, wonderful U! You're right, of course. I'm not sensible, I'm sick, I have a soul, I'm a microbe. But isn't blooming a sickness? Doesn't it hurt when the bud bursts open? And don't you agree that the spermatozoon is the most terrifying of all microbes?

I'm upstairs in my room. I-330 is sitting in the sprawling cup of the armchair. I'm on the floor, my arms around her legs, my head in her lap, and we're both quiet. Silence. My pulse. I'm a crystal, dissolving in her, in I-330. I feel with absolute clarity the way the polished facets that define me in space are melting, melting. I'm vanishing, dissolving in her lap, in her. I'm getting smaller and smaller, and at the same time wider, larger, off every scale. . . . Because she . . . she's no longer herself, she's the whole universe. And for one second I and this chair shot through with joy beside the bed—we are one; and the old woman with the marvelous smile at the gates of the Ancient House, and the wild wastes beyond the Green Wall, and the silver-on-black ruins that drowse like the old woman, and that door that just slammed somewhere, probably far away: All that is in me, with me, listening to the beating of my pulse and flying across the blessed second.

I try to tell her—in stupid, confused, drowned words—that I am a crystal, and that that is why the door is in me, and why I can feel how happy the chair is. But such balled-up nonsense comes out that I stop, I'm ashamed, I . . . and suddenly I say, "I-330, darling, forgive me . . . I don't understand, I'm talking such nonsense. . . ."

"What makes you think nonsense is bad? If they'd nurtured and cared for human nonsense over the ages the way they did intelligence, it might have turned into something of special value."

"Yes. . . ." (I think she's right. How, right now, could she not be right?)

"And for your nonsense alone, for what you did yesterday on the walk, I love you still more . . . still more."

"But then why did you torture me, why didn't you come, why did you send your tickets, why did you make me . . . ?"

"But maybe I had to test you? Maybe I had to find out whether you'd do everything I wanted? That you were completely mine?"

"Yes, completely!"

She took my face, all of me, between her palms and lifted up my head: "Well, but what about your 'duties of every honest Number'? What of that?"

Sweet, sharp, white teeth. Then, a smile. In the opened cup of the chair she was like a bee—she had both honey and a sting.

Yes, duties. . . . In my mind I quickly went through the most recent entries in these pages. The fact is that there wasn't anywhere the least thought of any duty that I should . . .

I keep quiet. There's an ecstatic (and probably stupid) smile on my face. I look into her eyes, now one, now the other, seeing myself in each. I am tiny, minuscule, jailed in these little rainbow prisons. And then more bees, lips, the sweet pain of blooming. . . .

Inside each of us Numbers there is an invisible metronome ticking away quietly, and we never have to glance at a clock to know the exact time to within five minutes. But now my metronome had stopped and I did not know how much time had passed. Frightened, I grabbed my badge with its clock out from under the pillow. . . .

Praise be to the Benefactor! I still had twenty minutes. But minutes . . . such stumpy little short things it's not even funny . . . were running, and I had so much to tell her—everything, all of myself: about O's letter, about the horrible evening when I gave her a child; about my own childhood, for some reason; about the mathematics teacher Pliapa; about $\sqrt{-1}$; about my first time at the Day of Unanimity and how hard I cried because on that day of all days I got a spot of ink on my yuny.

I-330 raised her head and propped herself on her elbow. At the corners of her lips were two long sharp lines, and the angle of her eyebrows made a cross.

"Maybe, that day . . ." She stopped, and her brows darkened even more. She took my hand and pressed it hard. "Tell me, you won't forget me? You'll always remember me?"

"Why do you say that? What are you talking about? Darling?"

I-330 said nothing, and her eyes were already looking past me, through me, far away. Suddenly I heard the wind whipping its huge wings against the glass (this had been happening all along, of course, but I only heard it now), and for some reason I recalled the shrill birds flying over the top of the Green Wall.

I-330 gave her head a shake as though to get rid of something. Once more, for one second, the whole length of her body touched me, the way an aero gives the earth one springy little touch before it lands.

"Right, then. Hand me my stockings. Hurry!"

The stockings had been thrown on my table, on page 193 of these notes, which were lying open there. In my hurry I knocked against the manuscript and the pages scattered and I couldn't put them back in order, but the main thing is that it wouldn't matter even if I did put them back in order, because there's no real order, anyway, there'll always be dangerous rapids and pits and unknowns.

"I can't go on like this," I said. "Here you are, here, next to me, and you still seem to be on the other side of some ancient wall that I can't see through. I hear rustling sounds through the wall, voices, but I can't make out the words, I don't know what's back there. I can't go on like this. You're forever stopping just short of telling me something. You've never told me where I was that time in the Ancient House, and where those corridors went, and how come there was a doctor . . . or, maybe that never happened?"

I-330 put her hands on my shoulder and looked slowly and deeply into my eyes.

"You want to know everything?"

"Yes I do. I have to."

"And you won't be afraid to follow me anywhere, to the very end, no matter where I lead you?"

"Anywhere!"

"All right. I promise you—when this holiday is over, if only . . . Oh, yes: How's your INTEGRAL? I keep forgetting to ask you. Is it soon?"

"No. What do you mean *if only*? You're doing it again. *If only* what?"

She was already at the door when she said, "You'll see. . . ."

I'm alone. All that's left of her is a slight hint of something that reminds me of the sweet, dry, yellow pollen of certain flowers on the other side of the Wall. That and the questions that stick in me like fishhooks, like those things the ancients used to catch fish (Museum of Prehistory).

. . . Why'd she suddenly ask me about the INTEGRAL?

# RECORD 24

*Limit of Function*

*Easter*

*Cross It All Out*

I'm like a machine being run over its RPM limit: The bearings are overheating—a minute longer, and the metal is going to melt and start dripping and that'll be the end of everything. I need a quick splash of cold water, logic. I pour it on in buckets, but the logic hisses on the hot bearings and dissipates in the air as a fleeting white mist.

Well, of course, it's clear that you can't establish a function without taking into account what its limit is. And it's also clear that what I felt yesterday, that stupid "dissolving in the universe," if you take it to its limit, is death. Because that's exactly what death is—the fullest possible dissolving of myself into the universe. Hence, if we let L stand for *love* and D for *death*, then L = f(D), i.e., love and death. . . .

Yes, that's it, that's it. That's why I'm afraid of I-330, why I fight against her, why I don't want . . . But why do those two exist side by side in me: *I don't want* and *I want*? That's just what's so horrible: What I want again is that blissful death of yesterday. What's so horrible is that even now, when the logical function has been integrated, when it's obvious that it contains, as a hidden component, death itself, I still want her, my lips, my arms, my chest, every millimeter of me wants her. . . .

Tomorrow is the Day of Unanimity. She'll be there, too, of course, and I'll see her, only from far away. From far away:

That's going to be painful, because I need her, I'm drawn irresistibly to be . . . next to her, to have her hands, her shoulder,
her hair. . . . But I want even that pain . . . let it happen.

Great Benefactor! How absurd—to want pain! Can there be
anyone who doesn't know that pain is a negative quantity, and
that if you add them up it reduces the sum we call happiness?
So, it follows . . .

But . . . nothing follows. The slate's clean. Naked.


## EVENING.

A windy, feverishly pink, alarming sunset comes through the
glass walls of the building. I turn my chair so that this pink-
ness won't stick up in front of me, and I leaf through these
notes. What I see is that once more I've forgotten that I'm not
writing for myself but for you, you unknown ones that I love
and pity, for you, who are still trudging somewhere in distant
centuries, down below.

About the Day of Unanimity, that great day. I've always
loved it, ever since I was a child. For us I think it's something
like what "Easter" was for the ancients. I remember how on
the eve you'd make yourself a little calendar of hours and
grandly cross them off, one at a time: one hour closer, one
hour less to wait. Honestly, if I were sure nobody would see,
I'd carry a little calendar like this around with me everywhere
even now and mark off how much time was left until tomorrow, when I'd see . . . even if from far away.

(I was interrupted. They just brought me the new yuny,
straight from the shop. It's the custom to issue new yunies for
the big day tomorrow. You hear footsteps in the hallway,
noise, happy shouting.)

To go on. Tomorrow I'll see the same sight that's repeated
from one year to the next, bringing new excitement each time:
the mighty chalice of harmony, the people's arms reverently up-
lifted. Tomorrow is the day for the annual election of the Benefactor. Tomorrow we once more place the keys to the unshakable
fortress of our happiness into the hands of the Benefactor.

It goes without saying that this has no resemblance to the disorderly, unorganized elections in ancient times, when—it's hard to say this with a straight face—they couldn't even tell before the election how it would come out. To establish a state on the basis of absolutely unpredictable randomness, blindly—could there be anything more idiotic? Still, it looks like centuries had to pass before this was understood.

I don't suppose it's necessary to say that here, as in everything else, we have no place for randomness; there can't be any surprises. And even the elections amount to little more than symbolism, to remind us that we are one, powerful, million-celled organism, that we are, in the words of the ancient "Gospel," one Church. Because the history of OneState does not know of a single instance when so much as one voice dared to violate the majestic unison of that glorious day.

They say the ancients somehow carried out their elections in secret, hiding like thieves. Some of our historians even say they carefully masked themselves before turning up at the election ceremonies. (I can just picture that fantastically gloomy spectacle: night, a city square, figures in dark capes creeping along the walls, the crimson flame of the torches guttering in the wind.) Why all this secretiveness was needed has never yet been fully explained. Most probably the elections were connected with some mystical, superstitious, or maybe even criminal rites.

But we have nothing to hide or be ashamed of; we celebrate our elections openly, honestly, in the daylight. I see how everybody votes for the Benefactor and everybody sees how I vote for the Benefactor. And how else could it be, since *everybody* and *I* add up to the one *We*? How much more uplifting, sincere, lofty this is than the cowardly, thievish "secret" of the ancients! And how much more expedient it is, too. Because even if you suppose the impossible, by which I mean some kind of dissonance in our usual monophony, you've still got the concealed Guardians right there in our ranks ready at a moment's notice to stop any Numbers that might have gotten out of line and save them from making any other false steps—as well as save OneState from them. And finally there's one more thing. . . .

I'm looking through the wall to the left. I see a woman in front of the mirror in the closet door hurrying to unbutton her yuny. I get a quick hazy glimpse of eyes, lips, the tips of two pink buds. Then the blinds go down and in an instant all of yesterday floods back over me and I forget what the "one more thing" was and I don't care, I don't want it! All I want is one thing: I-330. I want her to be with me every minute, each and every minute, only with me. And all that stuff I just wrote about the Day of Unanimity—nobody needs it, it's all wrong, I want to cross it out, tear it up, throw it out. Because I know (maybe this is blasphemy, but it's true) that the only holiday for me is being with her, only if she's there next to me, shoulder to shoulder.

Without her the sun tomorrow won't be anything more than a disk cut out of tin and the sky will just be tin painted blue, and I myself . . .

I grab the telephone: "I-330! Is that you?"

"Yes. Do you realize how late it is?"

"Maybe it isn't too late. I want to ask you . . . I want you to be with me tomorrow. Darling . . ."

I said "darling" very softly. And for some reason this made me think of a thing that happened this morning at the hangar: For a joke somebody had put a watch under a hundred-ton sledge. They'd swung the sledge with all their might, it made a wind in your face, and then stopped, a hundred tons of gentleness, just short of the little watch.

There was a pause. I imagine I hear someone in her room whispering. Then her voice says: "No, I can't. Listen, you know I'd also like . . . But no, I can't. Don't ask why. You'll see tomorrow."

## NIGHT.

# RECORD 25

*Descent from Heaven*

*History's Greatest Catastrophe*

*End of the Known*

Before the proceedings got under way, when everyone rose and the slow majestic canopy of the anthem began to sway above our heads (hundreds of the Musical Factory's pipes and millions of human voices), I forgot, for a moment, about everything. I forgot the disturbing things that I-330 had said about today's celebration, and I think I even forgot about her. All over again I was that little boy who had once burst into tears on this day when he found a tiny spot, visible to no one but himself, on his yuny. Maybe no one around me now can see the black indelible blotches all over me, but I know—I know that a criminal like me has no business being among all these wide innocent faces. Oh, if only I could stand up right this minute and—even if it choked me—scream out the whole truth about myself. So it would be the end of me, so what! At least for one second I'd feel that I was clean, I'd feel that all the thoughts had been swept out of my head, and I'd be like that tender blue sky.

All eyes were lifted upward into the blue immaculate morning still damp with the tears of night and focused on a barely visible dot that was dark at times and at others clad in the rays of the sun. It was He. He was descending from the heavens in His aero to be among us, the new Jehovah, as wise and as cruel in his love as the Jehovah of the ancients. Closer and closer He comes with every minute, while higher and higher reach millions of hearts to greet Him, and at last He sees us. In my thoughts I am up there with Him looking down: The concentric circles of the stands are traced by light blue rows of dots, like the circles of a spiderweb besprinkled with microscopic suns (our shining badges), a spiderweb in whose center the wise white Spider will now alight, the Benefactor, in white raiment, binding us hand and foot in His wisdom with the beneficial snares of contentment.

But now His majestic descent from the heavens had been accomplished, the brass anthem had fallen silent, everyone had sat down—and I instantly understood: All this in reality was an immensely delicate spiderweb, stretched to its limit and trembling, and at any moment it would snap and something beyond all imagining would happen. . . .

I rose slightly from my seat and looked round. My gaze met that of many other eyes, looking from face to face with love and terror. There's one who just raised his hand and made a sign to someone with a very slight movement of his fingers. And there's the answer in the same way. And another . . . Now I understood: These are Guardians. I understood that something's upset them. The web is stretched, it's trembling. And there's a responsive shudder inside me, like a radio receiver set on the same wavelength.

On the stage a poet was reading the pre-election ode, but I didn't hear a word of it, only the measured back and forth of the hexameter's pendulum, every swing of which brought nearer some fatal hour. And I'm still feverishly leafing through face after face in the ranks as if they were pages, though I still can't see that one thing I'm looking for, but I'd better find it quick, because one more tick of the pendulum and . . .

Him! It was him, of course. Down below, past the stage, slipping above the gleaming glass, rushed the pink ear-wings; the body reflected there was the dark double-looped letter S, hurrying somewhere in the maze of passages among the stands.

S, I-330—there is some sort of thread (between them; for me there's always been some sort of thread running between them—what kind I still don't know, but one day I'll untangle it). I clamped my eyes on him. He rolled on like a ball of wool, one thread paying out behind him. Now he's stopped, now . . .

I was shot through, tied into a knot, as though I'd been hit by a high-voltage bolt of lightning. S had stopped at our row, no more than 40 degrees away from me, and bent down. I saw I-330 and, next to her, the disgustingly grinning African lips of R-13.

My first thought was to tear down there and yell at her: "Why are you with him today? Why didn't you want me . . . ?" But some lucky spiderweb that I couldn't see held me tight, hand and foot. Gritting my teeth, I sat there like a lump of iron, keeping my eyes on them. I can feel the sharp, physical pain in my heart as though it were happening right now. I remember thinking, "If a nonphysical stimulus can produce the physical reaction of pain, it's clear that . . ."

Unfortunately, I didn't work the conclusion all the way out: All I remember is some passing thought about the "soul," and the pointless old proverb flashed through my mind: "His heart sank into his boots." And I froze as the hexameters went silent. Now it was starting . . . but what?

Custom called for a five-minute break before the election. Custom also called for silence before the election. But this was not the same genuinely prayerful, reverent silence as usual; this was the way it was in ancient times when they had no knowledge of our Accumulator Towers, when the untamed heaven still raged at times with "thunderstorms." This was the way it was for the ancients before a storm.

The air was like cast iron you could see through. You felt you had to hold your mouth wide open to breathe. Your hearing was so keen it hurt, and it registered from somewhere in the rear a kind of excited whispering, like mice gnawing. Without lifting my eyes all this time, I could still see those two—I-330 and R—next to each other, shoulder to shoulder, and those strange, shaggy, hateful hands of mine were trembling on my knees.

Everyone is holding his badge with his watch in his hands. One. Two. Three. Five minutes . . . and from the stage there comes a slow, cast-iron voice.

"Please raise your hands, those who vote Yes."

If only I could look him in the eye as before, I'd say, directly and devotedly, "Here am I. All of me. Take me!" But now I couldn't. My limbs felt all rusty. It was only with an effort that I raised my hand.

The rustle of millions of arms. I hear a smothered groan, "Oh!" I feel something has started, fallen, headlong, but I have no idea what, and I don't have the strength, or the courage, to look. . . .

"Those opposed?"

This was always the grandest moment of the celebration: Everyone would go on sitting quite still, bowing his head in joy to the beneficent yoke of the Number of all Numbers. But right at this point, to my horror, I heard another rustle, infinitely delicate, like a sigh. It was more audible than the brass pipes of the anthem had been. It was like the last sigh that a man breathes out in his life, almost inaudible, but everyone standing around him goes pale and cold drops start out on their brow.

I raise my eyes and . . .

All this took the hundredth part of a second, a hair's breadth in time. I saw a thousand hands shoot up—"opposed"—and come down. I saw the pale face of I-330, the cross on her brow, her raised hand. Things went black before my eyes.

Another hair's breadth, a pause, silence, heartbeat. Then— as though some insane director had given the cue—there was an instant uproar in all the stands, shouting, Numbers running, their yunies flying, Guardians tearing about in a frenzy, someone's heels in the air right in front of my face, next to the heels someone's wide face, his mouth stretched in a silent scream. That's the image that burnt itself into me deepest of all: thousands of silent mouths, screaming—like something projected on a monstrous screen.

And on another part of the screen, somewhere far down below, visible only for a second, the pale lips of O. She was pressed against a wall, standing with her arms crossed over her belly, trying to protect it. And she was gone, wiped out, or I forgot about her, because . . .

This now was no screen—this was inside me, this squeezed heart, these pounding temples. R-13 had suddenly jumped up on a bench that was above me, to the left; he was red, spitting, in a rage. He was carrying I-330 in his arms. She was pale, her yuny ripped open from her shoulders to her breast, blood showing on the white part. She had her arms round his neck and he was jumping from bench to bench in huge leaps, repulsive and agile as a gorilla, and carrying her toward the top.

Everything went red. It was like some ancient fire. And there was nothing for me to do but jump up and try to catch them. To this day I couldn't explain even to myself where I got the strength, but I blasted through the crowd like a battering ram, on people's shoulders, on benches, and as soon as I was close enough I grabbed R by the collar:

"Oh no you don't!" I yelled. "Oh no you don't! Put her . . ." (nobody could hear me, fortunately—they were all running and yelling themselves).

"Who the . . . ? What's happening? What?" R turned around, his lips wet and trembling. He probably thought one of the Guardians had grabbed him.

"What? I'll show you what! I won't stand for it. Put her down at once!"

But he only made an angry sound with his lips, shook his head, and started to run on. But at this point—it's incredibly embarrassing for me to write this down, but I've got to. It seems to me I've got to write it down so that you, my unknown readers, can make a full study of the history of my illness—at this point I let him have it with a blow to the head. You understand? I hit him! That I remember distinctly. And I also remember something else: something like liberation, a kind of lightness all through my body from this blow.

I-330 quickly slipped down out of his arms.

"Get out of here!" she shouted to R. "You see he's . . . he's . . . Get out of here, R, get away!"

R bared his white, African teeth, splashed some word in my face, dived downward, and vanished. And I picked I-330 up in my arms, held her tightly against me, and carried her off.

My heart felt huge inside me. It was pounding, and with each beat a wave of hot, wild joy whipped through me. And what did it matter that something had been smashed to pieces—who cared? Just so I could carry her like this, and carry and carry . . .

### EVENING.
### 22:00 HOURS.

I can hardly hold the pen in my hands; there's no describing how tired I am after the dizzying events of this morning. Surely it can't be true that our salvation, the age-old walls of One-State, have fallen? I can't believe we're homeless again, like our distant ancestors, living in the wild state called freedom. No Benefactor . . . it can't be. "Opposed"?—on the Day of Unanimity—"opposed"? I feel the shame they ought to feel, the pain, the terror. But who are they, anyway? And who am I? "They" . . . "We" . . . How am I to know?

Here she was, sitting on a glass bench, one hot from the sun, at the very top of the stands, where I carried her. Her right shoulder and, below it, the beginning of that marvelous incalculable curve, were all bare; there was a tiny little red snake of blood. She pretends not to notice the blood, or that her breast is bare—or rather, she sees it all, but it's just the way she wants it at the moment, and if her yuny had been buttoned up, she would have ripped it open, she . . .

"And tomorrow . . ." She was hungry to breathe through her shining white teeth, clenched tightly. "And tomorrow . . . what? Nobody knows. You understand? Neither I nor anyone else knows. It's unknown. You understand it's come to an end, everything that was known? Now it'll be new, never before seen, or imagined."

Down below us they were on the boil, rushing about and screaming. But all that was far away, and it got even farther away when she looked at me, slowly drawing me into herself through the narrow golden windows of her eyes. This went on for a long time, in silence. And for some reason I thought of how I once looked through the Green Wall and saw someone's incomprehensible yellow eyes, while birds whirled above the Wall (or was that at some other time?).

"Listen, if nothing out of the way happens tomorrow, I'll take you there. You know what I mean?"

No, I don't. But I nod my head slowly. I've dissolved, I'm infinitely small, I'm a point. . . .

When all is said and done, this being a point has its own logic (modern): A point contains more unknowns than anything else. All it has to do is move, budge a bit, and it can transform into thousands of different curves, hundreds of solid shapes.

I don't want to budge. . . . I'm afraid. What'll I turn into? And it seems to me that everyone is like me—they're all afraid of the slightest movement. Take right now, while I'm writing this. Everyone's sitting all closed up in his own glass cage waiting for something. Out in the hallway there's no noise from the elevator that you usually hear at this hour, no laughter, no footsteps. From time to time I see a couple walking down the hall on tiptoe, looking over their shoulders and whispering. . . .

What will happen tomorrow? What will I turn into tomorrow?

# RECORD 26

*The World Exists*

*A Rash*

*41° Centigrade*

Morning. The usual morning—strong, round, red-cheeked—comes through the ceiling. It occurs to me that I would have been less surprised to see overhead some kind of unusual rectangular sun, people dressed in animal skins of various colors, or stone walls you couldn't see through. So what does this mean? The world, *our world*, must still exist? Or is it just inertia? The generator's still plugged in, the cogwheels are still buzzing and twirling, they'll go on for two turns, three, and on the fourth they'll quit.

You know this strange condition? You wake up at night, open your eyes on the darkness, and suddenly you feel—you're lost, and you start groping around as fast as you can, looking for something familiar and solid, the wall, lamp, chair. That's just how I was groping, looking for something as fast as I could in the *State Gazette*. Here's what I found:

"The day long and impatiently awaited by everyone, the Day of Unanimity, took place yesterday. For the 48th time the unanimous election went to that same Benefactor who has so often given evidence of his unalterable wisdom. The solemn occasion was marred by a slight disturbance, caused by the enemies of happiness, who, in so doing, naturally forfeited their right to become bricks in the foundation, renewed yesterday, of OneState. Everyone clearly understands that to take their votes into account would be as absurd as to consider part of a great, heroic symphony the coughing of sick persons who merely chance to be in the audience. . . ."

Oh, how wise! Does it mean we're saved after all, in spite of everything? No, really—could there be any objection to this pellucidly crystal syllogism?

"Today at twelve there will be a joint session of the Administrative Bureau, the Medical Bureau, and the Bureau of Guardians. Important governmental action is impending in the next few days."

No, the walls are still standing, there they are, I can feel them. And I no longer have that strange feeling that I'm lost, that I don't know where I am, that I've strayed off somewhere, and I'm not the least bit surprised that I can see the blue sky and the round sun; and everyone is headed off to work, just as usual.

I was walking along the avenue with an especially firm, ringing tread, and everyone seemed to be doing the same. But then came the crossing, a turn round the corner, and I see everyone acting strangely, turning the corner of a building sideways, as though a pipe had burst in the wall and cold water was splashing all across the sidewalk, so that you couldn't use it.

I take another five, ten steps and also get a dousing with cold water that hits me and knocks me off the sidewalk. Stuck on the wall, about two meters up, I'd say, was a rectangular sheet of paper and on it some incomprehensible letters printed in poisonous green:

MEPHI

Beneath this was somebody's back bent in the shape of the letter S and a pair of transparent ear-wings that either anger or excitement had set flapping. He was jumping up, with his right arm extended and his left held back like a broken wing, trying to tear the paper down, but he couldn't do it—lacked just this much.

Everyone passing by probably had the same thought: "If I go up to him, just me out of this crowd, won't he think I'm guilty of something, which is the very reason I'm trying to . . . ?"

I won't deny the same thought was in my own head. But I remembered all the times he'd been my real guardian angel, how many times he'd rescued me—so I walked boldly up, reached out my hand, and tore down the sheet.

S turned around and quick as a flash his drills sank right down to the bottom of me, where they picked something up. Then his left eyebrow went up and made a sign toward the wall where "Mephi" had been hanging. And I thought I saw a little tip end of a smile, a kind of happy smile, to my astonishment. But what's so astonishing, after all? A doctor always prefers a rash and a fever of 40° to a long-drawn-out incubation period of rising temperature: At least he knows right off what kind of illness he's facing. The "Mephi" that broke out on the walls today—that's the rash. I see why he's smiling. . . .*

I head down into the subway, and under my feet, on the immaculate glass of the steps, there's another white sheet: "Mephi." And the same ominous white rash has broken out everywhere down there: on the wall, on the bench, on the mirror in the car (stuck on in a hurry, you can see, crooked and careless).

The hum of the wheels stands out against the silence—sounds like feverish blood. Someone feels a touch on the shoulder—he shudders and drops his roll of papers. This other one to my left . . . he's reading one and the same line in the paper over and over and over again, and you can see his paper trembling slightly. And I can feel it—in the wheels, in hands, in newspapers, in eyelashes—everywhere the pulse is quicker, and maybe today, when I-330 and I get there, the black line on the thermometer will show 39°, 40°, 41°.

At the hangar there's exactly the same silence, humming like some propeller so far away you can't see it. The lathes stood around frowning, saying nothing. All you could hear, and just barely, was the cranes slipping around on tiptoes, bending over, grabbing in their claws the light-blue blocks of frozen air

---

*I must confess that the real reason for this smile I learned only after many days, days packed with the strangest and most astonishing events.

and loading them into the INTEGRAL's lateral tanks: We're already setting it up for its test flight.

"What do you say—will we be done loading in a week?"

I was talking to the Second Builder. He has this porcelain face decorated with sweet little blue and tender pink flowers (his eyes and lips), but today they had a faded, washed-out look. We were counting out loud, but I suddenly broke off in the middle of a word and stood there with my mouth gaping: Way up under the cupola, stuck on one of the blue blocks being lifted by a crane, you could just make out a white square of paper. And something jolted me—maybe it was a laugh— yes, I was hearing myself laugh (that ever happen to you, when you hear yourself laugh?).

"No, listen," I say. "Imagine this. You're in an old aeroplane, the altimeter reads 5000 meters, you've lost a wing, you're going down like a tumbler pigeon, and on the way you're going over your schedule: Tomorrow from noon to two . . . then from two to six . . . dinner at six . . . Wouldn't that be crazy? But that's just what we're doing!"

The little blue flowers go into action. They goggle. What if I were made of glass and he could see that in about three or four hours . . .

# RECORD 27

*No Contents—Can't*

I'm alone in endless corridors—the same ones as before. A mute concrete sky. Water is dripping on stone somewhere. Same door, heavy and opaque, with a muffled humming coming from behind it.

She said she'd come out to me at 16:00, but I've watched 16:05, 16:10, 16:15 go by and . . . nobody.

For a second I feel like my old self, terrified that the door might open. Five minutes more and that's it . . . if she doesn't come.

Water dripping on stone somewhere. Nobody. I feel a kind of gloomy relief: I'm saved. I walk slowly back along the corridor. The quavering dotted line of lightbulbs on the ceiling gets dimmer and dimmer. . . .

Suddenly, from behind me, I hear the door open with a quick banging sound and then hurried footsteps reverberate softly from the ceiling and the walls and she comes flying, slightly out of breath from running, breathing through her mouth.

"I knew you'd be here, that you'd come! I knew it. Oh, you . . . you . . ."

The lances of her lashes move apart to let me pass inside . . . and . . . But how can I find words for what it does to me, this ancient rite, stupid and wonderful, of her lips touching mine? What formula could express how this whirlwind sweeps everything out of my soul, except her? Yes, yes—I said soul. If you want to laugh, go ahead.

With an effort she slowly raised her lids and managed to say, slowly: "No, enough . . . Later. For now, let's go."

The door opened. Steps, old and worn. A discordant racket, whistling, light . . .

---

Nearly twenty-four hours have passed since then, I've settled down a bit, and still it's extremely hard for me to describe what happened, even in rough outline. It's as if they set off a bomb in my head and all around, piled in a heap, are open mouths, wings, screams, leaves, words, stones . . .

I remember the first thing that went through my head was "Quick, clear out, get back!" Because I could see that while I was waiting there in the corridors they'd somehow blown up or destroyed the Green Wall—and the lower world that had always been kept out of our city was now beating and rushing over it.

I must have said something like that to I-330, because she gave a laugh: "Of course not! We've simply gone to the other side of the Green Wall."

Then I opened my eyes . . . and found myself in broad daylight face to face with what no living person had ever seen up to then except reduced a thousand times, weakened and dimmed by the cloudy glass of the Wall.

This sun . . . it wasn't our sun, evenly distributed over the mirrored surface of the sidewalks. This sun was all sharp fragments, alive somehow, constantly leaping spots, that blinded the eyes and made the head spin. And the trees were like candles sticking right up to the sky, or like spiders squatting on the ground with crooked legs, or like silent green fountains. . . . And all this was crawling about on all fours, shifting and buzzing, and out from under my feet some kind of shaggy tangle of something came slipping, and I . . . I was riveted to the spot, I couldn't move . . . because I wasn't standing on a

surface, you see, not a surface, but something disgustingly
soft, yielding, alive, green, springy.

I was deafened by all this, I was choked—that's probably
the word that comes closest. I was standing there hanging on
with both hands to some kind of swinging bough.

"Don't worry! Don't worry! This is only the beginning. It'll
pass. Hang on!"

Next to I-330 against the dizzying, leaping network of green
was someone's profile, very thin, like something cut out of
paper . . . no, not someone's—I know him. I remember him—
it's the doctor . . . no, no, I've got it now. I see that the two of
them have me by the arms and they're dragging me forward,
they're laughing, my legs are twisted, I'm slipping toward cawing sounds, moss, tufts of grass, screeching, branches, tree
trunks, wings, leaves, whistling . . .

And . . . now the trees give way and I see a bright clearing,
and in the clearing people . . . or, I'm not sure, maybe creatures is more like it.

And now comes the hardest part of all. Because *this* passes
all the bounds you'd think possible. And now I see why I-330
always insisted on holding something back: I wouldn't have
believed it anyway—not even her. Maybe tomorrow I won't
even believe myself, not even these notes.

In the clearing, around a naked stone that looked like a
human skull, there was a noisy crowd of some three or four
hundred . . . people. Let's say "people," otherwise I wouldn't
know what to say. And just as, when you see a whole lot of
faces on a platform, you always first of all pick out the ones
you know, so here the only thing I noticed at first was our
gray-blue yunies. A second later and I saw, all around among
the yunies I quite distinctly saw: jet black, reddish, tawny, bay,
roan, and white people . . . or they seemed like people. None
of them had any clothes on, and they were all covered with
short glossy fur, the kind anyone can see on the stuffed horse
in the Prehistoric Museum. But the females had faces just
like . . . yes, exactly the same as our women: tender, pink, and
hairless, and their breasts were also free of hair—large, firm,

and very beautiful in geometrical form. As for the males, only part of their faces had no fur—the same as with our ancestors.

This was so completely incredible, so totally unheard of, that I simply stood there. I'm telling you the truth, I simply stood there and looked. It's the same as with scales—you over-load one side and then you can put as much as you want there and the pointer won't budge.

Suddenly I find myself alone. I-330 is no longer next to me, and I have no idea how or where she disappeared. The only ones around me are those with coats glistening like satin in the sun. I grab someone by his hot, strong, jet-black shoulder: "Listen, in the name of the Benefactor, you didn't happen to see where she went? She was right here only a minute ago. . . ."

A pair of bushy, strict eyebrows turn toward me: "Sh-h-h! Be quiet!" And they made a busy wave toward the center, the place with the yellow stone that looked like a skull.

There I saw her, up high, over the heads, over everybody. The sun was right in my eyes, from behind her, which made her whole figure stand out sharply, coal-black against the blue canvas of the sky, a coal-black silhouette on blue. A little higher up the clouds were flying past, and it seemed it wasn't the clouds that were flying but the stone, and her on the stone, and the crowd behind her, and the clearing—it was all slipping silently away, like a ship, and the light earth beneath our feet was sailing away. . . .

"Brothers!" she was saying. "Brothers! All of you know that over there, beyond the Wall in the city, they're building the INTEGRAL. All of you know that the day has come when we will demolish this Wall, all walls, so that a green wind may sweep all across the earth, from one end to the other. But the INTEGRAL is going to carry these walls aloft, up there, to the thousands of other earths whose lights will rustle for you tonight through black nocturnal foliage. . . ."

Against the stone, beating like waves, foam, wind: "Down with the INTEGRAL! Down with the INTEGRAL!"

"No, brothers! Not down with it. The INTEGRAL must be ours. On that day when it launches out into the heavens for the first time—we will be on board. Because the Builder of the

INTEGRAL is with us. He has left walls behind, he has come here with me, to be among you. Long live the Builder!"

In a flash I'm somewhere up in the air and beneath me are heads, heads, heads, mouths wide open and screaming, hands shooting up and down. It was totally strange, intoxicating: I sensed myself above everyone; I was . . . myself, something separate, a world; I stopped being one of many, the way I'd always been, and became just one.

And then here I am back down, right beside the stone, my body rumpled, happy, crumpled as if it had just made love. Sun. Voices from above. I-330's smile. Some woman with golden hair, herself all gold and satin, smelling of grasses. She has a cup in her hands, a wooden cup, apparently. She drinks from it with her red lips and hands it to me and I shut my eyes and drink, I drink greedily, to douse the fire, I drink sweet, stinging, cold sparks.

And after that my blood and the whole world go a thousand times faster and the light earth races like a bit of fluff. And everything seems to me easy, simple, and clear.

Now I see the huge, familiar letters on the stone: "Mephi." And it somehow seems to me that it's just as it should be—that's the strong, simple thread tying everything together. I see a crude drawing (also on the stone, maybe) of a winged youth with a transparent body and instead of a heart he has a glowing coal, blindingly crimson. And again I feel I understand this coal, or rather, I feel it—just as I feel each word (she's speaking up there, on the stone) without actually hearing it—and feel everyone breathing in unison—and that it's everyone's fate to fly off together somewhere, just like the birds that time over the Wall. . . .

From behind, from the dense breathing thicket of bodies, there comes a loud voice: "But this is madness!"

And I think I—yes, I think that was my voice—I think I jumped up onto the stone, from where I see sun, heads, a jagged-toothed saw of green against the blue, and I shout:

"Yes, yes, that's right! And everybody has to go mad, everybody must absolutely go mad, and as soon as possible! This is crucial! I know it is!"

I-330 is beside me. Her smile is two dark lines from the corners of her mouth upward at an angle, and it sinks into me like a coal, and this instant is easy, almost painless, wonderful. . . .

After that, all I retain are a few scattered sharp remnants.

A slow, low-flying bird. I see it's alive, like me. Like a human, it turns its head right and left and bores into me with its dark round eyes. . . .

More. A back with glistening fur the color of old ivory. Across the back a dark insect with tiny transparent wings is crawling—the back shivers to drive the insect off, shivers again. . . .

More. The leaves cast a shadow—woven, crosshatched. People are lying about in this shadow and eating something that looks like the legendary food of the ancients: a long yellow fruit and a piece of something dark. A woman puts this in my hand and I feel funny, not knowing whether I can eat it.

And then the crowd, heads, legs, arms, mouths. Faces pop up for a second and then get lost, like soap bubbles that have burst. And for a moment I see, or maybe I think I see, transparent ear-wings that flit past.

I grab I-330's hand for all I'm worth. She turns to look at me: "What is it?"

"He's here. . . . I think I . . ."

"Who?"

"S. . . . Just now, in the crowd. . . ."

Thin coal-black eyebrows pulled toward the temples. The sharp triangle of a smile. I don't get it—why's she smiling, how can she smile?

"You don't understand, I-330. You don't understand what it means if he, or any of them, is here."

"You're funny! Do you really think anyone over there behind the Wall could ever dream that we are here? Just think of yourself: Did you ever really imagine it was possible? They're looking for us over there! Let them look! You're dreaming."

She gives an easy, gay smile, and I smile. The earth is drunk, merry, light—it's sailing. . . .

# RECORD 28

*Both Women*

*Entropy and Energy*

*Opaque Part of the Body*

Consider this. If your world resembles the world of our distant ancestors, then imagine that once upon a time you were sailing on the ocean and you bumped into a sixth or a seventh part of the world, some kind of Atlantis, and there you found unheard-of labyrinth-cities, people soaring about in the air without the help of wings or aeros, stones that you could lift just by looking at them—in other words, something that you'd never be able to imagine even if you had the dream sickness. That's just how I felt yesterday. Because, you see, ever since the 200-Years War none of us had ever been on the other side of the Wall—that I've already told you.

I know, my unknown friends, what my duty is before you. It is to tell you in greater detail about this strange and unexpected world that was revealed to me yesterday. But for the moment I'm in no condition to go back to that. New things keep happening so fast, there's such a downpour of events, that I'd have to be two people to catch it: I pull out my yuny like an apron, I cup my hands—and bucketfuls pour by me, splashing nothing but drops on these pages. . . .

The first thing that happened was that I heard loud voices outside my door. I recognized her voice, supple and metallic, and another, almost rigid, like a wooden ruler: the voice of U.

Next, the door swung open with a bang and the two of them shot into my room. And I mean shot.

I-330 laid her hand on the back of my armchair and, looking over her right shoulder, smiled at the other woman with nothing but her teeth. I would not like to have that smile aimed at me.

"Listen," I-330 said to me, "this woman seems to have made it her aim in life to protect you from me, as though you were a child. She have your permission on this?"

Then the other one, her gills quivering: "That's right. He *is* a child. Yes! That's the only reason he can't see what you're getting him into with all this . . . just to . . . that it's all . . . a farce. Yes! And it's my duty . . ."

In the mirror I get a glimpse of the broken, bouncing line of my eyebrows. I jumped up and (barely managing to stifle that other self in me with the shaggy fists) squeezed out between my teeth words that I shouted point-blank right into her face, into her very gills: "Get out of here! Right now! Out!"

The gills puffed out, brick red, and then collapsed and turned gray. She opened her mouth to say something, said nothing, clamped it shut, and left.

I rushed over to I-330: "I'll never forgive . . . I'll never forgive myself for that! She would dare to . . . to you? But surely you don't think that I think that . . . that she . . . It's all because she wants to be registered to me, and I . . ."

"Fortunately, she's too late for registering. And it wouldn't bother me if there were thousands more like her. I know you'll believe me, and only me, not those thousands. Because after what happened yesterday, so far as you're concerned, you have me exactly where you wanted me. I'm in your hands. At any moment, you can . . ."

"At any moment . . . what?" And then I immediately understood "what." Blood gushed into my ears, my cheeks, and I shouted, "Don't talk to me about that! Never mention that to me! You do understand, don't you—that was . . . that other me, the one before, but now . . ."

"Who knows who you really are? A person is like a novel:

Up to the very last page you don't know how it's going to end. Otherwise, there'd be no point in reading. . . ."

I-330 strokes my head. I can't see her face, but something in her voice tells me that she's looking very far away, that her eyes are fixed on a cloud floating by silently, slowly, headed no one knows where. . . .

Suddenly, pushing me away with her hand, she said in a firm, tender voice: "Listen, I came to tell you that it may be that these are already our final days. . . . You know all the auditoriums are closed, starting tonight?"

"Closed?"

"Yes. And I looked in as I was going past. They're getting something ready in the buildings where the auditoriums are, some kind of tables, with medics in white coats."

"But what does it mean?"

"I don't know. Nobody knows yet. Which is worst of all. I just have this feeling that they've thrown the switch, the power's on . . . so if not right away, then tomorrow. . . . But maybe they'll be too late."

I'd long ago lost track of who was *they* and who was *we*. I didn't know which I wanted: for them to be late or not. One thing only was clear to me, and that is that I-330 was walking right along the very edge, and at any moment . . .

"But this is crazy," I say. "You . . . and OneState. It's like putting your hand over the muzzle and thinking you can stop the shot. It's absolutely crazy!"

With a smile: "Everyone has to go mad . . . go mad as soon as possible. Someone said that yesterday. Remember? There . . ."

Yes, I have that written down. Which means it actually happened. I say nothing but merely look at her face: The dark cross on it is now especially vivid.

"I-330, darling, before it's too late . . . If you want, I'll throw it all away, I'll forget about it . . . and we'll go together, over there, beyond the Wall, to those . . . I don't know who they are."

She shook her head. Through the dark windows of her eyes, there, on the inside, I see the stove burning, sparks, tongues of flames leaping up, piles of dry resinous wood. And I see that it's already too late. My words can no longer do any . . .

She got up. She's about to leave. It may be that these are the final days . . . or final minutes. I grabbed her by the hand.

"No! Just a little while longer . . . for the sake of . . ."

Slowly she lifted my hand up into the light, my shaggy hand, which I so detested. I tried to pull back, but she held on tight.

"Your hand . . . You don't know, there are few who do know, that there are women from here, from the city, who have come to love those others over there. You, too, probably have a drop or two of that sunny forest blood. Maybe that's why I . . ."

There was a pause, and strangely enough, the pause, the blank, the nothing, made my heart race. And I shout:

"Oh good! You aren't leaving yet! You won't leave until you tell me about them, because you love . . . them, and I don't even know who they are, where they come from. Who are they? Are they the half we've lost—the $H_2$ to our O, that have to be joined as $H_2O$ to make streams, seas, waterfalls, waves, storms?"

I distinctly remember every movement she made. I remember her taking the glass triangle from my table and, all the while I was talking, pressing the sharp edge of it to her cheek, which raised a white welt that later was suffused with pink and then vanished. What is surprising is that I can't remember what she said, especially at the beginning. All I recall are various images and colors.

I do know that at first it had to do with the 200-Years War. There was something red against the green of the grasses, against dark clays, against the blue of the snow—pools of red that never dried up. Then yellow grasses, burnt by the sun, naked, yellow, ragged people, and ragged dogs beside them, next to bloated corpses—of dogs, or maybe of humans. . . . All this on the other side of the Wall, of course, because the city had already won, inside the city you could already find the kind of food we have now, made of petroleum.

And stretching almost from heaven to earth were the heavy black folds of some material, waving folds: It was columns of slow smoke above the forests, above the villages. A hollow wailing sound hung over the black endless lines of those who were being driven into the city, to be saved by force and taught happiness.

"You almost knew all this?"

"Almost, yes."

"But you didn't know, only very few knew, that a small part of them managed to survive and went on living there, on the other side of the Walls. They were naked and went off into the forest. There they learned from the trees, animals, birds, flowers, sun. They grew coats of fur over their bodies, but beneath the fur they kept their hot red blood. You had it worse. You grew numbers all over your body, numbers crawled about on you like lice. You all have to be stripped naked and driven into the forest. You should learn to tremble with fear, with joy, insane rage, cold—you should learn to pray to the fire. And we Mephi, we want . . ."

"No, wait. Mephi? What is Mephi?"

"Mephi? It's an old name. Mephi is one who . . . You remember, there on the stone, there was an image of a youth. . . . Or, no, I'd better put it in your language so you'll understand it sooner. Look—there are two forces in the world, entropy and energy. One of them leads to blissful tranquility, to happy equilibrium. The other leads to the disruption of equilibrium, to the torment of perpetual movement. Our—or rather, your—ancestors, the Christians, worshipped entropy as they worshipped God. But we anti-Christians, we . . ."

At this moment there came a knock at the door that you could hardly hear, like a whisper, and into the room rushed that same Number with the flat face and the forehead pulled down over his eyes that had often brought me messages from I-330.

He ran up to us and stopped, panting like a pneumatic pump, unable to get a word out—he must have been running as fast as he could.

"Well, come on! What's happened?" I-330 grabbed him by the arm.

The pump finally managed to pant out: "They're headed this

way . . . the guards . . . and he's with them, that one with the sort of hunch!"

"S?"

"Yes! They're right here, inside. They'll be here any minute! Hurry!"

"Relax . . . we've got time!" She laughed. There were sparks in her eyes, gay little tongues of flame.

Either this was stupid, irrational courage, or there was something else going on here that I didn't understand.

"I-330! For the Benefactor's sake! You've got to understand . . . this is . . ."

A sharp triangular smile: "For the Benefactor's sake . . ."

"Well, for my sake, then . . . Please!"

"Oh, by the way, I still have to talk with you about a certain matter. . . . But, never mind—it can wait till tomorrow. . . ."

She nodded to me gaily (that's right: gaily), and the other one came out from underneath his brow just long enough to give me another nod, and I was left alone.

Quick, sit at the table. Unrolled my notes, took out my pen—I meant for *them* to find me at work for the benefit of OneState. And all of a sudden it felt as if every hair on my head had come alive and stood up: "And what if they take and read a page, even one page, especially one of these last ones?"

I sat motionless at the table and saw the walls trembling, the pen in my hand trembling, the letters swaying and blending together. . . .

Stash them? But where? Everything's made of glass. Burn them? But they could see from the hall and from the rooms next door. Besides, I can't, I no longer have the strength to destroy this painful piece of myself, which might turn out to be the piece I value most.

Far down the corridor I could already hear voices and footsteps. All I had time for was to grab a bunch of pages and stick them under me and there I was, welded to a chair every atom of which was shaking under me, with the floor under my feet like a deck pitching and rolling. . . .

Hunching down into a ball and somehow looking out from the overhang of my brow, I watched stealthily and saw them

going from room to room, starting at the right end of the corridor and getting closer all the time. Some, like me, sat frozen
in their positions; others were jumping up to greet them and
throw their doors open wide—lucky them! If only I . . .

"The Benefactor is that most perfect disinfectant, necessary
for humanity, as a consequence of which no peristalsis in the organism of OneState . . ." —this absolute nonsense I was squeezing out with a pen leaping all over the paper as I bent lower and
lower over the table while some insane blacksmith was pounding an anvil in my head and behind me I heard the door handle
turn and felt a gust of wind and the chair beneath me began to
tap-dance. . . .

Only then did I manage to tear myself away from the page
and turn to face those who had come in (it isn't easy playing a
farce—oh, who was it talking to me today about a farce?). S
was in the lead—his gloomy, silent, quick eyes started drilling
wells in me, in my chair, in the pages shaking under my hand.
Then, for a moment, I saw some familiar, everyday faces on
the threshold, and one in particular stood out: It had puffed
out, brownish-pink gills. . . .

I recalled everything that had been going on in this room
half an hour ago, and it was clear to me that she now . . . My
whole being was beating and pulsing in that part of my body
(opaque, fortunately) with which I was hiding the manuscript.

U came up to S from behind, cautiously touched his sleeve,
and said very quietly: "This is D-503, the Builder of the INTE-
GRAL. You've heard of him, no doubt. He's always at his desk
this way. Absolutely no mercy on himself!"

And as for me? I was thinking: What a marvelous, astonishing woman!

S slunk up to me and peered over my shoulder at the desk. I
tried hiding my paper with my elbow, but he shouted sternly:
"You will show me that at once!"

Mortified, I handed him the paper. He read it, and I saw a
smile slip out of his eyes, slide down his face, and, with a flick
of its tail, take a seat on the right side of his mouth.

"Rather ambiguous, but still . . . Okay, go on; we won't
bother you further." He paddled off to the door, and with his

every step I got back more of my feet, hands, fingers—my soul spread evenly once more through my body, and I breathed again. . . .

The last thing was that U hung around long enough to come whisper in my ear: "Lucky for you that I . . ."

What she meant to say I don't know. Later that evening I learned they'd taken away three Numbers. Not that anyone talks about this, or anything that's going on (the edifying influence of the Guardians hiding everywhere among us). The talk is mostly about how fast the barometer is falling and the weather changing.

# RECORD 29

*Threads on the Face*

*Shoots*

*Unnatural Compression*

Strange—the barometer is falling, but there's no wind yet, just silence. Up there above, where we can't hear it, it's already begun, the storm. The rainclouds are racing along at full speed. There aren't many of them yet—scattered serrated fragments. It's as though some city had fallen up there and now the pieces of the walls and towers are flying down, the heaps of them grow with horrible rapidity before your eyes, and they come closer and closer, but still have days to fly through blue emptiness before they crash down here to the bottom, with us.

Down below it's quiet. There are thin, mysterious, almost invisible threads in the air. Every fall they blow in here from over there, beyond the Wall. They float slowly. Suddenly you feel you've got something strange, that you can't see, on your face, and you try to brush it off, but no, you can't, there's no way to get rid of it.

These threads are unusually numerous if you go near the Green Wall, where I was walking this morning. I-330 had asked me to meet her at the Ancient House, in our "apartment" there. [I was not far from the rust-red, opaque] mass of the Ancient House, when I heard behind me someone's hurried little steps and rapid breathing. I turned round and saw O trying to catch up with me.

There was something special about her person, how rounded

and softly full it seemed. Her arms and the cups of her breasts and her whole body, which I knew so well, rounded out her yuny and stretched it, as though the thin material was going to give at any minute and everything would be . . . outside, in the sun, in the light. It occurred to me that over there in the green thickets, in the springtime, shoots break their way up through the earth just as stubbornly, in order to put out branches and leaves as quickly as possible, to bloom as soon as they can.

She was silent for a few seconds while the blue of her eyes shone in my face.

"I saw you that time, on the Day of Unanimity."

"I saw you too." And I had a sudden recollection of her standing down below in the narrow passageway, her back pressed to the wall and her hands shielding her belly. I couldn't help glancing at her belly, round beneath her yuny.

She must have noticed this; she became all round and pink, and gave me a pink smile: "I'm so happy, so happy. . . . I'm full, you see. Full up to the brim. I walk about and I hear nothing going on around me—I'm forever listening on the inside, inside myself. . . ."

I said nothing. There was something on my face, it bothered me, I couldn't manage to brush it away. Then suddenly, her blue eyes still shining, she surprised me by grabbing my hand—and I felt the touch of her lips on my hand. . . . This was the first time in my life this ever happened. This was some kind of ancient caress that I'd never even heard of. . . . I felt such hurt and shame that I jerked my hand back (probably a little too roughly).

"Listen, you've lost your mind! And not only this . . . in general, you . . . what are you so happy about? Don't tell me you've forgotten about what's going to happen to you? Not right now, maybe, but in a month or two for sure. . . ."

She was like a candle that just went out. All the circles that made her up suddenly got lopsided and warped. And as for me, there was an unpleasant, even painful compression in my heart, the kind associated with the sensation of pity (that's all the heart is—an ideal pump; a pump sucking up a liquid—to call that compression, contraction, is a technical absurdity;

from which it follows how absurd, unnatural, diseased are all these "loves" and "pities" and anything else that's supposed to cause this compression).

Silence. The cloudy green glass of the Wall was on our left. The dark red mass ahead. And these two colors, blending together, combined in me to produce a resultant: what I considered a brilliant idea.

"Wait! I know how to save you. I can save you—you won't have to take one look at your baby and then die. You'll be able to feed it, you understand, you'll watch it grow in your arms, grow round and ripe like a fruit."

A shudder went through her whole body and she clung to me.

"You remember that woman, you know, a long time ago, on the walk? Okay, listen. She's here now, in the Ancient House. Let's go to her, and I promise—I'll settle everything right away."

I could already see us—the three of us, her, me, and I-330—going down the corridors, taking her to where the flowers and grass and leaves . . . But she took a step back away from me and the horns of her pink crescent were trembling and turning downward.

"You're talking about . . . her," she said.

"About? . . ." I was embarrassed, for some reason. "Of course, I'm talking about her."

"And you want me to go to that woman? You want me to ask her to . . . ? Don't you ever mention her to me again!"

She bent over and hurried away from me. Then, as if she'd remembered something else, she turned round and shouted: "So I'll die—so what! It's none of your business—what do you care?"                                                                    (

It's quiet. Pieces of the blue towers and walls keep falling from above and grow before your eyes with horrible swiftness, but they still have hours, maybe even days, to fly through infinity; the invisible threads float slowly past, settle on your face, and you can't brush them off, there's no way to get rid of them.

I walk slowly toward the Ancient House. In my heart is the absurd, agonizing compression. . . .

# RECORD 30

*The Final Number*

*Galileo's Mistake*

*Wouldn't It Be Better?*

Here's the conversation I had with I-330 yesterday in the Ancient House amid a colorful riot of reds, greens, bronze-yellows, whites, and oranges, which jammed any logical train of thought. And all the while we were beneath the frozen marmoreal smile of the ancient flat-nosed poet.

I reproduce this conversation verbatim, because in my opinion it is going to have an enormous, decisive meaning for the fate of OneState and, what is more, for the universe. And also because you, my unknown readers, might find here something that justifies me. . . .

I-330 wasted no time and hit me with everything immediately: "I know that you're making the first test flight of the IN-TEGRAL day after tomorrow. That's the day we take it over."

"What? Day after tomorrow?"

"Yes. Sit down and don't get excited. We don't have a minute to lose. There were twelve Mephi among the hundreds that the Guardians seized at random yesterday. If we wait two or three days, they'll be killed."

I didn't say anything.

"To observe how the test is going, they'll have to send you electricians, mechanics, doctors, meteorologists. And precisely at 12:00—remember this—when the bell rings for lunch and everyone files into the dining room, we'll stay behind in the corridor, lock them in the dining room, and the INTEGRAL is ours. You understand, it's got to be this way, no matter what. The INTEGRAL in our hands—with a weapon like that we'll finish the whole thing at once, quickly, painlessly. Their aeros will be a joke! Like midges against a shrike! And then if we need to, we can turn the blast from the engines against them and let that do the work. . . ."

I jumped up. "This is unthinkable! It's stupid! Can't you see that what you're plotting is . . . revolution?"

"Yes—revolution! Why is that stupid?"

"Stupid—because there can't be a revolution. Because our—this is me talking, not you—our revolution was the final one. And there cannot be any further revolutions of any kind. Everybody knows that. . . ."

Her brows make a sharp mocking triangle: "My dear, you are a mathematician. You're even more, you're a philosopher of mathematics. So do this for me: Tell me the final number."

"The what? I . . . I don't understand. What final number?"

"You know—the last one, the top, the absolute biggest."

"But, I-330, that's stupid. Since the number of numbers is infinite, how can there be a final one?"

"And how can there be a final revolution? There is no final one. The number of revolutions is infinite. The last one—that's for children. Infinity frightens children, and it's essential that children get a good night's sleep. . . ."

"But what's the point? What's the point of all this? In the name of the Benefactor, what point is there if everyone is already happy?"

"Let's suppose . . . Okay, good, let's even suppose that what you say is true. Then what?"

"That's silly! A completely infantile question. Tell something to children, tell them the whole thing right to the end, and they'll still ask: Then what? What comes next?"

"Children are the only bold philosophers. And bold philosophers will always be children. So you're right, it's a child's question, just as it should be: Then what?"

"Then nothing! Finished. All through the universe, evenly spread, everywhere . . ."

"Aha—evenly, everywhere! That is precisely what we're talking about—entropy, psychological entropy. You're a mathematician. Surely you see that only differences, differences of temperature, only contrasts in degree of heat, only that makes for life? And if throughout the universe all bodies are equally warm, or equally cool . . . You've got to smash them into each other—so there'll be fire, explosion, inferno. And we—we're going to smash them."

"But, I-330—remember, just remember: That's just what our ancestors did—during the 200-Years War. . . ."

"Oh, and they were right, they were a thousand times right. They made only one mistake: Afterward, they got the notion that they were the final number—something that doesn't exist in nature. Their mistake was the mistake of Galileo. He was right that the earth revolves around the sun, but he didn't know that the entire solar system revolves around yet another center; he didn't know that the real orbit of the earth, as opposed to the relative orbit, is by no means some naive circle. . . ."

"And you?"

"And we—for the time being at least we know there's no final number. Maybe we'll forget this. No—it's even probable that we'll forget it, when we get old, the way everything unavoidably gets old. At which time we, too, will inevitably go down, just as leaves fall from the tree in the autumn—just as, the day after tomorrow, you will . . . But no, no, darling—not you. Because you're with us, you're with us!"

A hot flashing whirlwind—I'd never seen her like this, and she was all around me, I vanished into her. . . .

The last thing she said, looking straight into my eyes: "Remember now: at 12:00."

And I said, "Yes, I remember."

She left. I was alone amid the noisy tumult of many voices—blue, red, green, bronze-yellow, orange. . . .

Yes, at 12:00. . . . —and suddenly the crazy feeling of something odd that's settled on your face, something you can't manage to wipe away. Suddenly, I recall yesterday morning, U, and what she was shouting in I-330's face. . . . Why? How absurd.

I rushed to get outside, and home, as soon as I could, home . . .

From somewhere behind me I heard the piercing squeal of the birds above the Wall. And ahead, in the light of the setting sun, crystallized crimson fire, were the globes of the cupolas, huge flaming cubes of buildings, the spire of the Accumulator Tower, like frozen lightning in the sky. And all that, all that unimpeachable geometrical beauty, I was with my own hands going to . . . I couldn't believe there was no way out, no other path.

I go past some auditorium (don't remember the number). Inside, benches have been piled up; in the middle are tables covered with sheets of snow-white glass; on the white the sunlight leaves a spot of blood. Hiding in all this is some kind of tomorrow—unknown and therefore terrifying. This is against nature: for a thinking, sighted creature to live among irregularities, unknowns, X's. Suppose they blindfolded you and forced you to walk by feeling your way along, stumbling, and knowing that right there, inches away, was the edge. Just one step, and all that's left of you is a piece of flattened dead meat. Isn't that just what I'm doing?

. . . And what if you don't wait? You just dive over the edge yourself? Wouldn't that be the only right thing to do, the one that would solve everything?

# RECORD 31

*The Great Operation*

*I Have Forgiven Everything*

*A Train Wreck*

Saved! At the very last moment, when it already seemed there was nothing to grab at, when it seemed everything was already over . . .

It was as if you'd already climbed the steps up to the Benefactor's terrible Machine, and the bell-glass had already come down over you with a heavy clank, and for the last time in your life you looked around—hurry!—to swallow the blue sky with your eyes . . .

And suddenly: It was only a "dream." The sun is pink and happy, and the wall—what a pleasure to run your hand over the cold wall, and the pillow, you can't get enough of looking at the dent your head has made in the white pillow . . .

That will give you at least some idea of what I felt this morning when I read the *State Gazette*. I'd had a terrifying dream, and it was over. And I—I'd had so little courage, so little faith, I was even thinking of taking my own life. I'm ashamed now to read the last lines that I wrote yesterday. But it doesn't matter: Let them be, let them stand as a reminder of that incredible thing that might have happened—and that now will not happen . . . that's right, will not happen!

Here's the headline that glowed from page one of the *State Gazette*:

## REJOICE!

For henceforth you are perfect! Up until this day your offspring, the machines, were more perfect than you.

## IN WHAT WAY?

Every spark of the dynamo is a spark of purest reason. Every stroke of the piston is an immaculate syllogism. But do you not also contain this same infallible reason?

The philosophy of the cranes, the presses, and the pumps is as perfect and clear as a circle drawn with a compass. But is your philosophy any less perfect?

The beauty of the mechanism is in the precise and invariable rhythm, like that of the pendulum. But you—sustained as you were from infancy on the Taylorian system—are you any less pendulum-perfect?

But think of this:

The mechanism has no imagination.

When you were at work did you ever happen to see a distant, idiotic, dreamy smile spread across the physiognomy of a cylindrical pump? At night, during the hours designated for rest, did you ever happen to hear the cranes toss restlessly and heave sighs?

## NO!

But—and you should be ashamed of yourselves!—the Guardians more and more frequently note that you yourselves smile and sigh in just this way. And—cover your eyes for very shame!—the historians of OneState are seeking to resign rather than record certain shameful events.

But you are not to blame. You are sick. The name of your illness is:

## IMAGINATION.

This is the worm that eats out black wrinkles on the brow. This is the fever that drives you to run farther and farther, even though that "farther" began in the place where happiness ends. This is the last barrier on the path to happiness.

But rejoice: It has already been demolished.

The path is free.

The latest discovery of State Science: The imagination is centered in a wretched little brain node in the region of the *pons Varolii*. Expose this node to three doses of X rays—and you are cured of imagination.


FOREVER

You are perfect, you are the equal of the machine, the path to 100 percent happiness is free. Hurry, then, all of you, young and old, hurry to undergo the Great Operation. Hurry to the auditoriums where the Great Operation is performed. Long live the Great Operation! Long live One-State! Long live the Benefactor!


. . . You—if you had only read all this not in my notes, which are like some ancient whimsical novel—if your trembling hands held, as mine now do, this sheet of newspaper still smelling of fresh ink—if you only knew, as I do, that this is all the most genuine reality, if not of today then of tomorrow—wouldn't you feel exactly what I feel? Wouldn't your head spin the way mine does now? Wouldn't you feel this prickling—scary, sweet, icy—along your arms and down your back? Wouldn't you also think you're a giant, an Atlas, and that if you stood up straight you'd be sure to hit your head against the glass ceiling?

I grabbed the telephone: "I-330 . . . Yes, I said 330." Then, choking, "Oh good, you're home. Did you read . . . you're reading it? Isn't that . . . It's astonishing!"

"Yes. . . ." Long, dark silence. I could barely hear a low sound in the receiver. She was thinking something over. . . . "I've got to see you today without fail. Yes, at my place after 16:00 hours. Without fail."

The darling. My precious, precious darling! "Without fail."

I felt myself smiling, and I couldn't help it, so now I was going to carry this smile through the streets like a torch, high over my head. . . .

Once outside, the wind hit me. It was twisting, whistling, cutting. But it made me even happier. Go on, howl: You won't knock over any walls now. Overhead, cast-iron gray clouds were tearing along. Go to it—you can't dim the sun. We've fastened it to the zenith with a chain forever—we Joshuas, sons of Nun.

At the corner was a dense little group of Joshuas standing with their foreheads pressed against the glass wall. Inside, one was already lying on a blindingly white table. The soles of his bare feet could be seen sticking out at a yellow angle from beneath the white; white medics were bending over his head; a white hand was passing to another hand a syringe filled with something.

"And you, how come you aren't going?" I asked no one in particular, or rather, all of them.

"And how about you?" Someone's globular head turned to me.

"I'm going later. First I've got to . . ."

I left, slightly embarrassed. I really did have to see I-330 first. But why "first"? I couldn't answer this.

The hangar. The INTEGRAL, pale icy blue, shone and sparkled. In the engine compartment the dynamo hummed— it lovingly repeated one and the same word over and over— some word of mine, I felt. Bending over, I stroked the long cold tube of the engine. Darling . . . what a precious darling. Tomorrow you will come to life, tomorrow for the first time in your life you will shudder from the fiery burning flashes in your womb. . . .

How might I have looked upon this mighty glass monster if everything had remained as it was yesterday? If I knew that tomorrow at 12:00 I would betray it—yes, betray it?

I felt a careful touch on my elbow from behind. I turned round. The Second Builder's flat platter of a face.

"You know, of course . . ." he said.

"What? The operation? Yes, how about that? How about the way everything, all at once . . . ?"

"No, not that. The test flight's been postponed, until day after tomorrow. All because of that operation. . . . We knocked ourselves out for nothing. . . ."

*All because of the Operation.* What a funny, limited person. He can't see over the edge of his platter. If only he knew that, except for this Operation, he'd be locked in a glass cage tomorrow at 12:00, thrashing about and climbing the walls. . . .

It's 15:30 and I'm back in my room. I came in and saw U. She was sitting at my table looking like a figure of ivory, hard and straight, her right cheek propped in her hand. She must have been waiting for a long time, since when she jumped up to meet me her fingers left five creases in her cheek.

For one second that most unfortunate morning flashed back to me, when we were here in the same spot next to the table, she next to I-330, in a rage. . . . But only for a second—it was instantly wiped away by today's sunshine. That's how it is if you walk into a room on a bright day and flip on the light switch absentmindedly: The lightbulb does in fact come on, but it might as well not be there, it's so silly, weak, useless. . . .

Without thinking about it, I stuck out my hand, I was forgiving everything—she grabbed both my hands in a firm, prickly grip while her sagging cheeks, like ancient ornaments, quivered with excitement: "I've been waiting. . . . I only came in for a minute. . . . I just wanted to tell you how happy I am, how glad I am for you! Tomorrow or the day after, you know, you'll be completely well, you'll be born all over again. . . ."

I saw a sheet of paper on the table—the last two pages of my notes from yesterday. They lay exactly where I'd left them last night. If she saw what I wrote there . . . But what difference did it make? That was only history now, it was now so far away it was funny, like something seen through the wrong end of the binoculars. . . .

"Yes," I said. "And do you know what, just now I was walking along the avenue, and there was a man in front of me, and he cast a shadow on the sidewalk. And the shadow, see, was glowing. And I think—no, I'm absolutely sure of it—that tomorrow there won't be any shadows, not from people, not from things. The sun will be—right through everything. . . ."

She was gentle but strict: "You are imagining things! I wouldn't allow my children at school to talk that way. . . ."

And she went on talking about the children, about how she'd taken them all, in a bunch, to the Operation, and about how they'd had to tie them down, and about how you had "to love without mercy, without mercy," and about how she would finally make up her mind to . . .

She smoothed out the gray-blue fabric between her knees, quickly plastered me with her smile, and, without saying anything more, left.

And . . . fortunately the sun did not stand still today but went running on and now it was already 16:00 and I was knocking on the door and my heart was knocking inside me. . . .

"Come in!"

I drop onto the floor beside her chair, put my arms around her legs, throw my head back, and look into her eyes, first into one and then into the other, to see myself in each, myself in wonderful captivity. . . .

There on the other side of the wall was a storm, there the clouds looked more and more like cast iron, but so what? Inside my head things were crowded, boisterous words were spilling over, and I was noisily flying somewhere, like the sun—no, wait, not somewhere, *now* we know where—and the planets were flying behind me, planets spurting flame and peopled with fiery singing flowers—and mute blue planets, where the rational stones are organized into societies—planets that, like our earth, have reached the apex of absolute, hundred-percent happiness. . . .

Suddenly a voice from above: "But don't you think that apex . . . is nothing more than stones united into an organized society?"

And, as the triangle got sharper and darker: "And happiness. . . what is it, after all? Desires are a torment, aren't they? And it's clear that happiness is when there are no longer any desires, not even one. . . . What a mistake, what a stupid prejudice it's been all these years to put a plus sign in front of happiness. Absolute happiness should of course have a minus sign, a divine minus."

I remember muttering distractedly: "Absolute minus is 273°. . . ."

"Minus 273°. Exactly. Rather cool, but doesn't that alone prove that we're at the apex?"

She was somehow talking for me, through me, the same as she did that other time, long ago, and spinning out my thoughts to the end. But there was something so eerie in this that I couldn't stand it, and with a great effort I forced out the word: "No."

"No," I said. "You're . . . you're joking. . . ."

She started to laugh, very loud . . . too loud. She laughed until, an instant later, she'd reached some kind of edge, from which she stepped back, and down. There was a pause.

She stood up. She put her hands on my shoulders. She gave me a long slow stare. Then she drew me to her and everything vanished except for her sharp burning lips.

"Farewell!"

This word came from far away above me and was a long time coming—a minute, maybe, or two.

"What do you mean, farewell?"

"You are sick. You've committed crimes on account of me. It was a torment for you, wasn't it? But now comes the Operation, and you'll be cured of me. So . . . farewell."

"No!" I began to shout.

A mercilessly sharp triangle, black on white: "What is this? Don't you desire happiness?"

My head was going in all directions. Two logical trains had crashed, piling on top of each other, crumpling, flying apart. . . .

"Well, how about it? I'm waiting. Choose: the Operation and 100 percent happiness, or . . ."

"I can't live without you, I don't want to live without you," I either said or thought, I don't know which, but I-330 heard me.

"Yes, I know," she answered. Then, with her hands still on my shoulders and her eyes still looking into mine: "In that case, I'll see you tomorrow. Tomorrow at 12:00. You remember?"

"No. It's been postponed one day. The day after tomorrow. . . ."

"So much the better for us. At 12:00 the day after tomorrow. . . ."

I was walking alone down the street in the twilight. The wind was twisting, carrying, driving me like a scrap of paper; fragments of the cast-iron sky were flying, flying—they had another day, or two, to fly through the infinite. . . . I was brushing against the yunies of those walking the other way, but I was all alone. I could see it clearly: All were saved, but there was no saving me, not any longer. *I did not want to be saved.* . . .

# RECORD 32

*I Do Not Believe*

*Tractors*

*The Human Chip*

Do you believe that you will die? Yes, man is mortal, I am a man, ergo . . . No, that isn't what I mean. I know that you know that. What I'm asking is: Have you ever actually *believed* it, believed it completely, believed not with your mind but with your *body*, actually felt that one day the fingers now holding this very piece of paper will be yellow and icy . . . ?

No, of course you don't believe it—which is the reason why, up to now, you haven't jumped from the tenth floor to the pavement, why you've gone on eating, turning pages, shaving, smiling, writing. . . .

It's the same—yes, exactly the same—with me today. I know that this little black hand on my watch is going to creep down to here, midnight, and that it will then climb slowly back upward, to cross at a certain moment some final point, at which time an incredible tomorrow will commence. This I know, but I somehow do not *believe* it—or maybe it seems to me that the twenty-four hours are going to be twenty-four years. And that is why I can still do something, hurry somewhere, answer questions, climb up the ladder to the INTEGRAL. I still feel it rocking on the water and understand that I have to hold on to the handrail and that it's cold glass I feel under my hand. I see the transparent living cranes bending their goose necks, sticking out their beaks, and carefully, tenderly feeding the INTE-

GRAL the terrible explosive food for its engines. And, down below on the river, I have a clear view of the blue watery veins and nodules inflated by the wind. But even so, all this is very separate from me, strange, flat—like a diagram on a sheet of paper. And it's also strange that the flat diagrammatic face of the Second Builder is suddenly talking: "So what do you say? How much fuel shall we take on for the engines? If you count three, or say, three and a half hours . . ."

Before me, in three-dimensional projection on the diagram, I see my hand, which is holding a calculator, the logarithmic dial of which points to the number 15.

"Fifteen tons. No, better make that . . . yes, make it 100 . . ."

This is because I do after all know that tomorrow . . .

And out of the corner of my eye I see my hand, the one holding the dial, begin almost imperceptibly to tremble.

"A hundred? But why such a lot? That's enough for a week. What am I saying? For much longer than a week!"

"There's no telling . . . who knows?" I know.

The wind whistles and all the air, right up to the sky, seems tightly packed with some invisible substance. I have trouble breathing, trouble walking, and down there at the end of the avenue, the hand on the clock of the Accumulator Tower has trouble slowly crawling along, never stopping for a second. The spire of the tower, dim and blue, is in the clouds, where it howls vacantly as it sucks electricity. The pipes of the Musical Factory are howling.

In rows, four across, same as always. But the rows seem to be unstable, somehow, maybe from the wind that's shaking and twisting them. More and more. Now they've bumped against something on the corner, recoiled, and now they're a dense, frozen, tight clot, breathing hard, and all craning their necks at once.

"Look! No, look there! Hurry!"

"Them! It's them!"

"Me? Never! Not for anything—stick my head in the Machine first!"

"Shut up! You're crazy!"

The door of the auditorium at the corner is wide open and

out of it is coming a slow, heavy column of about fifty men. Or rather, not "men"—that isn't the word. Those weren't feet but some kind of heavy, forged wheels, drawn by some invisible drive mechanism. Not men but some kind of tractors in human form. Above their heads, snapping in the breeze, was a white banner embroidered with a golden sun, in the rays of which was a device: "We are the first! We have already had the Operation! Everybody follow us!"

They were plowing through the crowd, slowly but irresistibly, and you could see that if there was a wall or a tree or a house in their way instead of us, they would plow right through the wall, tree, house without stopping. Now they're already in the middle of the avenue. Now they've stretched out into a chain, hand in hand, facing us. And we—a tense little clot of bristling heads—we wait. We crane our necks. Clouds. Whistling wind.

Suddenly the left and right wings of the chain quickly close in on us, faster and faster, like a heavy car running downhill, lock us in a ring, and . . . toward the wide-open doors, through the doors, inside . . .

Someone's piercing scream: "It's a roundup! Run for it!"

And there was a stampede. Right near the wall there was still a narrow little breach in the living ring. Everybody headed that way, heads out, heads momentarily sharpened into wedges, with sharp elbows, ribs, shoulders, sides. They were like a stream of water compressed by a fireman's hose—they fanned out and scattered stamping feet, swinging arms, and yunies all over the place. Out of somewhere my eyes caught sight of a body bent double like the letter S with transparent ear-wings—then he was gone, sunk into the earth, and I was alone in the midst of flailing arms and feet. I ran for it.

A stop for breath in some kind of entranceway, my back pressed up against the doors, and instantly, as if the wind was blowing it, a little sliver of humanity comes toward me.

"I've been behind you . . . the whole time. . . . I don't want it, see . . . I don't want it. I agree . . ."

Tiny round hands on my sleeve, round blue eyes: It's her, O. Then she sort of slips down the wall and settles on the ground.

There she bent over and made a small lump of herself on the cold stairs, and I, standing above her, caress her head, her face, with my wet hands. This made me look very big and her very small, like a small part of myself. This was totally different from the way it was with I-330, and it occurred to me that it was something like the way the ancients treated their own personal children.

I can hardly hear what she is saying down there, talking through the hands covering her face: "Every night I . . . I can't . . . if they cure me . . . every night, alone in the dark, I think about him—how he'll turn out, how I'll do for him . . . I wouldn't have anything to live for, see? . . . You've got to . . . got to . . ."

It was a stupid feeling, but I did in fact feel certain: Yes, I've got to. Stupid, because what I had to do was one more crime. Stupid, because white cannot be black at the same time, a duty can't also be a crime. Or else there's nothing in life that is black or white and color depends on some fundamental logical postulate. And if you start from the postulate that I gave her a child illegally . . .

"Okay, but just calm down . . . calm down . . ." I say. "You understand, I've got to take you to I-330 . . . as I wanted to earlier . . . so that she can . . ."

"Yes." (This in a low voice, her hands still over her face.)

I helped her get up. Then, without saying a word, each thinking his own thoughts, or maybe each thinking about one and the same thing, we go along the darkening street among the quiet leaden houses, through the wind's tense whipping branches. . . .

At one transparent, tense point I heard behind me, through the whistling wind, the familiar sound of feet squelching through puddles. At the turn I looked back through the upside-down reflection of the racing rainclouds in the dim glass pavement and saw S. Immediately I start waving my arms in some strange awkward way and yelling to O that tomorrow, yes, tomorrow, the INTEGRAL will make its first test flight, and that this will be something absolutely incredible, marvelous, terrifying. . . .

In her circular blue amazement, O looks at me, then looks at my loud, idiotically waving hands. But I don't let her get a word out—I go on talking and talking. But inside me, where only I can hear it, a separate feverish thought is humming and knocking: "You can't . . . somehow you've got to . . . You can't let him follow you to I-330. . . ."

Instead of heading left, I cut off to the right. The bridge obediently presented its slavishly bent back to the three of us: me, O, and him, S, who was following. From the brightly lit buildings on the opposite bank lights were sprinkling into the water and shattering into thousands of feverishly leaping sparks, spattered with mad white foam. The wind was humming—it sounded like a bass string made of ship's hawser and strung somewhere low overhead. And through the bass, all the time, behind me . . .

The building where I live. At the entrance O stopped and started saying something like: "No, you promised . . ."

But I didn't let her finish, pushed her quickly through the door, and we were inside, in the lobby. At the control desk—the familiar sagging cheeks, shaking with excitement; a dense clot of Numbers standing around and some argument in progress, heads are sticking through the banisters of the second floor; people are running down the stairs, one at a time. But that would wait. . . . For now, I hurried to take O to the opposite corner and sat down with my back to the wall (on the other side of the wall I'd seen a dark, large-headed figure slipping back and forth along the sidewalk) and took out a pad of paper.

O sank slowly into her chair as though her body, under her yuny, was melting, evaporating, leaving only an empty garment, and empty eyes that absorbed you with their blue vacancy. Her tired voice said: "Why'd you bring me here? You tricked me?"

"No . . . sh-h! Look! See there . . . on the other side of the wall?"

"Yes. A shadow."

"He's always behind me. . . . I can't. Look—I can't . . . I'm going to write a couple of words here and you're going to take the note and leave . . . alone. I know he'll stay here."

Beneath the yuny her burgeoning body shifted again, the belly grew slightly rounder, her cheeks showed a barely perceptible morning light, a dawn.

I stuck the note into her cold fingers, pressed her hand, and for the last time took a drink with my eyes from her blue eyes.

"Farewell! Perhaps there'll be another time. . . ."

She drew back her hand. Bent over, she slowly started off, took two steps, turned around quickly, and was at my side again. Her lips moved, her eyes, her lips, all of her, telling me one and the same, one and the same word over and over. . . . What an unbearable smile. What pain. . . .

Then there was a human sliver hunched over in the entrance, a tiny shadow on the other side of the wall, never glancing back, moving more and more quickly. . . .

I went up to U's desk. Puffing out her gills with alarm and outrage, she said: "Look . . . they're all crazy! That one swears he saw some kind of naked man covered all over with fur near the Ancient House. . . ."

A voice out of the tight little bunch bristling with heads: "Yes! And I say it again: I saw him. I did."

"How do you like that, eh? It's delirium!"

And this "delirium" of hers was so certain, so inflexible, that I asked myself: "Maybe it really is delirium—all that's been happening to me and around me in the last few days?"

But I glanced at my hairy hands and words came back to me: "You probably have a drop of forest blood yourself. . . . Maybe that's why my feeling for you is . . ."

No, fortunately, it isn't delirium. No, unfortunately, it isn't delirium.

# RECORD 33

*(No Time for Contents,
Last Note)*

This day has arrived.

Get the paper quick, maybe it's there. . . . I read the paper with my eyes (that's no mistake: My eyes are like a pen now, or a calculator, something you hold in your hand, something you feel is not you—a tool).

There it is in big print all across page one:

> The enemies of happiness are not asleep. Hold on to happiness with both hands! Work will be suspended tomorrow— all Numbers will report for the Operation. Those not in compliance will be subject to the Machine of the Benefactor.

Tomorrow! Is there really going to be some kind of tomorrow?

By force of daily inertia I extended my hand (a tool) to the bookshelf and inserted today's *Gazette* into the gold-embossed binder along with the others. Halfway to the shelf, I think: "How come? What difference does it make? I'm never coming back to this room, not ever again. . . ."

And the paper falls out of my hand onto the floor. And I stand up and look round the room, every square centimeter of it, quickly gathering stuff up, feverishly jamming into some invisible suitcase everything I'd be sorry to leave behind—table, books, chair. That's the chair I-330 sat in that time, with me down there on the floor. . . . The bed . . .

Another minute passes, two . . . maybe I'm waiting for some stupid miracle—the telephone will ring, maybe, and she'll say that . . .

No. There isn't any miracle. . . .

I'm leaving . . . for the unknown. These are my last lines. Farewell to you, my unknown, my dear readers, with whom I've lived through so many pages, to whom, when I came down with "soul," I revealed all of myself, right down to the last pulverized screw, the last busted spring. . . .

I'm leaving.

# RECORD 34

*Those on Leave*

*A Sunny Night*

*Radio-Valkyrie*

Oh, if only I had really smashed myself and everyone into smithereens, if only I had really turned up with her somewhere on the other side of the Wall, among beasts baring their yellow tusks, if only I really had never come back here. It would have been a thousand, a million times easier. And now what? Go and strangle that . . . ? But what good would that do?

No, no, no! Get hold of yourself, D-503. Line yourself up on a strong logical axis . . . even if it won't be for long, bear down on the lever with all your weight . . . and, like an ancient slave, keep on turning the millstones of syllogisms until you've written, thought through, everything that's happened. . . .

When I boarded the INTEGRAL, everyone had already assembled, each in his place, and all the honeycombs of the gigantic glass beehive were filled. Down below through the glass decks one could see tiny antlike people beside the telegraphs, dynamos, transformers, altimeters, valves, dial-pointers, engines, pumps, and pipes. In the wardroom were some types leaning over tables and instruments—no doubt on assignment from the Scientific Bureau. Next to them was the Second Builder with two of his assistants.

These three all had their heads retracted into their shoulders like turtles, their faces gray, autumnal, dim.

"Well, how goes it?" I asked.

"Oh . . . fairly grim," one of them answered with a dim gray smile. "No telling where we might have to land. In general, there's no telling. . . ."

I couldn't bear to look at them—to look at men whom I would, in an hour's time, with these very hands, cast out forever from the cozy figures of the Table of Hours, whom I would tear away forever from the maternal breast of OneState. They reminded me of the tragic figures of "The Three on Leave," a story known to every schoolboy. This story tells of how three Numbers, as an experiment, were given leave from work for a whole month: Do as you like, go where you like.* The poor things hung around the place where they usually worked and kept on looking inside with starved eyes. They would dawdle around the square and for hours at a stretch they would go through the motions that their organisms had begun to require every day at a certain time: They would saw and plane the air, bang invisible hammers, clobber crude castings of iron that no one could see. After ten days of this, they finally couldn't take it any longer. They all joined hands, went into the water, and, in step with the March, went in deeper and deeper until the water put an end to their torment. . . .

I repeat, it was painful for me to look at them. I was in a hurry to get away.

"I'll just check in the machine room," I said, "and then— we're on the way."

They were asking me about this and that—what voltage to set for the blast-off, how much water ballast was needed for the aft tank. There was a sort of phonograph in me that answered all questions quickly and precisely, while, on the inside, I never ceased to concentrate on my own business.

And suddenly, in a narrow little gangway, one thing got to me there, inside, and that was in fact the moment from which it all started.

Gray yunies, gray faces, were passing by in that narrow little gangway when, for one second, one stood out—tousled

---

*This was a long time ago, in the Third Century of the Table.

hair low on a forehead above deep-set eyes: him. I understood: They were here.

And there was nowhere I could go to escape from all that. And there were only minutes left, a handful of minutes. . . . There began an infinitesimal, molecular trembling throughout my body (from that point to the very end it never left me)—as though a huge motor had been turned on and the structure of my body was too light to bear it and all the walls, partitions, cables, girders, lights—everything was trembling. . . .

I still don't know whether she's here. But there's no time now—they've sent for me to come up to the bridge at once: It's time for take-off. . . . Take-off to where?

Gray, dim faces. Down below, on the water, tense blue veins. Ponderous, cast-iron layers of sky. And my hand seems made of cast iron when I lift the command phone.

"Lift-off—45°!"

Dull explosion—jolt—aft, a green-and-white mountain of water goes berserk—deck, soft and spongy, vanishes beneath the feet—and everything below, all of life, forever . . . In one second everything around shrank as we fell into a sort of funnel: the icy blue convex cityscape, the round bubbles of the cupolas, the lonely leaden finger of the Accumulator Tower. Then—a momentary curtain of cotton-wadding clouds—through it— and the sun was shining in a blue sky. Seconds, minutes, miles— and the blue was quickly becoming firm and suffused with darkness, the stars were emerging like drops of cold silver sweat.

And here it was—the anxious, unbearably bright, black, starry, sunny night. It was how it might be if you suddenly went deaf: You can still see the trumpets blaring, but you only see them; the trumpets are mute. There's only silence. That's how the sun was—mute.

This was natural, this was to be expected. We'd left the earth's atmosphere. But it somehow happened so quickly, so abruptly, that everyone suddenly turned shy and got quiet. But as for me—I somehow felt even easier under this fantastic mute sun: as though I had done with cringing, I had crossed some unavoidable threshold, leaving my body down there somewhere while I was speeding in a new world where you expected everything to be unprecedented, upside down. . . .

"Hold this heading!" I shouted into the intercom, or rather, this shout came from the phonograph in me—and the same phonograph, with a mechanical, hinged movement, handed the intercom phone to the Second Builder. And I, my whole body covered with this thin molecular trembling that only I knew about, headed below, looking for . . .

The door to the wardroom—the very one: In an hour from now it would slam shut and lock tight. Next to the door was someone I didn't know—shortish, with a face you'd never pick out of a big crowd, with one unusual feature: His arms were uncommonly long and reached to his knees—looked as though they'd been taken by mistake from a different set of human parts.

One of these long arms reached out and barred the door: "Where are you going?"

I could see he didn't know that I knew everything. But so what—maybe it's better that way. I drew myself up to my full height and said, with deliberate bluntness: "I am the builder of the INTEGRAL. I am in charge of the tests. You understand?"

The arm vanished.

The wardroom. Heads bent over the instruments and maps, some of them sprouting a gray bristle, others yellow, bald, ripe. I gather them all into a bunch with one quick glance and head back along the gangway, down the companionway, to the engine room. There, pipes that were glowing from the explosions gave off heat and racket, glistening levers were going through a desperate drunken dance, and the dial pointers never for a moment ceased their barely perceptible trembling. . . .

Finally, at the tachometer, him—the one with the overhanging brow—bent over a notebook. . . .

"Listen . . . !" I had to shout over the racket right into his ear. "She here? Where is she?"

There was a smile in the shadow under his brow: "Her? Over there. In the radio telephone room."

I go there. I find three of them. All of them in winged headphone helmets. She looked a head taller than usual, winged, gleaming, flying—like one of the ancient Valkyries—and there seemed to be huge blue sparks overhead, on the radio antenna: This came from her, and so did the faint whiff of ozone, lightning.

"Could someone . . . or you," I said, speaking to her and panting (from running), "could you take a transmission back to earth, to the hangar? Come with me, I'll dictate it."

Next to the equipment room was a small cabin the size of a drawer. We sat at the desk, next to each other. I found her hand and pressed it.

"Well? What do we do now?"

"I don't know. Do you have any idea how marvelous this is— just to fly, not knowing, no matter where. . . . And soon it'll be 12:00 and no one knows what? And tonight . . . where'll we be tonight, you and I? On the grass, maybe, on dry leaves. . . ."

Blue sparks from her, and the scent of lightning, and my trembling gets faster and faster.

"Take this down," I say to her in a loud voice, still panting (from running). "Time 11:30. Speed 6800 . . ."

From beneath her winged helmet, keeping her eyes on the paper, she says quietly: "She came to me last night with your note. . . . I know, I know everything, be quiet. But her baby . . . it's yours, right? So I sent her . . . she's there already, on the other side of the Wall. She's going to live. . . ."

I'm back on the bridge. Back with the insane night of black star-studded sky and blinding sun. Back with the crippled hand of the clock on the wall slowly going from minute to minute and everything clothed in a fog of infinitely fine, all but imperceptible trembling, known to me alone.

Why, I don't know, but it struck me that it would be better for all this to take place not here, but somewhere down there, closer to the earth.

"Stop engines!" I shouted into the intercom.

Still moving forward, by inertia, but slower, slower. Then the INTEGRAL snagged on some hairbreadth second of time, hung for an instant motionless, till the hair snapped, and the INTEGRAL dropped downward, faster and faster, like a stone. Thus silently for minutes, for dozens of minutes, my pulse audible, the minute hand before my eyes nearer and nearer to 12. And I saw that I was the stone, that I-330 was the earth, that I was a stone thrown by someone, and that the stone had an intolerable need to fall, to smash into the earth, into a thousand fragments. . . . But what if . . . below you could already see the firm blue smoke of clouds . . . But what if . . .

But the phonograph inside me, with the smooth precision of a hinge, grabbed the phone and gave the order: "Ahead slow!" The stone stopped falling. Now only the four lower engines, two aft and two forward, were wearily panting just enough to counter the INTEGRAL's weight, and the INTEGRAL, barely trembling, as though riding at anchor, stood still in the air, some bare kilometer from the earth.

Everyone spilled out onto the deck (the twelve o'clock mealtime bell was due), and, leaning over the glass railing, drank in, in great hurried gulps, the unknown world down there, beyond the Wall. Amber, green, blue; the woods in autumn, meadows, a lake. At the edge of the blue saucer were some yellow ruins, like bones, from which a dried yellow finger rose menacingly—the steeple of an ancient church, probably, that had survived by a miracle.

"Look! Look! Over there, to the right!"

There across the green desert a quickly moving spot flew like a brown shadow. Mechanically I moved the binoculars in my hands to my eyes: Chest-high in the grass a herd of brown horses galloped, their tails flying, and on their backs were those creatures, dark bay, white, black. . . .

A voice behind me: "But I tell you I saw it—a face."

"Go on . . . tell that to someone else."

"Well here . . . you take the binoculars."

But they'd already vanished. Endless green desert . . .

And in the desert, filling all of it and me and everyone, the piercing vibration of the bell: mealtime in one minute, at twelve.

Instantly the world scattered in disconnected bits. Someone's resonant golden badge lay on the steps, and it meant nothing to me; it crunched beneath my heel. A voice: "But I tell you, it was a face!" A dark rectangle: open door to the wardroom. White teeth clenched in a sharp smile . . .

And at that moment, when the clock began to strike with infinite slowness, not breathing between one stroke and another, and the lines in front had already begun to move, the rectangle of the door was suddenly barred by two familiar, unnaturally long arms:

"Halt!"

Fingers dug into my palm—this was I-330, who was next to me.

"Who's this? Do you know him?"

"Isn't . . . but isn't he . . . ?"

Now he was on someone's shoulders. Above the hundreds of faces his face, the face of hundreds and thousands but uniquely his.

"In the name of the Guardians . . . Those to whom I'm speaking are listening, each one of them is listening. And what I'm telling you is this: We know. We don't know your numbers yet, but we know everything. The INTEGRAL will not be yours. The test flight will be carried out to the end, and as for you— you dare not make a move—you will carry it out with your own hands. And then . . . but I've finished. . . ."

Silence. The glass paving beneath my feet was soft, quilted, and my feet were soft and quilted. Next to me an absolutely white smile, frantic blue sparks. Into my ear, through her teeth:

"So it was you? You 'did your duty'? Well . . . so be it. . . ."

Her hand tore out of mine and the Valkyrie helmet with its angry wings was already far ahead of me. Frozen, silent, like all the others, I walk alone into the wardroom. . . .

But it wasn't me—it wasn't! I told no one about this—no one except these mute white pages. . . .

Inside myself I was screaming this at her—this desperate, loud, inaudible scream. She was sitting opposite me across the table and not once did her eyes brush me. Seated beside her was someone's ripe yellow bald spot. I could hear I-330 talking:

"'Nobility'? But my dear professor, a simple philological analysis of this word shows that it is a prejudice, a survival from ancient feudal epochs. But we . . ."

I felt myself turning pale, and in a moment everyone would

see this. . . . But the internal phonograph counted off the fifty statutory chews for each morsel, I locked myself inside myself as in an ancient opaque house, I blocked my door with rocks, I closed the drapes. . . .

Then the command phone was in my hands and . . . flight, in frozen, final misery—through dark clouds—into the night of sun and stars. Minutes, hours. And evidently inside me all this time, feverishly, at full speed, unheard even by me, the logical motor had been running. Because all of a sudden at some point in blue space I saw my desk and above it the gill-like cheeks of U, on it a forgotten sheet of my records. And I saw it all clearly: nobody but her . . . I saw it all. . . .

Oh if only . . . if only I could make it to the radio. . . . Winged helmets, the smell of blue lightning. . . . I remember—I was talking to her in a loud voice about something, and I remember how she looked straight through me as if I were glass and said absently:

"I'm busy. I'm getting a transmission from below. You can dictate yours to her over there. . . ."

In the tiny box of the cabin I thought for a second and dictated in a firm voice:

"Time: 14:40. Prepare for landing! Stop all engines. It's all over."

Bridge. The mechanical heart of the INTEGRAL has stopped, we're falling, but my own heart can't fall fast enough, keeps lagging, rises higher in my throat. Clouds—and then in the distance a green spot, greener, more and more clear, rushes whirling at us—this is the end. . . .

The porcelain-white, distorted face of the Second Builder. It was probably him who shoved me with all his might. I hit my head against something and just as I was falling, going dark, I vaguely heard:

"Aft engines! Ahead full!"

There was a sharp leap upward. . . . That's all I remember.

# RECORD 35

*In a Hoop*

*Carrot*

*Murder*

I didn't sleep all night. All night long I thought about one thing. . . .

After what happened yesterday, my head's been in tight bandages. Or rather, no—it isn't a bandage, but more like a hoop, a merciless hoop made of glass steel and riveted to my head. And I myself am in just such a forged hoop: Kill U. To kill U, and then go to her, to I-330, and say, "Now do you believe me?" But the most revolting thing is that killing is somehow dirty and archaic; to take something and smash someone's skull in—this gives me a sensation of something disgustingly sweet in my mouth and I can't swallow my own spit, I'm forever spitting in my handkerchief, my mouth's dry.

In my locker lay a heavy piston rod that had broken after casting (I needed to examine the structure of the fracture under a microscope). I rolled my notes up into a cylinder (let her read all of me, right down to the last letter), shoved the broken end of the piston rod inside, and headed below. The stairway seemed endless, the steps disgustingly slippery somehow, and watery, and I had to keep wiping the sweat away with a handkerchief. . . .

Below. Heart pounding. I stopped, took out the rod, went to the control desk. . . .

But U wasn't there. The board was vacant, frozen. I remem-

bered that all work had been canceled for today; everybody
had to go for the Operation. So it made sense: She had no reason to be here, there wouldn't be anybody to register. . . .

On the street. Wind. Sky made of racing cast-iron plates.
And, just as it happened yesterday at a certain moment: The
whole world was divided up into separate, distinct, indepen-
dent pieces, and each of them, falling headlong, would stop for
a second and hang in the air in front of me—then evaporate
without a trace.

Just as if the precise black letters on this page were to shift
suddenly, were to be startled into flying off every which way,
and not a single word remained, only nonsense: artl-ngoffichwa—.
That's just the sort of scattered crowd that was on the street—
no rows, but forward, back, across, cater-cornered.

Then there was no one. And for one second everything froze
in headlong motion: Up there on the second floor, in that glass
cage hanging out in the air, is a man and a woman, kissing,
standing up, her whole body leaning bent over backward.
That's forever, for the last time.

At a certain corner I come on a prickly shrub of heads waving about. Up in the air above this, all by itself, is a banner
with the words: "Down with the Machines!" "Down with the
Operation!" And something in me (not me) has a momentary
thought: "Can it be that everyone harbors the kind of pain
that can be extracted only along with the heart, and that everyone has to do something before . . . ?" And for one second the
world contains nothing except (my) animal hand with its cast-
iron weight in a roll of paper. . . .

Now a boy turns up, all of him straining forward, a
shadow beneath his lower lip. His lower lip is inside out, like
the cuff of a rolled-up sleeve—his whole face is inside out—
he's yelling—running from someone as fast as he can—footsteps
behind him. . . .

From the boy my mind jumps to the conclusion: "That's
right, U must be at the school now. Better get there quick." I
ran to the nearest subway entrance.

At the entrance someone running past yelled: "They aren't
running! The trains aren't running today! There . . ."

I went down. Absolute delirium below. The glitter of faceted crystal suns. Platform rammed full of heads. An empty, stationary train.

And in this silence, a voice: hers. I can't see her, but I know it, I know this resilient, pliant voice, like a slashing whip. There, somewhere, is the sharp triangle of brows drawn back to the temples. . . .

I shouted: "Let me through! Let me through! I've got to . . ."

But my arms and shoulders were clamped in someone's grip, and in the silence I heard a voice: "No, run upstairs! You'll be cured there—they'll stuff you tight with good rich happiness and when you're full, you'll dream peaceful organized dreams, snoring in time with everyone—can't you hear that great symphony of snores? You silly people—they want to rid you of these question marks that squirm like worms and gnaw at you like worms. And here you stand and listen to me. Get upstairs quick to the Great Operation! What difference is it to you if I stay on here alone? What difference is it to you if I don't want others to do the wanting for me? If I want to want for myself? If I want the impossible?"

Another voice, slow and heavy: "Aha! The impossible? That means running after your imbecilic fantasies so they can wag their tails in front of your nose? No—we're going to grab that tail and stamp on it, and then . . ."

"And then—stuff it in your face and snore away—and there'll have to be a new tail to put in front of your nose. They say the ancients had an animal called the donkey. In order to make him keep on going forward, they tied a carrot to the shaft in front of his face so that it was just out of his reach. But if he did reach it, he ate it. . . ."

Suddenly the clamp let me go and I pitched forward into the middle, where she was speaking—and just at that moment everyone shoved forward, there was a crush, and from behind someone shouted: "They're coming! They're headed this way!" The light surged and went out—someone had cut the wire—and there was an avalanche, screams, howling, heads, fingers. . . .

How long we were rolling along like this in the underground

tube I do not know. Finally we came to some steps, a dim twilight, it got lighter, and we fanned out on the street again, everyone going in different directions. . . .

And here I am alone. Wind and, just above my head, a low gray twilight. Very deep in the wet glass of the sidewalk are reflections of lights, walls, and people walking with their legs in the air. And the incredibly heavy paper roll in my hand is pulling me downward toward the bottom.

Again U was not at the desk downstairs, and her room was dark and empty.

I went up to my place and turned on the light. Compressed inside the tight hoop, my temples were pounding, and I was still walking locked into the same circle: table, on the table the white rolled paper, bed, door, table, white roll . . . The blinds were down in the room to the left. In the one to the right, bent over a book, was the bumpy bald spot and the forehead like a huge yellow parabola. The wrinkles on the forehead make a row of yellow illegible lines. At times, when our eyes meet, I have the feeling that these yellow lines are about me.

. . . It happened precisely at 21:00. U herself walked in. I remember with clarity only one thing: I was breathing so loud that I could hear it and kept trying to turn it down—but couldn't.

She sat down and smoothed out her yuny on her knees. The pinkish-brown gills trembled.

"Oh, my dear, so it's true—you were hurt? As soon as I heard about it, just now . . ."

The rod was in front of me on the table. I jumped up, breathing even louder. She heard this, stopped in the middle of what she was saying, and also, for some reason, stood up. I could already see the spot on her head, it was disgustingly sweet in my mouth, I reached for my handkerchief, had no handkerchief, and spat on the floor.

He was there beyond the wall on the right, with his yellow intense wrinkles—about me. He mustn't see it. It would be even more repulsive if he was watching. . . . I pressed the button—so what if I had no right, what difference could that make now?—and the blinds went down.

She evidently sensed something, understood, and threw herself toward the door. But I beat her to it, still breathing loudly, and never for a moment took my eyes off that spot on her head. . . .

"You . . . you've gone crazy! Don't you dare . . ." She backed away and sat or rather fell down on the bed and put her clasped hands, trembling, between her knees. I was pure compression. Still holding her tethered with my eyes, I slowly stretched my hand out to the table—only one arm moved—and closed it on the rod.

"I'm begging you! A day—just one day! Tomorrow, I promise you, tomorrow, I'll go and do everything. . . ."

What was she talking about? I swung the rod. . . .

And I consider that I killed her. That's right, my unknown readers, you have every right to call me a murderer. I know I would have brought the rod down on her head, if she hadn't shouted: "In the name of . . . don't . . . I agree . . . Give me a second . . ."

And with shaking hands she tore off her yuny—and her large, yellow, flabby body fell over backward on the bed. . . . And only then did I understand. She thought the blinds . . . that I'd let them down to . . . that I wanted to . . .

This was such a shock, so stupid, that I suddenly howled with laughter. And the tight spring that I'd become suddenly burst, my arm lost all its strength, the rod clattered on the floor. And that was when I learned from my own experience that a laugh can be a terrifying weapon. With a laugh you can kill even murder itself.

I sat at the table and laughed—a desperate, ultimate laugh. I couldn't see any way out of this whole idiotic situation. I don't know how it would have ended if it had taken its natural course—but at this point a new, external ingredient suddenly popped up: The phone rang.

I dashed to the phone and lifted the receiver—maybe it was her. Someone's unfamiliar voice said: "One moment, please. . . ."

A merciless eternal hum. From somewhere far off I could hear heavy footsteps coming nearer, more resonant, more cast iron . . . and then: "D-503? Ah . . . You're speaking to the

Benefactor. Report to me immediately!" Dink: He hung up.
Dink.

U was still lying on the bed, her eyes closed, her gills spread
wide in a smile. I swept her clothes up off the floor, flung them
to her, and said, through my teeth: "Come on! Hurry up!"

She lifted herself on her elbows, her breasts flopped to the
sides, her eyes were round and the rest of her waxy.

"What . . . ?"

"Never mind what. Come on, get dressed!"

Clutching her clothes, she went through contortions, and
said in a crushed voice: "Turn away. . . ."

I turned away and leaned against the glass with my forehead. Lights, figures, sparks trembled on the black, wet mirror. No, it's not the mirror trembling, it's me. Why'd He call
me? Could He already know about her, about me, about everything?

U is at the door, already dressed. In two steps I'm by her
side, squeezing her hand as if I could squeeze out of it, drop by
drop, what I needed: "Listen to me. . . . Her name—you know
who—did you give them her name? No? Tell me the truth, I've
got to know. It doesn't matter, just tell me the truth. . . ."

"No."

"No? Then how come . . . once you'd already gone there to
report . . . ?"

Her lower lip suddenly turns inside out, like that boy's, and
down her cheeks ran drops. . . .

"Because I . . . I was afraid that if I gave them her . . . that
you might . . . that you'd stop lov . . . Oh, I can't—I couldn't
have!"

I understood. This was the truth. The stupid, ridiculous
human truth! I opened the door.

# RECORD 36

*Blank Pages*

*The Christian God*

*About My Mother*

Here's something strange. My head's like a blank, white page. How I went there, how I waited (I know I waited)—none of that do I remember, not a sound, not a face, not a gesture. As if all the lines between me and the world had been cut.

When I came to myself, I was already standing in front of Him, and I was too terrified to raise my eyes. All I could see were His huge cast-iron hands, resting on His knees. These hands were heavy even on Him, His knees gave under them. He moved His fingers slowly. His face was up there somewhere in a mist, and the only reason why His voice didn't roar like thunder, didn't deafen me, and sounded like an ordinary human voice, was that it reached me from such a height.

"So . . . you too? You, the Builder of the INTEGRAL? You, to whom it was given to become greatest among the conquistadors. You, whose name was to have begun a new, brilliant chapter in the history of OneState. . . . You?"

The blood rushed into my head, my cheeks—and again the page is blank except for a beating pulse in my temples and, above, that echoing voice—but not a word remains. Only when he'd stopped talking did I come to. I saw the hand move as though it weighed a thousand pounds, slowly creep up, and point a finger at me.

"Well? Why are you silent? Is it so or isn't it? Is *executioner* the word?"

"It is," I answered meekly. And from that point I clearly heard His every word.

"What? You think I fear this word? But have you ever made the experiment of removing its outer shell to examine what is inside? I shall now show you. Remember the scene: a blue hill, a cross, a crowd. Some are up on top, bespattered with blood, nailing the body to the cross; others are below, bespattered with tears, looking on. Does it not strike you that those above are playing the most difficult, the most important role of all? If it weren't for them, would this magnificent tragedy ever have been mounted? They were hissed by the vulgar crowd, but this very fact should earn them even more munificent rewards from God, the author of the tragedy. And this same Christian, all-merciful God—the one who slowly roasts in the fires of Hell all those who rebel against him—is he not to be called *executioner*? And those whom the Christians burned at the stake, are they fewer in number than the Christians who were burnt? But, all of this notwithstanding, you see, this is still the God who has been worshipped for centuries as the God of love. Absurd? No, on the contrary. It is the patent, signed in blood, of man's indelible good sense. Even then, in his savage, shaggy state, he understood: A true algebraic love of mankind will inevitably be inhuman, and the inevitable sign of the truth is its cruelty. Just as the inevitable sign of fire is that it burns. Can you show me a fire that does not burn? Well? Prove it! Put up an argument!"

How could I argue? How could I dispute what were (formerly) my own thoughts? Not that I would ever have been able to clothe them in such forged, gleaming armor. I didn't say anything. . . .

"If this means you agree with me, then let's talk like grown-ups after the children have gone to bed, holding nothing back. I ask this question: What is it that people beg for, dream about, torment themselves for, from the time they leave swaddling clothes? They want someone to tell them, once and for all, what happiness is—and then to bind them to that happiness with a chain. What is it we're doing right now, if not that? The ancient dream of paradise . . . Remember: In paradise they've lost all knowledge of desires, pity, love—they are the blessed, with their imaginations surgically removed (the only reason why they are blessed)—angels, the slaves of God. . . . And now, at the very moment when we've achieved this dream, when we have seized it like this (He squeezed his hand shut so tight that if a rock had been in it, juice would have shot out), when all that remained was to dress the kill and divide it into portions—at this very moment you—you . . ."

The cast-iron rumble suddenly broke off. I was red as a lump of pig-iron on the anvil under a striking hammer. The hammer drew back in silence and . . . the wait is more agoniz . . .

Suddenly: "How old are you?"

"Thirty-two."

"And as naive as a sixteen-year-old—half your age! Listen—did it really never once cross your mind that they—we don't know their names yet but we're certain to get them out of you—that they need you only as the Builder of the INTE-GRAL, only so that through you . . ."

"Don't! Don't!" I shouted.

Like hiding behind your hands and shouting "don't" to a bullet: You could still hear your "don't" after the bullet's gone through and you're twitching on the floor.

Yes, yes. Builder of the INTEGRAL . . . Yes, yes . . . and immediately I had a picture of the infuriated face of U with its trembling brick-red gills—that morning when both of them were together in my room. . . .

I remember it very clearly: I burst out laughing and lifted my eyes. In front of me sat a bald man who resembled Socrates and whose bald pate was covered over with tiny drops of sweat.

How simple it all was. How magnificently banal and ludicrously simple it all was.

Laughter was choking me, tearing itself out of me in clumps. I clamped my hands over my mouth and rushed out in headlong confusion.

Steps, wind, wet, leaping fragments of lights, faces, and, on the run, I think: "No! To see her! To see her just once more!"

Another blank white page comes right here. All I remember is—feet. Not people but just—feet, hundreds of feet, a heavy rain of feet, falling out of somewhere onto the sidewalk, stamping every which way. And some sort of song, playful, not very nice, and a shout: "Hey! You! C'mon over here!"

After this comes a deserted square, filled to the top with a tense wind. In the middle of it: a dim, ponderous, ominous mass—the Machine of the Benefactor. And from it—there is a sort of surprising echo in me: a blindingly white pillow; on the pillow is a reclining head with half-closed eyes; a sharp, sweet band of teeth . . . And this is all somehow idiotically, horribly connected with the Machine—I know how it is connected, but I still don't want to see it, to say it aloud—I don't want to, I mustn't.

I closed my eyes and sat down on the steps leading up to the Machine. It must have been raining: my face was wet. Somewhere far off I hear muffled shouting. But no one hears me, no one hears me shouting: Save me from this—Help!

If only I had a mother, the way the ancients had. I mean *my own* mother. And if for her I could be—not the Builder of the INTEGRAL, and not Number D-503, and not a molecule of OneState, but just a piece of humanity, a piece of her own self—trampled, crushed, outcast. . . . And suppose I do the nailing or they nail me—maybe that's all the same—but she would hear me, she would hear what no one else hears, and her old lips, her old wrinkled lips . . .

# RECORD 37

*Infusorian*

*Doomsday*

*Her Room*

In the morning in the dining room my neighbor to the left whispered to me in a frightened voice: "Eat, will you! They're watching you!"

It took all my strength to smile. And at that it felt like some kind of rupture across my face: I smile, the rupture cracks open wider, and it hurts all the worse. . . .

So it went. I'd just manage to spear a cube on my fork when the fork would start shaking in my hand and clink against the plate—whereupon everything started shaking and ringing, the tables, walls, dishes, air, and outside a huge round iron clamor reached all the way, over heads, over houses, to the sky, and then petered out far away in barely noticeable little rings like ripples on water.

I looked up to see faces instantly drained of all color, mouths paralyzed in mid-action, forks frozen in the air.

Then everything went haywire, shot off the familiar rails, everybody jumped up from his place (without singing the Hymn) every which way, out of time, still chewing, choking, groping one another: "What was that? What happened? What?" And these disorderly splinters of the once-great sleek Machine—they all scattered downstairs, to the elevators—down the stairs—steps—stamping—fragments of words—like bits of a shredded letter whipped away by the wind. . . .

From all the neighboring buildings they came scattering out in the same way, and after a minute the avenue looked like a drop of water under the microscope: infusoria locked in the transparent glassy droplet going berserk—sideways, up, down.

"Aha!" goes this triumphant voice, and I see in front of me the back of someone's head and a finger pointed up at the sky. I very vividly remember the yellow-pink fingernail and at the base of the nail a white crescent, like the moon creeping above the horizon. And this finger was like a compass: Hundreds of eyes followed it and looked at the sky.

There, rainclouds were tearing along trying to escape some invisible thing chasing them, crushing and leaping across one another, and, tinted with the color of the clouds, the dark aeros of the Guardians, dangling the black elephant snouts of their spy-tubes, and farther still, in the west, something that looked like . . .

At first nobody understood what it was. Even I, who'd found out a lot more (alas) than anyone else, didn't understand. It looked like a huge swarm of black aeros—quick little dots that you could hardly see at some incredible altitude. They get closer and closer. Hoarse, guttural droplets of sound come down to us. Finally there are birds overhead. They fill the sky: sharp, black, piercing, falling triangles. Beaten down by a storm, they swarm on cupolas, on roofs, on pillars, on balconies.

"Aha-a." The triumphant head turned round, and I saw who it was—him, the beetle-browed one. But little remained of his old self—he was like a book that had vanished except for the title. He had somehow crawled out from underneath that eternal overhanging brow and now on his face around his eyes and his lips lines were sprouting like hairs and he was—smiling.

"Do you understand?" he shouted to me through the whistling of the wind, the wings, the cawing. "Do you understand? They've broken through the Wall! The Wall, I'm telling you!"

Somewhere off in the background, figures with their heads stretched out were flitting past and hurrying to get inside the buildings. In the middle of the sidewalk there was a quick avalanche of postoperative cases (who nevertheless seemed slowed by their weight); they were headed over there, to the west.

. . . Hairy tufts of rays around his lips, his eyes. I grabbed his hand: "Listen! Where is she—where is I-330? Is she on the other side of the Wall? I need to—do you hear what I'm saying? Right now, I can't . . ."

"Here!" he shouted through his strong yellow teeth, like a grinning drunk. "She's here in the city, she's doing it! Hoo-ha! We're pulling it off!"

Who is this "we"? Who am I?

Around this one were some fifty others, exactly like him, who had crept out from underneath their brows—loud, happy, with sets of strong teeth. Their mouths open to gulp down the storm, waving around their lethal electric weapons (inoffensive enough to look at, but where did they find them?), they were moving west, the same as the postoperatives, but flanking them along Avenue 48, which ran parallel.

I was stumbling over taut hawsers woven out of wind and running toward her. Why? I don't know. I was stumbling, the streets were empty, the city was strange and wild, the triumphant clamor of the birds would never cease—it was Doomsday. In several buildings I could see through the glass walls (this sank in) that male and female Numbers were copulating without the least shame, without even lowering the blinds, without so much as a ticket, in broad daylight. . . .

The building . . . her building. The door seemed lost and was standing wide open. The control desk downstairs was empty. The elevator was stuck somewhere in the middle of the shaft. I ran gasping for breath up the endless stairwell. The hallway. The numbers of the doors fly past like the spokes of a wheel: 320, 326, 330 . . . I-330!

Through the glass door. Everything in the room was scattered, mixed up, crushed. Someone in a hurry had flipped a chair over and it was lying there with its four legs in the air like a dead cow. The bed was crazily pulled out at an angle from the wall. Pink tickets were scattered around the floor like fallen petals that had been trampled on.

I leaned over and picked one up, then another and another: All were marked D-503—I was on all of them—drops of me, melted, spilled over. That was all that was left. . . .

It somehow seemed impossible to leave them like that, on the floor, to be walked over. I gathered another handful, put them on the table, spread them out carefully, looked at them—and started laughing.

I'd never known this before, but now I do, and so do you: Laughter comes in different colors. It's only the distant echo of an explosion inside you. It might come in holiday colors—red, blue, golden rockets. Or it might be the bits of a human body flying out.

On the tickets I glimpsed a name I'd never heard of. I don't recall the number, only the letter, which was F. I swept all the tickets off the table onto the floor and stepped on them, on myself, like this, with my heel, and left. . . .

I sat in the hallway on a windowsill opposite her door and waited, vacantly and long, for I don't know what. Shuffling footsteps came from the left. An old man with a face like a punctured bladder that had collapsed and folded up, with some kind of clear stuff still oozing slowly out of the puncture. I finally formed the vague idea that these were tears. He'd already moved on a piece when I came to and called him: "Excuse me . . . listen, do you happen to know Number I-330?"

The old man turned, waved his hand in despair, and shuffled on.

At dusk I went back home to my place. In the west the sky, every second, was going through a pale blue spasm—this was what caused the dull muffled rumble. Birds perched here and there on roofs like black smoldering firebrands.

I lay down on the bed—and sleep fell on me instantly, like an animal, and smothered me. . . .

# RECORD 38

*(I Don't Know What Goes Here,
Maybe Just: A Cigarette Butt)*

I woke up—the light was so bright it hurt my eyes. I squinted. There was a sort of corrosive blue smoke in my head, everything was in a fog. And through the fog I hear myself saying, "But . . . I never turned the light on—how . . . ?"

I jumped up. Sitting at the table, her chin resting in her hand, I-330 was looking at me with an ironic grin. . . .

I'm sitting at the same table now, writing. They're behind me already—ten or fifteen minutes of time savagely compressed into the tightest of springs. But it seems to me she only just this moment shut the door behind her, and I might still catch up with her, grab her hand and—maybe she'll laugh and say . . .

I-330 was sitting at the table. I rushed to her.

"It's you, you! I was—I saw your room—I thought you'd . . ."

But I'd covered only half the distance when I found myself up against the sharp, immovable javelins of her eyelashes and stopped. I remembered her looking at me just the same way that time on board the INTEGRAL. And now I had one second in which to figure out a way to tell her everything so she'd understand . . . otherwise there'd never be . . .

"Listen, I-330 . . . I've got to . . . I've got to tell you all . . . No, wait—I need a sip of water. . . ."

My mouth was as dry as if it'd been lined with blotting

paper. I tried pouring some water, but couldn't, so I set the glass on the table and grabbed the pitcher with both hands.

Now I saw the blue smoke came from a cigarette. She put it to her lips, took a drag, greedily inhaled the smoke, just as I was drinking the water, and said: "Don't bother. Don't say anything. It doesn't matter—you see I came anyway. They're waiting for me downstairs. And you want these last few minutes of ours to be . . ."

She tossed the cigarette on the floor and leaned far over the arm of the chair (the button was on the wall, hard to reach) and I remember how the chair teetered and two of its legs lifted off the floor. Then the blinds fell.

She came up and threw her arms around me, hard. I could feel her knees through her dress—the slow, tender, warm, all-embracing poison. . . .

And suddenly . . . It sometimes happens that you're completely sunk in sweet, warm sleep—and suddenly something stabs you, you jump, and your eyes pop wide open again. . . . That's what happened now: I suddenly saw the floor of her room covered with the trampled pink tickets, with the letter F and some kind of figures on one of them . . . and they all rolled up inside me into one ball, and even now I can't say how that made me feel, but I held her so tight that she gave a cry of pain. . . .

One minute more—out of those ten or fifteen—her head thrust back on the gleaming white pillow, her eyes half closed; the sharp sweet band of her teeth. And the whole time this reminded me of something, something I couldn't shake off, stupid, painful, something I shouldn't have thought of—shouldn't even now think of. And I hold her still more tenderly, more cruelly, my fingers leave still more vivid blue marks. . . .

She said (and I noticed that she didn't open her eyes): "They say you were at the Benefactor's yesterday. Is that true?"

"Yes, it's true."

Then her eyes opened wide, and I was glad to see how quickly her face blanched, faded, and vanished, leaving only her eyes.

I told her everything. And there was only one thing—I don't

know why, no, that's not right, I do know—only one thing I held back: what He said at the very end, about them needing me only for . . .

Gradually, like a photograph in the developer, her face began to appear: her cheeks, the white band of her teeth, her lips. She got up and went over to the mirrored door of the wardrobe.

My mouth was dry again. I poured myself a glass of water, but the thought of drinking it disgusted me. I put the glass on the table and asked: "Is that why you came—because you had to know that?"

She looked at me in the mirror—the sharp mocking triangle of her brows lifted up toward her temples. She turned to say something to me but said nothing.

She didn't have to. I knew.

Say goodbye to her? I moved my—or somebody's—feet, hit the chair, it fell over and lay there dead, like the one in her room. Her lips were cold—as cold as the floor here in my room, next to the bed, had once been.

But when she left, I sat down on the floor and bent over the cigarette she'd thrown there. . . .

I can't write any more—I don't want to!

# RECORD 39

## *The End*

All this was like the final grain of salt added to a saturated solution: The crystals, bristling with needles, quickly began to appear, harden, and set. It was clear to me that everything had been decided. Tomorrow morning *I would do it*. It was the same thing as killing myself—but maybe that's the only way for me to be resurrected. Because you can't resurrect something unless it's been killed.

In the west the sky was going through a blue spasm every second. My head was on fire and pounding. I sat up the whole night like this and fell asleep only around seven in the morning, when the darkness was starting to thin out and turn green and you could see roofs dotted with birds.

I woke up and saw it was already ten o'clock (no bell this morning, apparently). The glass of water left over from yesterday was still standing on the table. I thirstily drank the water and ran out: I had a lot to do in a hurry, as soon as possible.

The storm had reamed out the sky, leaving it blue and empty. The shadows had sharp corners all cut out of the blue autumnal air and were so fragile you were afraid to touch them for fear they'd shatter into glass powder and blow away. It was the same inside me: no thinking, do not think, do not think, or else . . .

And I was not thinking, maybe not even seeing, actually, but merely registering. There on the sidewalk: branches from somewhere with green, amber, crimson leaves. Overhead: birds and aeros rushing about, crossing each other's paths. There: heads, open mouths, hands waving branches. That must be what is howling, cawing, humming. . . .

Then, streets as vacant as if some plague had swept through them. I remember stumbling over something unbearably soft and yielding though I still couldn't move it. I bent over: a corpse. It was lying on its back, legs spread, knees bent, like a woman. The face . . .

I recognized the thick African lips that even now seemed to be laughing juicily. His eyes were squinted shut and he was laughing right in my face. It took me one second to step over him and run on, because I couldn't wait, I had to do everything quickly, or else, I felt, I'd break, I'd bend out of shape like an overloaded rail. . . .

Luckily I only had some twenty steps to go before I came to the sign with the golden letters: BUREAU OF GUARDIANS. At the entrance I stopped, took as big a breath of air as I could, and went in.

Inside in the hallway was an endless line of Numbers, some with sheets of paper, some with thick notebooks in their hands. They were slowly moving forward—one step, two steps—then stopping.

I ran along this line, my head killing me, pulling at their sleeves, begging them, the way a sick man pleads with the doctor to give him something that would end it all with an instant of infinite pain.

Some woman wearing a tight belt over her yuny and above the two fat hemispheres of her buttocks, which she kept moving from side to side as if she had eyes in them, snorted at me: "He's got a stomach ache! Take him to the toilet—over yonder, second on the right!"

I got laughed at. This laughter made something rise up in my throat, and I was just about to start shouting or . . . or . . .

Suddenly someone grabbed my elbow from behind. I turned around: transparent ears like wings. Except they weren't pink as usual, but crimson, and his Adam's apple was bobbing up and down as though it might break out of his thin neck.

"Why are you here?" he asked, his eyes boring into me.

I grabbed hold of him: "Hurry! Let's go to your office. . . . Everything—I've got to . . . right now! I'm glad it's you. . . . Maybe it's terrible that it's you of all people, but it's good, I'm glad. . . ."

He also knew *her*, which was all the more painful for me, but maybe he'd also shudder when he heard, and we could do the killing together, and I wouldn't be all alone for that last second. . . .

The door slammed. I remember that some piece of paper got caught under the door and scraped across the floor when the door was closing, and then a sort of special, airless silence covered us like a bell-jar. If he'd said one word, no matter what, the most meaningless word, I'd have spilled everything right there. But he said nothing.

I was so tense all over that my ears were ringing. I said (not looking at him): "I think I always hated her, from the very beginning. I was fighting. . . . But no, no, better you don't believe me: I could have saved myself and didn't want to, I wanted to die, that meant more to me than anything. . . . I mean, not to die, but for her to . . . And even now, even now that I know everything . . . You know, do you know that I was called before the Benefactor?"

"Yes, I know."

"But what He told me . . . You know, it was like having the floor suddenly jerked out from under you—and you, along with everything on the table there, the paper, the ink . . . and the ink splashing out and making spots. . . ."

"Get on with it! And hurry. Others are waiting."

And then I told him the whole breathless, confused story— everything that's written down here. About the real me and the shaggy me, and about what she'd said that time about my hands—yes, that was how it all started—and about how I then didn't want to carry out my duty, and about how I fooled myself, and how she got the phony medical certificates, about how I got more corrupt from one day to the next, and about the corridors down there, and about how . . . on the other side of the Wall . . .

All this in incoherent lumps and chunks, with me out of breath, and not able to think of words I needed. The twisted lips with the double bend would smile ironically and pass me the words I wanted and I would thank him and say, Yes, yes . . . So then (what was going on?). So he was doing the talking for me and I was just listening: "Yes, and then? That's just how it was, yes, yes!"

I felt the skin around my collar getting cold, as if someone had daubed ether on it, and I could hardly bring myself to ask: "But how . . . there's no way you could have . . . ?"

The ironic smile, with no words, got more bent. . . . Then: "You know—you've been trying to hide something from me. Here you've named over all the ones you happened to see over there on the other side of the Wall, but you forgot one. You say you didn't? But don't you remember seeing over there—just for a second, just in passing—seeing me? That's what I said. Me."

A pause.

And suddenly it hit me with shameless clarity, like a bolt of lightning to the head: He was one of them. And everything I'd done, all my pains, everything I'd brought here with my last ounce of strength, my great heroic feat—it was all a joke. It was like the ancient story about Abraham and Isaac. Abraham, in a cold sweat, had already raised the knife over his own son, over his very own self, when suddenly there came a voice from on high: "Forget it! I was only joking!"

Without moving my eyes away from the ironic smile that was getting more and more crooked, I propped my hands against the edge of the table and slowly, slowly, pushed my chair backward, then, all of a sudden, I picked myself up in an armful and dashed out of there, past shouts, steps, mouths. . . .

How I got downstairs to one of the public washrooms in the subway station I do not remember. Up there above, everything was in ruins, the greatest and most rational civilization in all history had collapsed, but down here someone had had the ironic notion of keeping everything as it was, in splendid shape. And to think that all this was doomed, that it would all be grown over in grass, that nothing would be left of all this but "myths."

I groaned out loud. At the same moment, I felt a consoling touch on my shoulder.

It was my neighbor, who was in the seat to my left. His forehead was a huge bald parabola, written over by the yellow indecipherable lines of his wrinkles. And these lines were about me.

"I understand you, I understand you completely," he said. "But still, calm down. Don't carry on so. This'll all come back, it'll come back, no question. The only thing that matters is that everyone should hear about my discovery. You're the first one I'm telling. I've calculated that infinity does not exist!"

I gave him a wild look.

"Yes, it's true what I'm telling you. There is no infinity. If the world were infinite, then the average density of matter in it would equal zero. But since it is not zero—this we know—it follows that the universe is finite. It is spherical in shape and the square of its radius, $y^2$, is equal to the average density, times the . . . I've just got to calculate the numerical coefficient, and then . . . You see, everything is done, everything is simple, everything is calculable. And then we'll win philosophically, don't you see? But you, sir, are preventing me from finishing this calculation, your shouting . . ."

What shook me more I don't know—his discovery or his firmness in this apocalyptic hour. In his hands (I hadn't seen this until now) he held a notebook and a logarithmic dial. And I understood that even if everything was going to perish, my duty (before you, my unknown readers) was to leave my records in finished form.

I asked him for some paper, and on it I wrote down these final lines. . . .

I wanted to put a period, the way the ancients would set a cross over the pits where they piled their dead, but suddenly the pencil jerked and fell out of my hand. . . .

"Listen!" I grabbed my neighbor. "Listen to me, I tell you! You have to tell me this. There where your finite universe ends—what's there . . . beyond?"

He didn't have time to answer. From overhead, on the steps, the pounding of feet . . .

# RECORD 40

*Facts*

*The Bell*

*I Am Certain*

It is day. Clear. Barometer at 760.

Could it be that I, D-503, actually wrote these 225 pages? Could it be that I ever actually felt this—or imagined that I did?

It's my handwriting. And it goes on, in the same hand, but fortunately only the handwriting is the same. No delirium, no ridiculous metaphors, no feelings. Just the facts. Because I'm well, I am completely, absolutely well. I'm smiling—I can't help smiling: They extracted a kind of splinter from my head, and now my head is easy and empty. Or I should say, not empty, but there's nothing strange there that keeps me from smiling (a smile is the normal state of a normal person).

The facts are as follows. That evening they seized my neighbor, the one who'd discovered that the universe is finite, and me, and everybody who'd been with us, and charged us with not having the certificate of the Operation, and took us off to the nearest auditorium (the number of which, 112, was familiar for some reason). Here we were strapped to the tables and put through the Great Operation.

The following day I, D-503, reported to the Benefactor and told him all I knew about the enemies of happiness. Why could this have seemed hard for me before? I don't understand. Only one explanation: my former illness (soul).

That same evening, at one and the same table with Him, the Benefactor, I was sitting (for the first time) in the famous Gas Room. They brought in that woman. She was supposed to give her testimony in my presence. The woman was stubbornly silent and kept smiling. I noticed that she had sharp, very white teeth, and that this was beautiful.

Then they put her under the Bell. Her face got very white, and since she had eyes that were dark and big, this was very beautiful. When they started pumping the air out of the Bell, she threw her head back, and half closed her eyes and pressed her lips together, and this reminded me of something. She was looking at me, holding on tight to the arms of the chair, until her eyes closed completely. Then they pulled her out, quickly brought her to with the help of electrodes, and put her back under the Bell. This happened three times, and she still didn't say a word. Others that they brought in with that woman turned out to be more honest. Many of them began talking right after the first time. Tomorrow they'll all go up the steps of the Machine of the Benefactor.

It can't be put off, because in the western quarters there is still chaos, roaring, corpses, animals, and, unfortunately, quite a lot of Numbers who have betrayed reason.

But on Fortieth Avenue, which runs crosstown, they've managed to build a temporary wall of high-voltage waves. And I hope we'll win. More—I'm certain we'll win. Because reason has to win.

# NOTES

11. *the Taylor exercises*: In the absence of conclusive evidence, this was long thought to be Brook Taylor (1685–1731), a British mathematician noted for his contributions to the calculus. It now seems far more plausible that Zamyatin is referring to the American efficiency expert Frederick Winslow Taylor (1856–1915), the father of scientific management, whose famous time-and-motion studies were much discussed at the time *We* was being written.

16. *Maclaurin*: Colin Maclaurin, Scottish mathematician (1698–1746).

42. *"archangels"*: Thus in the available Russian text, though both Zilboorg and Cauvet-Duhamel have the more plausible "Guardian Angels" (*anges gardiens*).

145. [*I was not far from the rust-red, opaque*]: There is an omission at this point in the only full and reliable Russian text (NY, 1952). Noting this, the editors of the Soviet edition (M. 1988, p. 541) supply Russian words they arrive at by translating from the French translation of B. Cauvet-Duhamel (*Nous autres*, 1929): "J'apercevais déjà de loin la masse opaque et rouge" (172). I have used the English translation by Gregory Zilboorg (*We*, New York, 1924), that being the first published version of the phrase in any language.